THE VALANCOURT BOOK OF VICTORIAN CHRISTMAS GHOST STORIES

VOLUME FOUR

THE VALANCOURT BOOK OF

VICTORIAN CHRISTMAS

GHOST STORIES

VOLUME FOUR

Edited with an introduction by
CHRISTOPHER PHILIPPO

VALANCOURT BOOKS
Richmond, Virginia
2020

The Valancourt Book of Victorian Christmas Ghost Stories, Volume Four
First published December 2020

Introduction © 2020 by Christopher Philippo
This compilation copyright © 2020 by Valancourt Books, LLC

Published by Valancourt Books, Richmond, Virginia
http://www.valancourtbooks.com

ISBN 978-1-948405-80-5 (hardcover)
ISBN 978-1-948405-81-2 (paperback)
Also available as an electronic book.

Set in Bembo Book MT Pro

CONTENTS

Introduction

The earth did tremble and quake,
  And graves did open wide
Dead men's ghosts walked up and down
  In a frightful manner beside.

"The Twelve Apostles,"
an English Christmas carol

Unsettled History

I F IT MAY HAVE SEEMED that Americans didn't write Victorian Christmas ghost stories, it's no wonder. Stephen Nissenbaum's and Penne Restad's histories of the holiday in America, both fairly thorough, don't mention the tradition—apart from the embrace of Charles Dickens' *A Christmas Carol*.

It's impossible not to mention Dickens. The first American edition, by Harper's, was issued in January 1844. Wrote the *New York Commercial Advertiser,* "As everybody knows Dickens, and everybody, no matter how skeptical on the subject, likes ghost stories, the present work will doubtless be greeted by a great sale." By later that year, the book was being advertised, mentioned, and praised in Washington, D.C., the Wisconsin Territory, across at least twenty of the twenty-six states, published in an illustrated edition by Carey & Hart of Philadelphia, and adapted for stage in New York City by December 1844.

It's to *A Christmas Carol* that people turn to explain the lyrics of the 1963 American song "It's the Most Wonderful Time of the Year." After that, some might mention Dickens' other Christmas ghost stories, or the British tradition of that genre, or if thinking outside of the box maybe even German author E. T. A. Hoffmann's "The Nutcracker and the Mouse King" (1816), or Danish author Hans Christian Andersen's "The Little Match Girl" (1845). But . . . *American* stories?

There have been *some*, of course. "But American examples of the Christmas ghost story are few and far between," wrote anthologist Edward Wagenknecht in 1949. *The Valancourt Book of Victorian Christmas Ghost Stories, Volume 1* had included Francis Marion Crawford's "The Doll's Ghost" (1896), and though Italy was both the place of that author's birth and death, he'd lived for many years in Boston, and was published by Americans. Scattered through other anthologies are some more stories, but no more than a few collected in any one. Consequently, it has not been manifest that Americans had indeed widely embraced the tradition.

The cultural amnesia may also have been due to the lack of a single iconic American book, author, or image closely associated with the tradition. Washington Irving had mentioned it in *The Sketch Book of Geoffrey Crayon, Gent.* (1819), but he did not prominently feature Christmas ghosts.

Many of Edgar Allan Poe's fantastic stories like "William Wilson" first appeared in the 1830s and '40s in the annual *The Gift: A Christmas and New Year's Present,* published by Carey & Hart, but they were not set during the season. In his youth, Poe did impersonate a ghost on Christmas Eve, though. He'd tried startling men at a gentlemen's whist club that included Dr. Philip Thornton and Gen. Winfield Scott, and Poe had laughed heartily when caught.[1]

Illustrator Thomas Nast, so influential in the development of traditions around Santa Claus, had drawn the goblin for an American edition of Dickens' "Gabriel Grubb" and ghosts for William Douglas O'Connor's *The Ghost: A Christmas Story.* However, given the great variety of ghosts' manifestations

1 James Albert Harrison, "New Glimpses of Poe." *The Independent.* September 6, 1900.

even when "ghost" is narrowly defined, it might be impossible for any one picture to ever become representative of the genre as a whole. Nast, amusingly, had a son who'd requested a skeleton for Christmas, because he had so appreciated the one his father used as an artist's model.[1]

Even as some memories and records are lost over time, new ways of looking sometimes arise. Initially it had been anticipated that state and university libraries would be visited to physically flip through publications for possible inclusions for this volume, as there is still much that has not yet been digitized. Closures and limited services due to the COVID-19 pandemic, however, kiboshed that. The majority were found through aggressive, persistent, creative keyword searching in online databases of periodicals. Nevertheless, some reference librarians generously provided remote aid when possible.

For this fourth volume, everything is American authored, translated, or published. Most are explicitly set in America or American territories. Many of them are being republished for the first time; to our knowledge, none have ever been included in any Christmas ghost anthology before.

Moreover, everything is set at Christmas, save for two poems printed in special Christmas editions. While the term "Christmas ghost story" gets applied both to ghost stories taking place during the Christmas season and those published during the season, the former satisfy the name better.

Because the majority were found in newspapers, as opposed to other anthologies that mostly relied on Christmas gift books and Christmas numbers of journals, the nature of the stories may be different in some ways. Many of them are shorter, for one. Additionally, the audience the authors had in mind would have differed: not someone splurging on a fancy book for a loved one for a holiday, but someone spending just a nickel or less; not a readership across the country or the world, but on occasion a town of perhaps 400 people or so.

1 "Thomas Nast," *Watertown Daily Times* (N.Y.), Jan. 24, 1874: p. 1, col. 5.

Content ranges in date from 1841—thus predating *A Christmas Carol*—to 1917, for which final year an explanation is necessary. The Victorian Era was 1837 to 1901, when narrowly defined. More broadly defined, it is sometimes extended through the Edwardian Era to 1910, or even to the onset of WWI for Britain in 1914. Given the lesser relevance of Queen Victoria to America, for the purpose of this volume the period has been extended to 1917, the year the United States joined the war.

Something else to note, which may horrify you: *not every story is a "ghost" story*. After the reader has recovered from his or her fainting couch with the help of some smelling salts or a restorative brandy, be assured that there *are* more ghost stories than anything else. The exact count will vary, depending. Just as "fairy tales" needn't have *fairies* specifically to meet the definition, a "ghost story" in standard references like the Oxford English and American Heritage dictionaries includes ones with "ghostly" or "supernatural" elements. Merriam-Webster allows even just "a tale based on imagination rather than fact"; we don't go that far! One specialist's definition of "ghost story" is a similarly broad one, that of Julia Briggs in *Night Visitors: The Rise and Fall of the English Ghost Story*: "not only stories about ghosts, but about possession and demonic bargains, spirits other than those of the dead, including ghouls, vampires, werewolves, the 'swarths' of living men and the 'ghost-soul' or *Doppelgänger*." Even the Grinch and Heat Miser could potentially find a home in such company.

There is a history to such broader definitions that is consistent with Christmas ghosts in particular. Consider the things mentioned in the run-on title of a Georgian-era book from 1730: *Round About Our Coal-Fire: or Christmas Entertainments: Containing, Christmas Gambols, Tropes, Figures, Etc. with Abundance of Fiddle-Faddle-Stuff; Such As Stories of Fairies, Ghosts, Hobgoblins, Witches, Bull-Beggars, Rawheads and Bloody-Bones, Merry Plays, &c. for the Diversion of Company in a Cold Winter-*

Evening, Besides Several Curious Pieces Relating to the History of Old Father Christmas; Setting Forth What Hospitality Has Been, and What It Is Now. All that "Fiddle-Faddle-Stuff": ghost stories.

Nineteenth-century American newspapers even catered to a public curiosity about other Christmas bugbear traditions around the world: Knecht Ruprecht, Hans Trapp, Klapperbock, Habersack, Mari Lwyd, Perchta, Krampus, Jultomten, La Befana, Gryla, Kallikantzaroi, and more.[1] However, these do not seem to have featured in American short stories or poems, for the most part, only in journalism.

As for stories with endings where the supernatural aspects are explained away rationally, as in old "Scooby-Doo" cartoons, there is hardly anything of that sort here. That noted, the presence of some stories where ghosts have rational explanations in the end can help the genre have a greater air of suspense, which is arguably an asset. Such stories can still be satisfying as well. Ebert's Law that "a film is not what it is about, but how it is about it" applies to stories too. A rational ghost story might involve some good detective work, clever motivation for the gaslighting of a character, vivid local color, or any number of other saving graces.

One of the more amusing definitions for a ghost story comes from Sara Maitland's introduction to *Modern Ghost Stories by Eminent Women Writers:*

> It is an extraordinarily open genre: perhaps the only proper answer is that a real ghost story is one that doesn't make you protest when you find it in a collection of ghost stories.

It is greatly hoped that the reader finds the majority of the inclusions meet Maitland's definition. As for any of the stories that may not, feel free to consider those bonus content, historical context providing a wider portal into the Victorian era.

1 See Rene Bach, "German Soldiers in Trenches Will Get Visits from Christmas Hobgoblins." *El Paso Herald* (Tex.), Dec. 19, 1914, and "Weihnachtsmummenschanz," *Scranton Wochenblatt* (Penn.), Dec. 23, 1892: p. 1, cols. 3-5.

Speaking of bonus content, the manner in which the stories were found also lent itself to finding other items that decidedly were not ghost stories (even by Merriam-Webster's standards) but which it was thought the reader might nonetheless appreciate seeing. For example, social notices about Christmas ghost story parties or readings that provide evidence of the embrace of the tradition in America beyond just the existence of the stories and poems themselves. Telling of stories was a big part of the tradition, told extemporaneously, or from memory, or read aloud from a text. There are also Christmas news stories that highlight some of the real horrors of the season, like the flammability of Christmas trees and the cotton beards and batting on Santa Clauses. More people could die in a Christmas fire, particularly if accompanied by a public panic, than in most Christmas movies, be it *Black Christmas* or *Gremlins* or *Die Hard*. Surprisingly common too were news items about people dressed as Santa Claus or Belsnickle getting shot, or shooting others. Such material ranges from amusing to macabre and also includes Christmas poems hung on the frame of Poe's "The Raven" or "The Bells," short fiction or poems about Santa being dead, or killing others, and advertisements that made reference to the Christmas ghost story tradition.

Unsettling History

The variety of things that were found having been detailed, something must also be mentioned about what was not found, what was excluded, and other difficult matters.

It was not hard to find stories and poems by women; the prevalence of their ghost stories has long been observed. It *was* hard to find ones by authors who weren't white.

It hadn't been taken as a given that that would be the case. In what would become the United States, within the current fifty states, Washington, D.C., Puerto Rico, and other territories, the first Christmases celebrated would have been in New

Spain and New France, not New England or the New Nether-
lands. Beyond the French and Spanish explorers and colonists
involved, there were enslaved people, African, Native American, converts either willing or compelled.

There are some Christmas ghost-like traditions that date
back to that time, or nearly as far. In some places in the South
and Southwest there were Christmas plays begun by the Spanish Catholics that have continued long after Spain withdrew.
Los Pastores tells a story of the shepherds going to visit baby
Jesus, and the attempts of the Devil and demons to interfere
with them. There are mentions of it in some late nineteenth-
century newspapers, but no relevant story or poem could be
found. One way to become better acquainted with it would
be to watch PBS Great Performances' *La Pastorela: The Shep-
herd's Tale* (1991), starring Paul Rodriguez as Satanas, and also
featuring Linda Ronstadt, Robert Beltran, "Father Guido
Sarducci," and Cheech Marin.

Another unrepresented tradition is *Junkanoo*, a Christmas-
time festival with elements akin to mumming and hodening,
with some bugbear-like figures. Junkanoo has roots in Africa,
Haiti, and Jamaica, and was taken through the islands to the
American South. Also called "John Canoe," it shows up in
some early Victorian-era American newspapers in connection with reports of riots and violence abroad and fears of
slaveholders of the same at home. News items from the 1860s
and later are few and brief and treat it as a sort of curiosity;
there is also some brief description in Harriet Jacobs' semi-
autobiographical *Incidents in the Life of a Slave Girl* (1861), where
she called it the Johnkannaus:

> They consist of companies of slaves from the plantations,
> generally of the lower class. Two athletic men, in calico
> wrappers, have a net thrown over them, covered with all
> manner of bright-colored stripes. Cows' tails are fastened to
> their backs, and their heads are decorated with horns. A box,
> covered with sheepskin, is called the gumbo box. A dozen

> beat on this, while others strike triangles and jawbones, to which bands of dancers keep time. For a month previous they are composing songs, which are sung on this occasion. These companies, of a hundred each, turn out early in the morning, and are allowed to go round till twelve o'clock, begging for contributions.

There is more detailed discussion of the festival in Restad's chapter "Christmas in the Slave South," Nissenbaum's chapter "Wassailing Across the Color Line," and in May's *Yuletide in Dixie*.

Easier to find—without even looking for them specifically—were instances of white authors writing stories about Black characters, or writing what were called "Negro dialect poems." None of them will be printed here.

Dialect poems of all kinds were popular during the Victorian era. There were at least three renditions of "A Visit from St. Nicholas" into "Pennsylvania Dutch" alone. Some are written by actual speakers of the dialect, some can represent sincere attempts at accuracy by others, and if intended to be humorous in nature may sometimes be done with affection. However, much dialect poetry is rife with nationalism or racism. That was particularly true of stories or poems featuring both Christmas ghosts and Black characters, whether in dialect or not. The stereotype of Black people as especially afraid of ghosts was pretty frequently employed, as was the trope of "Mammy" telling ghost stories to doting white children.

One of the dialect poems found warrants mentioning: "G'wine back to Georgy," depicting a Black person or family leaving the North to return to the old Southern plantation and find the old slaveholders' family. The author was James R. Crowe (1838-1911) of Sheffield, Alabama, who was one of the founders of the Klan, known for its use of ghostly imagery—as he himself acknowledged.

Crowe's 1910 poem has the Black narrator recounting how

they'd listen to "mammy" telling stories of ghosts, witches, goblins, the Devil, Rawhead and Bloodybones, but the only people depicted as badly scared were the white sons of the slaveholder. As an example of Lost Cause mythologizing, in romanticizing antebellum times, he would have avoided recounting in that context how ghost imagery was used to terrorize Black people.

At any rate, the fact that ghost stories could have such a negative association may account for why few examples of anything like a Victorian Christmas ghost story could be found by people of color. Sean Ferrier-Watson in "The Missing Phantom in Early African American Children's Literature" had written:

> As the desire for uplift grew, so did the desire to separate from harmful stereotypes, particularly stereotypes that cast the African American community in a superstitious light, which led to an active effort to separate African American identity from superstitious beliefs in American popular culture. This is not meant to say that a campaign was being waged against the ghost and other superstitious tales in African American literature of the time—many fine ghost stories did appear during the Harlem Renaissance [ca. 1918-1937] by famous African American authors like Zora Neale Hurston—but rather that an attempt to create some distance between those traditions was actively being explored in African American literature, particularly in African American literature designed for children.

By the time of the Harlem Renaissance, Christmas ghost stories were on the wane (though never quite extinct), ghosts were increasingly associated with Halloween instead, and Halloween was becoming celebrated much more widely.

Nonetheless, two of the authors herein are African-American: Paul Dunbar and Amorel Sterne. (As for the demographics of the anonymous authors, it is of course impossible to say.)

Dunbar's poem "The Haunted Oak" has a depth and res-
onance in its tackling of a serious problem in a creative way.
His book *Speakin' O' Christmas and Other Christmas and Special
Poems* is worth a look; the photos it includes of people in
winter scenes, possibly friends and family of the author, are
particularly charming and interesting.

Amorel Sterne's poem "Xmas" is representative of many
Victorian poems that depict a parent for whom every Christ-
mastime is a time of grieving for the children who did not live
to see it. Some poems of the kind feature good spirits visiting
the children before they die as in "The Little Match Girl," or
the ghosts of the children returning to observe. Possibly for
Sterne the subject was not ripe for such fictitious whimsies;
she had in fact lost three of her children.

Two poems by Black authors that lacked anything fearful
or deathly that are not included still might be worth mentioning should someone else wish to investigate the subject
further. Priscilla Jane Thompson (1871-1942) in the poem
"A Christmas Ghost" from her 1907 book *Gleanings of Quiet
Hours,* had a boy maintain belief in Santa Claus by deciding
a noise heard early on Christmas Eve must have been a ghost,
rather than Santa catching him disobediently being out of
bed. Rosalie M. Jonas' (1861-1953) "Black 'Santy'" was one of
several dialect poems published in the *New York Daily Tribune*
for a Hell's Kitchen mission fund drive; it has points of interest
but is painful in the way it tried to appeal to potential wealthy
patrons.

Earlier Valancourt volumes at times have had to acknowl-
edge difficult content, and this one is no exception. The
anonymous author of "The Frozen Husband" carelessly refers
in passing to "America, which was peopled after the world
became round," which ignores the millions living here long
before Columbus arrived. It's regrettable he or she never took
the time to get to know any of their many descendants, as otherwise the author had shown a familiarity with and interest

in a range of cultural traditions. Honoré Beaugrand's "The Werwolves" is set in 1706 at Fort Richelieu, Quebec and its treatment of the indigenous people, though perhaps an accurate reflection of 18th-century colonial attitudes, is itself part of a spectrum of wrongful treatment. Just three years ago Prime Minister Trudeau, in speaking to the United Nations General Assembly, said the original inhabitants "were victims of a government which sought to rewrite their unique history, to eradicate their languages and their cultures, by imposing traditions and ways of colonial life." One hopes that Victorian Christmas ghost stories by Native American authors might still be located, but regrettably those will have to wait for some later volume.

As weighty as some of these remarks are, it is hoped the selections will prove to be the sort of escapism readers have anticipated (with some surprises), be it some variety of horror or, at times, humor. Remember, too, that in the days before radio, television, film, and Internet, that many of these stories would have been read aloud to others and very likely enhanced thereby. Consider doing that with some of your favorites, be it by the light of a fire or the glowing screen of a video chat. "Haunt it forward," as it were, and perhaps some of your listeners will like it enough to get their own copy and do the same for others. Ghosts represent a sort of connection from beyond the grave, ghost stories a human connection not to be neglected.

Christopher K. Philippo
Bethlehem, New York
October 2020

ABOUT THE EDITOR

CHRISTOPHER K. PHILIPPO was born in the city where "A Visit from St. Nicholas" was first published and the author of "Jingle Bells" had married. As a child he visited Santa's Workshop in North Pole, New York and at Christmas the fireplace at home had not just stockings but wooden shoes. A Trustee of the Bethlehem Historical Society, a former volunteer for the NYS Historian, and a gravestone conservationist, he finds figuratively or literally unearthing and then sharing the forgotten to be intensely satisfying. His future books will examine the complete works of H. C. Dodge, women horror directors' movies, and the early film career of Alfred Hitchcock.

Works Cited

Bach, Rene. "German Soldiers in Trenches Will Get Visits from Christmas Hobgoblins." *El Paso Herald* (Tex.) Dec. 19, 1914.

"Christmas Then and Now." *The Home-Maker* 9(3). Dec. 1892. 226-228.

Crowe, James R. "Origin of the Klan; One of the Founders of the Famous Organization Tells of Its Organization and Purposes." *The [Nashville] Tennessean.* July 10, 1905: 11.

Ferrier-Watson, Sean. "The Missing Phantom in Early African American Children's Literature." *The Children's Ghost Story in America.* McFarland, 2017.

Fry, Gladys-Marie. *Night Riders in Black Folk History.* University of North Carolina Press, 2001.

Harrison, James Albert. "New Glimpses of Poe." *The Independent.* Sept. 6, 1900.

May, Robert E. *Yuletide in Dixie: Slavery, Christmas, and Southern Memory.* University of Virginia Press, 2020.

Miles, Tiya. *Tales from the Haunted South: Dark Tourism and Memories of Slavery from the Civil War Era.* University of North Carolina Press, 2017.

"Poe's Writings in *The Gift.*" The Edgar Allan Poe Society of

Baltimore, March 31, 2012. https://www.eapoe.org/works/editions/agftoo1c.htm

"Thomas Nast." *Watertown Daily Times* (N.Y.), Jan. 24, 1874: p. 1, col. 5.

"New Publications." *Buffalo Courier*, Jan. 30, 1844: p. 2, col. 1.

Nissenbaum, Stephen. *The Battle for Christmas: A Cultural History of America's Most Cherished Holiday.* Vintage Books, 1997.

Restad, Penne L. *Christmas in America: A History.* Oxford University Press, 1996.

Smith-Wright, Geraldine. "In Spite of the Klan: Ghosts in the Fiction of Black Women Writers." *Haunting the House of Fiction: Feminist Perspectives on Ghost Stories by American Women,* edited by Lynette Carpenter and Wendy K. Kolmar. University of Tennessee Press, 1991.

Wagenknecht, Edward. "American Christmas Ghost Tales." *Chicago Tribune.* Dec. 4, 1949: IV, 37.

"Weihnachtsmummenshanz." *Scranton Wochenblatt* (Penn.), Dec. 23, 1892: p. 1, cols. 3-5.

Note on the Texts

MOST OF THE TEXTS presented in this volume were originally published in early American newspapers. Oftentimes, a story or a poem would appear first in one of the larger newspapers in a bigger city like Cleveland or Detroit before being reprinted over the course of the holiday season by newspapers in smaller towns throughout the region or the country. In a number of cases there are discrepancies among the various versions of a single text, sometimes the substitution of a single word (did she raise her hand to her "heart" or her "throat"? did her garment show her to "advantage" or to "disadvantage"?), but sometimes involved the addition or deletion of whole paragraphs. Where possible, we have compared multiple versions of the stories in an attempt to arrive at the most logical and accurate reading; however, because this volume is intended for a general public rather than a scholarly one, we have not included a list of textual variations.

The texts are presented here as they were originally printed, except that the occasional obvious typographical error—the texts were probably hastily typeset by newspaper printers, and errors were not uncommon—has been silently corrected.

Joseph Holt Ingraham

The Green Huntsman; or, The Haunted Villa

A Christmas Legend of Louisiana

REV. JOSEPH HOLT INGRAHAM (1809-1860) *was a prolific author from Maine; one critic cited in John Sutherland's* The Lives of the Novelists *"estimated that in the early 1840s, 10 percent of the new novels produced in the U.S. were Ingraham's."* His novel The Pillar of Fire *was a source for Cecil B. DeMille's* The Ten Commandments. *"The Green Huntsman" first appeared in the* The Ladies' Companion [N.Y.] *of June 1841, an example of how a Christmas ghost story could be printed any time of the year. A reprint in the* Huddersfield Chronicle *and* West Yorkshire Advertiser *appeared on December 24, 1858, though: an American story getting an English stamp of approval.*

———

"Is it a true and honest tale, fair master?"
"Nay—I vouch not. I give it thee as I had it."

IN THE UPPER *faubourg* of New-Orleans and conspicuous from the river on which it fronts, stands a vast, square mansion, gray and ruinous through neglect rather than time. A few old moss-stained oaks of a century's growth, rear their majestic heads above its rank lawn, and the hedges and walls that once enclosed it are broken down or utterly destroyed. Every where are the marks of its having been, in a better day, the abode of affluence and aristocratic pride. Lonely, in dilapidated grandeur, stately and imposing even in its ruin, it has for years attracted the eye of the curious stranger as he sailed past it. But vainly does the traveller seek to learn from those about him, the history of the spot. All that he can ascertain is, that it is called "The Haunted Villa."

Less than half a mile above this dilapidated edifice on the estate adjacent also stands a mansion, which is no less striking for its beauty, adorned as it is with verandahs, porticos and latticed conservatories, and half-hid in the most luxuriant foliage, with well-appointed hedges of the rose-thorn interspersed with lemon, acacia and pomegranate trees enclosing a lawn of the softest green. It seems the abode of taste, refinement and graceful affluence—the home of domestic bliss and social happiness. Never two mansions or grounds presented stranger or more remarkable contrasts, made still more striking by their juxtaposition.

At the latter villa on the evening of our story, there was held a Christmas festival, of a gayer and more brilliant description than usual, for it was a bridal night also—and the bride and bridegroom with the joyous train mingled merrily in the holiday festivities. The bride! How shall her matchless beauty be given to the eye of the reader! She was of stately stature, and graceful as the swan in her movements. Her eyes were dark, and burning with the light of love. There was an unfathomable well of feeling in their dangerous depths, and though they could occasionally flash fire and sparkle, their usual aspect was soft and timid as the gazelle's. She was called Ephèse, and men's eyes have seldom looked on a more beautiful woman, or a bridegroom's worshipping glance adored a fairer bride. She was wedded the night of our story, in the gorgeous rooms of the mansion just described. The owner of this mansion was a French gentleman, and had been a widower for many years.

He called Ephèse his child. Some said she was his daughter, others that she was not. There was evidently a mystery about her. She was just eighteen the night of her bridal, which was as well both her birth-day and wedding-day, a Christmas eve. The bridegroom was a rich young creole of Orleans, handsome, chivalrous and well-born, and every way worthy to wear so bright a jewel as Ephèse in his bosom.

It was a happy and merry night. All the youthful cavaliers for many leagues around were gathered there to grace the nuptials, and three score maidens, with the dark eye and raven hair of that sunny clime, presented their rival charms in the presence of the incomparable bride. In the wanton waltz and stately dance, amid never ceasing strains of ravishing music, and with the numerous scenes and changes of a bridal festival conjoined with a Christmas merry-making, the silvery hours flew swiftly on. Midnight at length approached, and the blushing bride, half-reluctant, half-consenting, was borne from the hall by a group of laughing virgins, to the nuptial chamber. At the instant the door closed behind her, the festive halls were strangely illuminated by a sudden light of a pale-green cast that out-shone the brilliant candelabra in the rooms and threw over every face the ghastly pallor of death. At the same instant a loud, heavy, rumbling noise, like underground thunder, appalled every ear.

"Look! the Haunted Villa!" shouted several voices on the verandah.

In an instant the halls were deserted, and the verandah and lawn looking in the direction of the ruined mansion, were crowded with terrified gazers. Terrific spectacle! The whole interior of the ruin, towards which their eyes were turned, seemed to be on fire. Through every aperture of door and window and gaping crevice, the fire shone out as if from a furnace, with an intense glowing heat. Yet there ascended no smoke from it, nor could there be heard any sound of crackling flame. But what was most fearful was a tongue of green flame, which rising from the midst of the molten mass, flung itself, lapping and curling high into the air, like a serpent, and then contracted and coiled down upon the surface of the bed of fire, again to unfold and dart upward, and shed its baleful glare a wide league around. The most death-like silence pervaded the groups of banqueters as they looked upon this spectacle. To all the name of the Haunted Villa was familiar, and to every mind supernatural terror was associated with it. No one breathed. Expectation and alarm sat on every face. Gradually the intensity of the glowing interior lessened, and in a few minutes all became dark as before, save the tongue of flame which continued to curl and writhe above the central tower with fiercer strength. All at once it disappeared, like a lamp blown out, and in its place a small globe of green fire, that shone with a steady light, was alone visible upon the summit of the tower.

Awed and full of conjectures and trembling apprehensions, the company instantly broke up. In a few minutes, nearly all were on their way to their homes, anxious to place the widest distance between themselves and this spot of supernatural sounds and spectacles. Five or six young men alone remained in the deserted verandah. They were intimate friends of the bridegroom, who himself stood among them as they discoursed together on the event.

"Did you notice that it was just as the door closed behind the bride?" remarked Don Antonio Baradas, one of the group upon the colonnade.

"I did, signor," replied Eugene Brissot, with animation, "for my eye was following her departure, surrounded by her bridesmaids, and methought I had never seen woman so lovely, and I mourned so bright a star should set to every eye but Henride's."

"You all noticed it was just as she left the room, signors?" repeated young Don Antonio, looking round with a marked manner and speaking in a solemn tone.

"We did," all answered, "but has Ephèse any thing to do with—"

"Speak, Don Antonio! what evil threatens or is connected with my beloved bride?" demanded the young husband, earnestly grasping his friend's hand.

"Listen, signor," answered Don Antonio Baradas.

The young cavaliers, joined by one or two ladies, now grouped closer about the young Spaniard as he leaned gracefully against a column, his arms folded within his silk mantle across his breast. His attitude was striking and commanding. His age appeared not less than thirty, but care or deep and active thought had worn in his face strong lines, which, while they added to its intellect, took from his youth. He had been very handsome and was still striking for his manly appearance. His figure was tall and slender and finely shaped. His complexion was so dark as to approach a swarthy hue. His features were finely acquiline, and his large dark eyes beamed with the fire of intelligence. Sometimes there was in them a strangeness of expression terrible to look upon, while ere it could be commented on by those who observed it, passed away, instantly followed by the sweetest smile human lips ever wore. With the early history of Don Antonio, none were acquainted. He had come to New-Orleans on a Christmas eve, eight years before, a traveller and as the heir of a noble Cuban family. After a sojourn of a few weeks, he gave out that he had become so much pleased with the city as to determine to abide there permanently. His lodgings were magnificently furnished, and in his horses and equipage, he rivalled the wealthiest Creoles. He soon found friends, and the halls of the oldest and best families of the land were thrown open to him. He was admired for his wit, accomplishments, and manly graces, and every where courted for his wealth. Thus for seven years had Don Antonio lived among the hospitable and refined Orleanois. During all this while it was remarked that he never had drank wine nor spoken to a woman—though the loveliest in the world were alluring him with their smiles. Between him and Henride Claviere, the bridegroom, there had existed a long and close intimacy. He had now been invited to wait on him as a groomsman, but had singularly and strangely to his friend, declined, saying he could be present only as a guest.

"Listen, signor," he said, in an impressive manner, as his friends gathered around him, their curiosity aroused by the tone and emphasis of his words. "It is twenty-one minutes yet to midnight! There will be full time 'till twelve for me to speak. Patience, Henride! thy bride hath not been gone ten minutes and thou must wait for the cathedral bell to toll midnight ere thou leave us."

"The Cathedral bell! It was never heard this distance," exclaimed several.

"It will be heard here to-night, as if swinging within the dome of this hall," he answered, in a deep voice that with his words made each heart weigh heavier in the bosom against which it audibly throbbed. "Yonder mansion, my friends, was built by a Castilian noble, in whose veins flowed the best blood of Spain. His wealth was inexhaustible. He possessed also boundless ambition, and never did human life stand between him and his object. His passions were evil and indulged at any sacrifice. He lived solitary in a lonely castle amid the most fertile and lovely region of Castile. There he associated only with his gold, which he kept in coffers in his vaults, and with his horse and black hounds, with which he used to hunt every Christmas eve, from sunset to sunrise, in company, it is said, with the free spirits of the air, with whom, riding like the wind, they traversed the kingdom in its breadth and length ere the dawn. And what think you he hunted, my friends? A Castilian maid who should be both *perfectly beautiful* and *perfectly blind!*—for there is a tradition in Spain, that such a maiden shall become the mother of an Emperor who shall unite all the kingdoms of Europe into one Empire. But it was not for this he would possess this blind beauty. He was in person the ugliest and most hideous man in all Spain. Men looked upon him with disgust and women with fear. He wanted a wife and forsooth, one that was beautiful too, for next to his money and hounds he admired women. But no female could be found to marry him, so hideous was his visage, for all the gold in his coffers. He had heard of this tradition, and the idea of having a bride who should be perfectly beautiful and yet be blind, was highly gratifying to his vanity, for he could feast upon her charms while she would be ignorant of his ugliness."

"And why should he seek her by night!" demanded Don Antonio's listeners.

"It is said he had a talisman purchased by a mint of golden zecchino of Pius VI., by which he would be guided to the abode of such a maiden, who could be borne off, says the tradition, only at the midnight hour and while buried in deep sleep.

"At length, one Christmas eve, when this Castilian noble was thirty years of age, he sallied forth with hound and horse and horn to seek the blind and beautiful maiden for his bride. It was a few minutes before midnight, that the priests who were chaunting prayers in a monastery in the Pyrenees valley, heard the unusual sound of huntsmen and the hoarse bay of hounds approaching in full cry. The sounds came nearer and nearer, and grew louder and yet louder, and all at once the wide doors of the chapel were burst open, and this young Castilian noble rode in at top speed, followed by his pack, and galloped straight towards the altar. The horror-stricken priests seized the golden crucifix that stood upon it and held it up between the sacred place and the intruders, whom they believed to be the spirit of the "Wicked Huntsman" of the Pyrenees, and no mortal man.

"Without heeding the priests or their crucifix, Don Rolando Osormo—for that was his name—leaped from his coal-black steed and passed through a small wicket that led into the cloisters of the nunnery. With a rapid step he traversed the corridor and stopped before a cell, the door of which was closed. It flew open at his touch. On a low couch, her features faintly visible by a lamp burning beside it, slept a nun of the most perfect symmetry of limbs and features. Don Rolando knelt beside her and lifted the lamp so as to obtain a more perfect view of her face. It was transcendantly lovely. He smiled with satisfaction, and lifting her in his arms, bore her forth into the corridor."

"How knew he that a maiden slept there?" asked one of the group.

"By the talisman on his whip, it is said."

"What was that, Don Antonio?"

"A lock of the Virgin Mary's hair braided in the snapper, says the legend. The pliant lash would straighten and point forward as he held it in his hand in the direction he should proceed. Its touch opened all barriers, and gave him ingress to the inmost closet of castle or cot. But the impious noble was soon to learn that he could not enter, even with such a talisman, a consecrated temple and bear off with impunity a bride of the church. His punishment, though long deferred, came. He returned into the chapel with his prize ere the terrified monks had recovered from their astonishment. Leaping upon his steed and followed by his hounds, he spurred down the echoing aisles again, and left the convent as the bell tolled midnight, the noise of his riding and the bay of his hounds breaking far and wide upon the stillness of the night, as he coursed homeward down the valley.

"Don Rolando soon reached his castle and laid his intended bride upon a gorgeous couch. Then sending for musicians, he placed them in a concealed alcove and bade them play the softest strains 'till she awoke."

"How was he certain that she was blind as well as beautiful, Don Antonio?" asked one of the group.

"He believed in the faithfulness of his talisman."

"And how could she be beautiful if she were blind, Don

Antonio?" asked Eugene Brissot. "Methinks a lady's beauty lieth mostly in her eye."

"The tradition saith that the maiden in question is to be *perfectly beautiful* still *perfectly blind*. She must have, therefore, perfect eyes to the observer though useless to herself as instruments of vision."

"Poor lady," sighed the young cavalier.

"I prythee proceed with thy story, Signor Antonio," said the impatient bridegroom.

"It indeed becomes me to hasten, for the midnight hour is near at hand. Don Rolando having arrayed himself magnificently and perfumed himself with the costliest essences of Persia, stood concealed behind the curtains of her couch to witness her awaking. At length the music stole into her senses, and slowly she began to open her eyes and throw off the deep sleep that had weighed upon the fringed lids. Don Rolando watched her with the most intense interest. He trembled lest he should have been deceived—for, already he passionately loved her. She rose in her couch and gazed around. Her eyes were blue as heaven, large, liquid and full of love and feeling. But whether they had vision he was unable to determine. He was about to show himself to make the trial, but restrained the impulse and remained still concealed, feeling assured that a few moments would decide it. She looked around her upon the damask hangings that on all sides enveloped her couch, but there was no individual object about her to arrest and fix the eye. She now threw back her golden hair from her forehead, as if perfectly awake, and gazed around with intelligent surprize, too visibly depicted on her features and in the enlargement of her dilating eye to be mistaken. Don Rolando's heart began to sink within him. She looked each moment more bewildered and alarmed.

" 'Holy Virgin, where am I?' she cried at length, in a voice which alarm had made most sweetly touching. 'These silken hangings—this heavenly music—this gorgeous chamber—'

for she had now put aside the curtains. 'Whither have I been borne in my sleep? It were heaven did not yonder lattice with a view of the distant stars through, tell me I am yet on earth.'

" 'She *sees*, and the talisman has played me false! Accursed be it and the head it grew upon!' muttered Don Rolando through his clenched teeth.

"He was about to rush forward and bury his dagger in her heart, for his vanity and pride would not allow him to permit her to see his features, inasmuch as he already loved her, and the thought of seeing her shudder at their ugliness was madness to him. He had rather slay her with his own hand. This he was about to do, when suddenly his arm was arrested by a light touch. He turned and beheld a low black figure, with a body no higher than his knees, with a prodigious head, in the brow of which was set a single eye of green flame like a shining emerald, and with hands and arms of supernatural length.

" 'Avaunt, fiend!' he cried, starting back with horror and affright.

" 'Fear me not, Don Rolando,' said the dwarf in a hoarse low tone. 'I know thy disappointment, ha, ha, ha! She has eyes brighter than stars.'

" 'By heaven she hath! How know you my thoughts and purposes?' demanded he with surprize.

" 'It matters not. I can aid thy purpose!'

" 'How?'

" 'Destroy her vision!'

" '*Thou*, hell-hound! would'st thou mar such glorious beauty? She shall die first by my own hand.'

" 'I will not mar it. I will take away her sight nor lay hand upon her.'

" 'Give me proof of it and thou shalt attempt it. I would give half my wealth could it be so. Give me proof.'

"The demon-dwarf fixed upon him his single eye for an instant with such a steady gaze, that Don Rolando's eyes were irresistibly riveted upon it as if fascinated. In vain he tried to take them off. They were no longer subservient to his will. The demon's eye grew larger and larger, brighter and brighter each moment, 'till the light of it became painfully intense, and seemed to Don Rolando's eyes to fill the whole space before him and to pervade the whole room. By degrees it then faded away, lessening and growing dimmer and dimmer until it left the place to his vision dark as midnight.

" 'Where art thou, fiend, that thou hast charmed me thus and left me in darkness?'

" 'Ha, ha, ha! Don Rolando, dost thou find thyself in darkness?' said the dwarf, speaking from the self same spot where Don Rolando had last seen him.

" 'Art thou here, demon? Who hath extinguished the lights?'

" 'No lights are extinguished, Don Rolando. The darkness is in thine own vision. Thou art stone blind.'

" 'Thou liest. Ho, lights, lights, knaves! bring lights!'

" 'Thou mayest call for lights 'till they rival in brightness the sun, and thou shalt not see their brilliancy.'

" 'Fiend, hast thou done this?'

" 'With a single glance of my eye. I have given thee but the proof thou didst seek. Look upon me once more.'

" 'I see thee not.'

" 'Be patient and I will restore thy vision.' The demon then placed a finger upon each eyelid of Don Rolando, and pressing upon them asked him if he saw two golden rings.

" 'I do,' answered Don Rolando.

" 'Fix thy inward gaze upon them as steadily as but now you fixed your external gaze upon my eye.'

"Don Rolando with an effort did so and by degrees the golden rings enlarged until he seemed to be in a universe of roseate light. The dwarf then removed his fingers and he opened his eyes. All around him then seemed an atmosphere of pale light but no object was visible. Gradually the light assumed a delicate blue shade, and then a green color, and seemed to gather itself into a circle opposite to him. This circle gradually lessened in size and increased in brilliancy. He kept his eyes steadily upon it as if by a supernatural energy, until it diminished to a small orb. That orb was the *dwarf's eye*, whom he now beheld standing in his presence as before.

"'It is enough! Thou shalt make use of thy power,' said Don Rolando. 'She is on yonder couch.'

"'The terms are the souls of the children she may bring thee,' said the dwarf, without moving.

"Don Rolando started. He saw that his visitor was resolute. 'It is but a contingency at the best,' thought he. 'I consent,' he said hesitatingly.

"'Lay thy thumb and forefinger upon my eyelid and it shall be thy oath,' said the demon.

"Don Rolando did so. The dwarf then placed himself at the foot of the couch in shadow, so that his bright green eye alone was visible from it. It instantly arrested the maiden's eyes and her glance was fascinated. In a few moments her vision was for ever darkened.

"The demon departed as suddenly as he had appeared, and Don Rolando stood by the couch of the blind maiden. He watched her motions. Her gaze was vacant and her hands moved like one who is in the dark.

"'Alas, alas! whither am I borne? To what fate am I doomed? A moment since all was bright and gorgeous, and now all is dark as midnight. *Ay de mi!* Hapless vestal!'

"'Nay, sweet lady,' said Don Rolando, in a gentle tone, for though his visage was hideous his voice was soft and harmonious; 'you are brought from the damp cells of a cloister to the halls of luxury and affluence—to a noble castle that waits to hail you as its mistress, and to a true knight's home, who is ready to lay his heart and honor at your feet.'

"Thus and in like manner spoke Don Rolando. His soothing voice and tender speech at length won her ear, and she listened to him with pleasure. But the story of his wooing and nuptials, and of her submission to her blindness, for which she could not account, and which, be it mentioned here, did nothing mar her beauty, must be passed over. Years rolled by and Don Rolando had become the father of seven beautiful daughters, every one of whom had been born on a Christmas eve. He loved his lovely and sightless wife each succeeding year more and more. Blessings seemed to flow in upon him on every side. The only desire he now had, to complete his happiness, was for a son, that he might have him heir to his name and vast estates. But this wish he was never destined to see fulfilled.

"At length his eldest daughter reached her eighteenth year, and a neighboring young noble who had won her heart was to lead her to the altar on her birth-day eve. The bridal party were assembled, the rites were performed, and the hours of festivity flew on with joy and hope. The bride, who was scarcely less lovely than Henride's, was in the midst of a waltz, when the castle clock tolled twelve. Ere the last stroke had ceased vibrating upon the ears of the banqueters, there entered the hall a tall dark stranger, in a green velvet dress richly studded with emeralds. In his bonnet was a sable plume fastened by an emerald that glowed like fire, and at his belt was a hunting horn. His aspect was noble and his face intellectual. His entrance drew nearly all eyes upon him. But there was something about him that made Don Rolando's heart shrink with ominous foreboding. He strode across the hall to the spot where Don Rolando was seated, and said in a low tone—

" 'Don Rolando, I have come for thy daughter.'

"Don Rolando started back and looked him in the face for an instant, and then with a shriek fell backward in the arms of his attendants.

"Leaving him, the stranger then approached the bride as she yet circled in the waltz, for while in its giddy mazes she had not yet noticed his entrance. He stood near her and sought to catch her eye. He succeeded! Instantly she stopped as if paralyzed, and then, without turning her glance aside from his steady gaze, approached him. He receded from her as she did so, still keeping upon her his riveted gaze, which seemed to fascinate her like a serpent's, for as he moved across the hall she followed him as if irresistibly drawn along solely by the power of his eye. He now took his way through the hall in the direction of the outer gate of the castle, steadily looking back towards her over his shoulder, while like a hound she continued to follow, step for step. All arrayed in her bridal robes and sparkling with jewels, with a face like death's and eyes supernaturally dilated, she went on after him, looking neither to the right nor to the left. Poor maiden—without once removing his glance from her terrified eyes, the stranger passed out of the hall, descended the marble steps to the court below and crossed the court to the outer gate; and through hall, corridor, and court-yard, the charmed bride followed him, keeping the same distance behind until she disappeared after him through the portal. Of the guests all were at first paralyzed, and followed them at a distance, the boldest, nor even the bridegroom himself, having power to attempt her rescue. Slowly behind her they followed, with silent amazement and horror, 'till the ill-fated bride had disappeared through the gate when the spell that seemed to have bound all present was broken.

"'Ho! cavaliers and gentlemen! To the rescue!' was the universal cry.

"Ere they reached the gate they heard the receding foot-steps of a horseman and the full cry of hounds as if a huntsman was scouring the country at the head of his pack. The sounds soon died away in a distant glen, and from that night forward nothing was ever heard of the bride that had been so strangely charmed away.

"The next day Don Rolando, who alone could unravel this mystery, sent ten thousand golden pistoles to the convent from whence he had abducted his wife nineteen years before, praying that masses might be nightly offered for his daughter's soul.

"Two years elapsed, and time, which heals all things, had in some degree thrown over this event its oblivious veil, when the second daughter, not less lovely than the eldest, attained her eighteenth year, and on her birth-night was led to the altar by a noble Arragonese cavalier. As before it was a night of mirth and festivity. Alas, for it! When the clock struck twelve, the bride was just entering her bridal chamber. On the threshold she looked back to receive Don Rolando's blessing when her eye encountered the fixed glance of the swart stranger. With a shudder she turned back from the very threshold of the bridal chamber and followed him at a short distance behind, through hall, court and corridor, to the outer gate of the castle. Again were heard, a moment afterwards, the huntsman and his hounds coursing up the glen, again the cavaliers present, 'till now spell bound, rushed forth to the rescue. But never from that time forward was there intelligence of the fate of the second daughter of Don Rolando Osormo.

"By a strange fatality the bridal night was always on the birthday night, which happened ever on Christmas eve, the anniversary of the night on which Don Rolando committed the sacrilege of abducting the novice."

"Doubtless Holy Church had something to do with his terrible punishment in the loss of his daughters," said Eugene Brissot.

Don Antonio Baradas smiled coldly and significantly and without replying continued—

"That these nupitals should be suffered to take place a second and a third time, after such a horrible consummation of them, is no less strange, than that the parties should be so little affected by circumstances that ought to have made a lasting impression on every mind. It would seem that Don Rolando and his friends and his daughters' wooers, were, one and all afflicted with a judicial blindness. A third, a fourth, and a fifth bridal took place, with two years interval between each, with precisely the same results—the nightly appearance, at the

stroke of twelve, of the dark stranger—the fascination of the
bride—her submissive following, and disappearance, with the
retiring sound of horse and hounds winding up the glen. What
is most remarkable connected with this affair, was, that at each
visit of the dark stranger, the sightless mother recovered her
vision during the time he was present, but immediately lost it
on his departure. At the loss of her fifth daughter she died of a
broken heart for her bereavements.

"At length Don Rolando roused himself at this series of
judgments, and resolved to avert the fate of his two remaining
daughters, one of whom was sixteen and the other and youngest of all but six years of age. For this purpose he secretly left
his castle and his native land, and came hither, as if the wide sea
were a wall between justice and the adjudged. He built yonder
solitary and gloomy mansion, and defended its portals with
iron gates. He consecrated every stone with holy water, and
in every threshold sunk a silver cross. The two years elapsed
as before, and strange infatuation, he suffered his daughter
to be led to the altar on her eighteenth birthday. A wealthy
and high-born young Creole had wooed and won her. Don
Rolando gave his consent, believing the power he dreaded
would not reach him here. He wished too, with a resistless
curiosity, to relieve his mind by the trial. He incurred the risk,
and *sacrificed his daughter!*"

"Did the green stranger appear?" asked every voice.

"True to the hour and stroke of midnight. The bride followed him from the drawing rooms and across the lawn, and
a moment afterwards the sound of horse and horn resounded
along the winding shore 'till lost in the dark cypress forests to
the south. The guests fled from the fatal halls in terror. But
none could afterwards tell the tale or describe the scene. A spell
seemed to have been laid upon their memories. All was confused and indistinct when they would recall it, but the impression of a supernatural presence there on that night remained
uneffaced. From that time the 'Haunted Villa' became the

scene of mysteries no man could unravel. The morning after
this supernatural event, M. Vergniaud, at present our noble
host, was surprized at the entrance of Don Rolando leading in his youthful daughter, a beautiful child in her eighth
year. To him Don Rolando consigned her, after telling him
the strange story you have heard me relate. With him he left
keys to coffers of gold in the vaults of his mansion, and then
blessing his daughter, took his leave of her for ever! He is now,
as a rigid and holy monk, doing penance day and night in the
monastery which he had so sacriligiously violated. Where is
M. Vergniaud? Methinks I have not seen him present among
you."

A low groan now arrested every ear. A figure lay upon the
ground in a kneeling posture—it was M. Vergniaud. He had
fainted there at the first sight of the spectacle the Haunted
Villa had presented. Ephèse had been to him as an own child.
He felt that the curse had not departed from her race, and had
fallen forward insensible, with a cry for mercy, mercy! for her
on his lips. They lifted him up and laid him upon an ottoman.
Those who assisted him were scarce more alive than himself.
Don Antonio's tale had filled the soul of every one that listened to it with horror. Henride Claviere, the bridegroom,
stood before Don Antonio like a statue of stone, and all eyes
were fixed upon the young Spaniard in silence. They expected
something, they knew not what—but something that would
harrow their senses and chill their blood. The connection of
the fearful tale with the bride, was too plain to be mistaken.

"Let us save her or die with her, good Don Antonio," cried
Eugene Brissot.

"Hark! it is twelve o'clock!" they cried, in the deep voice of
fearful expectation.

"It is the Cathedral bell! The saints preserve us!" fell from
every pallid lip.

At the last stroke Don Antonio cast aside his silken cloak
from his tall figure and stood before them the Green Huntsman

—the Swart Stranger of his tale. Without a word he left them, and entering the drawing room from the verandah, crossed it to the door through which Ephèse had gone with her bridesmaids. It opened ere he touched it. Passing on he traversed a suite of lighted rooms until he came to the door of the nuptial chamber. Disrobed of her rich bridal attire, Ephèse was standing among her bridesmaids in a *robe de chambre* and cap of snowy white, that made her look, if possible, still more lovely than ever. The door swung open and Don Antonio instantly fixed his eye upon hers and turned to leave the chamber. She clasped her hands together in agony, as if instinctively she knew her fate, and followed him. He did not keep his eyes upon her constantly, but strode forward without looking behind, as if satisfied she followed. Twice she stopped and stood still, wringing her hands supplicatingly. He had only to glance back over his shoulder, at such times, and she came crouching along close to his feet. Thus he led the ill-fated bride into the hall and forth upon the verandah. Here stood Henride—here stood Eugene Brissot and their friends. They beheld him advancing and saw him pass by close to the spot where they stood. They saw— oh, horror! oh, Heavenly pity! they saw too, the poor Ephèse following him—now stopping and wringing her snowy hands as he took his eyes from her, now as he turned and fixed them upon hers crouching and moving on mournfully in his fatal footsteps. Yet they could move neither hand nor foot to save her. Henride's eyes followed his bride with a glassy stare, and the brave Eugene Brissot seemed divested of every vital function and sense save the single sense of horror. Thrice she tried to turn and look upon her husband, but each time his eye arrested the movement of her head and drew her still on after him. From the verandah they traversed the lawn, reached the gate and passed through it. The next moment was heard the galloping of horse, the sound of hounds, and those on the verandah distinctly beheld the Green Huntsman riding like the wind in the direction of the Haunted Villa, bearing before him in his saddle the hapless victim bride. As he rode they saw his form change, (for he seemed to emit a horrid shining light that exhibited him as plainly as noon day to their vision) and assume the form of a hideous dwarf. On rode the demon and his victim, and on followed the pack of black hounds, baying in full cry. All at once the Haunted Villa became illuminated as before, with a red glare through window, portal and crevice, while again the writhing tongue of green flame lapped the air and shed a baleful light a league around.

The demon with his victim borne before him and followed by his whole sable pack, now turned into the lawn and rode towards the infernal mansion, at the wildest speed. Without pausing they all, rider, victim, horse and hound, dashed through the yawning portal and leaped into the midst of the glowing furnace. Shrieks and yells most piercing and appalling rent the air; the flames were suddenly extinguished, and in an instant darkness and terrible gloom shrouded the spot where a moment before seemed to yawn the sulphurous mouth of hell.

Such is the legend of the "Haunted Villa;" and such is the penalty of a parent's crime, which sooner or later Heaven will punish, even to making wicked spirits the instruments of its just vengeance. This will be more apparent when the end of the wicked Don Rolando is seen, which will be narrated in a subsequent legend.

Bill Bramble

Burt Pringle and the "Bellesnickle"

European traditions had various punitive companions to Santa Claus, most of which did not seem to travel to the United States before or during the Victorian era. One exception was Belsnickel, who remained part of celebrations by the "Pennsylvania Dutch" (i.e. Deutsch) from Germany's Rhineland. In appearance, Belsnickel is something like a rustic Santa but sometimes incorporating traits more closely related to Krampus. Descriptions of the tradition are not uncommon in English, but stories featuring him are. "Bill Bramble" wrote poetry and short fiction for the Syracuse, New York newspapers the Star *and the* Republican *in the mid-1850s, occasionally reprinted by other papers. The following piece originally appeared in the* Syracuse Republican *on November 11, 1853.*

A s THE HOLIDAYS ARE COMING ON, and election is fairly over, the following anecdote may not be uninteresting to many of the readers of the [Syracuse] Republican. But before I go any farther let me explain to those who are unacquainted with the word, the meaning of "Bellesnickle." As to its origin or derivation I have little to say. I know not whether it be Hog Latin or Lop-eared Dutch—perhaps a mixture of both—but this I do know: that it is used in the Pennsylvania German dialect to designate a very singular sort of a being: a great terror to "bad children," and consequently a terror to all.—He is a kind of a Dutch Santa Claus but with this difference: Santa Claus is said to ride in a beautiful cutter drawn by reindeers,

40

while Bellesnickle crams his pants in his boot-tops and jour-
neys on foot; Santa Claus is said to make his entry by the chimney flue, and chooses the hour of midnight when everyone
is soundly sleeping, for his visits, while Bellesnickle comes
boldly in at the door, and is never later than nine; Santa Claus
distributes his gifts according to age and merit, placing them in
stockings which are hung up for that purpose; to the good, his
gifts are appropriate, but sometimes the significant apparition
of a rawhide peering from their pendant hosiery will strike
terror into the hearts of "little disobedients;" but Bellesnickle
seldom brings gifts but never fails to find a pretext for rigor-
ously dusting the jackets of every "young one" he can lay his
hands on, but they also have the right to defend themselves
against his merciless castigations in any manner they may deem
expedient. As the children of neighboring families generally
congregate together on such occasions it not unfrequently
happens that Bellesnickle's visit is attended with some rare and
exciting sport, for sometimes one or two of the party will "get
their Dutch up" and a regular rough and tumble will ensue frequently to the entire discomfiture of poor Bellesnickle, often
obliging him to make his exit rather hastily and sometimes
minus a horn or a portion of his ghostly attire.

It is circumstance something similar to this of which I am
about to speak and of which I was an eye witness.

In the little village of Wadsworth in Medina County, Ohio,
there resided an honest, good hearted Pennsylvania Dutchman
by the name of Peters—Daniel Peters. He was a tanner by
trade but also owned and worked a large farm. Peters had in his
employ an apprentice whose parents, while living, had resided
at Akron, a large and flourishing village some twelve or fifteen miles from Wadsworth, and the county seat of Summit
County; but they died and he was thrown upon the world,
an orphan. But he was no drone, he had been taught to labor
and he would not sit despondingly down now. The world was
before him and he felt certain that where there was a will there

was a way. So he gathered together all he owned in the world, which was but a small bundle at best, and praying Heaven to direct his steps, he set out, he knew not whither. But by good luck or a kind intervention of Providence, whichever you choose to call it, he had not proceeded far when he was overtaken by this Peters who it seems had been to Akron with a load of grain and was returning home. He invited the boy to ride and as they journied along the young man informed Peters of his circumstances and told him that his name was Burt Pringle. Peters agreed to take him home and if he wished, he would learn him the tanning trade; so Burt became his apprentice.

The village of Wadsworth, where Peters resided, was settled almost entirely by Pennsylvania Dutchmen, who, though they are an honest, and kind hearted people, are dreadfully ignorant and superstitious. Their children were frightened into obedience by stories of "spooks," ghosts and goblins, or threats that the next Bellesnickle that came should carry them off.—Even the venerable Peters himself was tainted with this disease and would tell of many a horrid night, when things strange and unaccountable had happened and no consideration whatever could induce him to forego the observance of "signs." But Burt was a philosopher. There was no superstition about him.—He was a regular harum scarum, devil may care sort of a boy, and for the matter of fear, he would as soon sleep in a graveyard as in his bed.

Christmas was drawing near and Burt was often reminded by the neighbor's boys in the settlement that when a newcomer appeared among them he was sure to get "broken in;" and consequently he might expect that Bellesnickle would give him a regular walloping on that occasion. But Burt kept his own counsel and only occasionally muttered to himself "just let old Bellesnickle wallop if he wants to, and see who'll get broken in, that's all. These boys here are regular thick heads; they believe, and try to make me believe that this Bellesnickle is a ghost. Ghost!—humph! just let him lay his finger on me and see how quick I'll take his ghostliness out of him. They can't fool me. I know all about that great pair of horns and that whopping big cow hide they hid upstairs in that pile of hair, and didn't I hear Jake Burkman last night telling Peters that it was all right, that Phoebe Stoffer had agreed to make him a dough face and that he had some red ink at home that he could make himself look as if his throat was cut? and didn't I pry a clapboard off of the old mill last Sunday and ketch him practicing, with Stoffer's big chain tied to his leg? Now Jake is a darned clever feller and I like him first rate, but if he goes to playing up ghost and tries to maul me with that big gad he's hung up in the mill, I'm a-thinking he'll wish he *was* a ghost, before he gets through with me. Ghosts! ha! ha! I wonder if ghosts can swim?"

The day before Christmas at last arrived and Peters loaded his wagon with grain and leaving Burt to take care of the children and everything else in general, went with his wife to Akron to make their usual Christmas purchases. Nearly all day Burt was busily occupied in the tan yard. There was an old vat in the middle of the yard that had long before been condemned and filled up with tan. This tan Burt had removed and had pumped the vat full of water, after accomplishing which he spread some hide over the top of it and slightly covered the whole with tan. He then distributed the remainder of the tan which he had taken from the vat, evenly about the yard, causing it to present the same appearance as it did before he had touched it.

"There," said he, as he gave it the finishing touch, "now let him wallop, and see who'll get broke in!"

Just at dusk, Peters came home and Burt was called to put out the team, which duty he performed and then got out the old lap stone and hammer and while supper was cooking he and Peters cracked nuts and talked over the adventures of the day and speculated upon the probability of a visit from the Bellesnickle.

"Now what sort of a looking critter is he, any how?" asked Burt.

"Well Burty, I don't know as I could tell you exactly, but I suppose he'll have great horns, and perhaps be covered with hair like an ox, and they generally go about with chains tied to their feet and their throats cut."

"Can they swim?" asked Burt with a singular expression of countenance.

"Swim!" echoed old Peters in astonishment, "why no! spooks don't swim!"

"*Don't* they, well I think they'd better learn then," said Burt.

"Why what do you mean, Burt?"

"Nothing, only I was thinking the Bellesnickle might take it into his head to cross the pond and you know the ice is very thin."

"Oh, he couldn't break through if it was ever so thin. Spooks ain't like other folks."

"Glad to hear it said," said Burt, "but let's drop the subject and go to supper."

After supper the neighbors' boys began to gather in and among them came George Burkman, a brother of Jake's.

Burt's quick eye soon informed him that Jake was not with them and therefore might soon be expected in the capacity of Bellesnickle. But to be certain, he asked George where Jake was, and why he did not come over with the rest of them?

"He said he did not feel well enough to get out to-night," was the reply.

"He feels just well enough to get *in*, then," thought Burt.

"But I say, Burt," continued George, "if the Bellesnickle comes are you going to show fight or take your thrashing quietly?"

"Neither," said Burt.

"How are you going to get around it?" asked George somewhat puzzled.

"I shall run!" said Burt.

"Run!" echoed George. "Why Burt, that's cowardly; besides it won't do you any good, for he will certainly chase you."

"Do you think so? How far do you suppose he will chase me?"

"He would chase you to Texas and back but what he would catch you," said George.

"Well, now, I'll bet he gives up the race before we get half way across the tan yard," said Burt.

"My knife against yours that he won't," said George.

"Done!" said Burt.

The stakes were put in Peters' hands, who evidently began to smell a mice, for he nudged Burt in the ribs and whispered with a wink, "ah, Burty, you rogue, what you been up to?"

"Up to!" echoed Burt, "why, just what your Bellesnickle will soon be *in to!*"

Just then the rattle of a chain was heard on the porch and a general stampede was made by the timid portion of the assembly. Some dodged under the table and some under the beds; others crawled into the corners, each one endeavoring to get behind his neighbor. Burt sat alone unnerved. The apparition advanced towards him and raised its huge baton to strike, but Burt slipped out of its way and sprang out of the door calling on George to follow, if he wished to see who won.

On went Burt and the Bellesnickle followed close in his wake, and George, old Peters and all the rest came tearing along in the rear. But now Burt has reached the tan yard and the Bellesnickle————

"Ha! ha! ha!" Hear Burt laugh! "Ha! ha! ha! the Bellesnickle has tumbled into the old vat. Ah! ha! Jake, who's broke in now?—" asked Burt tauntingly. Jake has forgiven but never can forget Burt.

Anonymous

Worse Than a Ghost Story

This anonymous tale was apparently originally published in the
Grand Rapids Enquirer *around Christmas 1856, but both
the Public Library and Museum there lack issues for the entire
winter of '56-57. It was reprinted in the* Cleveland Plain
Dealer *of January 17, 1857, where it was titled "A Tale of
Horror and Facts: A New Phase of Spiritualism," and reprinted
again under the more compelling title used here, in the December 25, 1858 issue of the* Evansville Daily Journal *in Indiana.
Part of a tradition of stories where an editor or narrator provides
assurances to the reader of the authenticity of the story, with
its purported reproduction of notarized statements it goes to an
extreme not often seen elsewhere.*

A Most Wonderful Narrative.

Strange Development of Spiritualism.

The Dead Rising from the Grave.

WE HAVE RECEIVED THE FOLLOWING LETTER from Dr.
John Moreton, a gentleman of veracity and profes-
sional understanding. We think its perusal will convince every
one of our readers of the entire truth of all that is said about
Modern Spiritualism.

GRAND TRAVERSE, Michigan,

May 24, 1858.

EDITORS: I send you the following account of a most

extraordinary event or transaction—or what you will—
because, in my opinion, it ought not to be suppressed, but,
on the contrary, thoroughly investigated. In the midst of the
excitement here, such a thing as calm and unbiased examination is altogether out of the question; nor would it be safe to
attempt it, in as much as the determination of the people is
strongly to "hush up." As I myself am one of the chief characters concerned in the affair, I dare not attempt, if I possessed
the ability, to determine the character of what I am about to
relate.

I left Cleveland to establish myself here, as you will remember, some time last June—a young and inexperienced physician. Almost the first patient I was called to see was a Mrs.
Hayden—a woman thirty-five years of age, a strong constitu-
tion, and a well-balanced mind (apparently), and (apparently)
with little or no imagination. She was, however, a "spiritual-
ist," with the reputation of being a superior "medium." Her
usual physician, Dr. J. N. Williams, was absent—hence her
application to me. I found her laboring under a severe attack
of typhus fever, which threatened to prove fatal. Having prescribed for her, I left, promising to send Dr. W. as soon as he
returned.

This was on Saturday morning. At night Dr. W. took the
patient off my hands, and I did not see her again until Friday
evening of the ensuing week. I then found her dying, and
remained with her until her decease, which took place precisely at midnight. She was, or appeared to be, rational during
the whole of my visit, though I was informed that she had
been delirious the greater part of the week. There was nothing
remarkable about her symptoms; I should say the disease had
taken its natural course.

At the time of her decease there were in the room besides
myself, her husband, Mrs. Green (her sister), and Mrs. Miles
(a neighbor). Her husband, whom I particularly noticed, was
very thin and weak, then suffering from a quick consumption,

already beyond recovery. He bore the character of a clear minded, very firm, illiterate but courteous man, and a most strenuous unbeliever in spiritualism.

There had been some subdued conversation, such as is natural in such scenes, the patient taking no part in it except to signify, in a faint and gradually diminishing voice, her wants, until about an hour before her death, when a sudden and indescribable change came over her features, voice and whole appearance—a change which her husband noticed by saying, with, as I thought, wholly unwarranted bitterness:

"There goes those cursed spirits again."

The patient hereupon unclosed her eyes, and fixed a look of unutterable emotion upon her husband—a look so direct, searching and unwavering that I was not a little startled at it. Mr. Hayden met it with something like an unhappy defiance, and finally asked of his wife what she wanted. She immediately replied, in a voice of perfect health, "you know."

I was literally astonished at the words and the voice in which they were uttered.

I have often read and heard of a return of volume and power of voice just preceding dissolution; but the voice of the patient had none of the natural intonation of such—it was, as I have said, perfectly healthy. In a few moments she continued in the same voice, and with her eyes still fixed upon her husband:

"William, in your secret soul, do you believe?"

"Wife," was the imploring reply, "that is the devil which has stood between us and Heaven for so many months. We are both at the very verge of the grave, and in God's name let him be buried first."

Apparently without hearing or heeding him she repeated her words:

"You dare not disbelieve."

"I do," he replied, excited by her manner, "while you are dying—nay, if you were dead, and should speak to me, I dare not believe."

"Then," she said, "I will speak to you when I am dead! I will come to you at your latest hour, and with a voice from the grave I will warn you of your time to follow me!"

"But I shall not believe a spirit."

"I will come in the body, and speak to you; remember!"

She then closed her eyes and straightway sank into her former state.

In a few moments—as soon as we had somewhat recovered from the shock of this most extraordinary scene—her two children were brought into the room to receive her dying blessing. She partially roused herself, and placing a hand on the head of each, she put a faint prayer to the throne of grace, faint in voice, indeed, but a prayer in which all the strength of her great unpolished soul, heart and mind was exerted to its utmost dying limit—such a prayer as a seraph might attempt, but none but a dying wife and mother could accomplish. From that moment her breathing grew rapidly weaker and more difficult; and at 12 o'clock she expired, apparently without a struggle.

I closed her eyes, straightened and composed her limbs, and was about to leave the house, when Mrs. Green requested me to send over two young ladies from my boarding house to watch with the dead. All this occupied some ten minutes.

Suddenly Mrs. Miles screamed, and Mr. Hayden started up from the bedside where he had been sitting.

The supposed corpse was sitting erect in the bed, and struggling to speak. Her eyes were still closed; and, save her open mouth and quivering tongue, there were all the looks of death in her face. With a great heave of the chest, at last the single word came forth:

"Remember!"

Her jaw fell back to its place, and she again lay down as before. I now examined her minutely. That she was dead there could be no further possible shadow of a doubt; and so I left the house.

On the following day Dr. Williams made a careful and minute post mortem examination of the body. I was prevented by business from attending, but I was informed by the doctor that he found the brain but slightly affected—an unusual fact in persons dying of typhus fever—but her lungs were torn and rent extensively, as if by a sudden, single and powerful effort, and suffused partially with coagulated blood. These were all the noticeable features of the case. She was buried on the afternoon of the same day.

★ ★ ★

About two weeks after the death of his wife I was called to visit Mr. Hayden. On my way I met Dr. Williams and told him my errand, expressing some surprise at the preference of the family for myself, as I knew him to be a safe and experienced practitioner. He replied that nothing could induce him to enter that house. He had "seen things that—well, I would find out when I got there."

I was considerably amused by the Doctor's manner and warmth, and beguiled my way by fancying what had alarmed him, a physician, from his duty.

On my arrival I found no person present with the patient except Mrs. Green, who informed me that the spirits had been playing such pranks that not a soul, Dr. W. included, could be induced to remain. The children had been gone for some time; they were at her house.

I found the patient very low, and with no prospect of surviving the attack. He was, however, quite free from pain, though very weak.

While I was in the house I noticed many manifestations of the presence of the power called spiritualism. Chairs and tables were moved and removed, billets of wood were thrown upon the fire, and doors opened and shut without any apparent agency. I heard struggles and unaccountable noises, too, and felt an unusual sensation, caused, no doubt, by the mysteries which surrounded and mocked me.

Noticing my manner, the patient observed:

"It is nothing. You must get used to it, doctor."

"I should not be content unless I could explain them, as well as become indifferent to them," I replied.

This opened the way to a long conversation, during which I probed my patient's mind to the bottom, but without detecting a shadow of belief. Speaking of his wife, he said:

"You heard Hellen promise to warn me of my time to die?"

"I did—but you do not believe her?"

"No. If it is possible, she will keep her word, in spite of heaven or hell. But it is simply impossible. She promised to come in the body and speak to me. I shall accept no other warning from her, save the literal meaning of her words."

"And what then?"

"How much of her body is there left, even now, doctor? and she has not come yet. She promised to come from the grave. Can she do it? No; it is all a humbug—a delusion. Poor Hellen! Thank God, doctor, the devilry which so haunted her life, and stood between her soul and mine, cannot reach her now."

"But if she should come? You may be deceived."

"I cannot. Others may see her, too, and hear her. I shall believe no spectre, if there are such things. Her body as it is, or will be, let that speak if it can!"

From that day up to the hour of his death I was with him almost constantly, and was daily introduced to some new and startling phenomenon. The neighbors had learned to shun the house, and even the vicinity, as they would the plague; and strange stories traveled from gossip to gossip, acquiring more of the marvelous at every repetition. Nevertheless, my practice increased.

On the morning of March 20th I called earlier than usual. During the visit the manifestations of a supernatural presence were more frequent, wild, and violent than ever before. I was informed that they had been exceedingly violent during the preceding night. Their character, too, had been greatly changed. Beside the moving of all movable articles, the tinkling of glasses, and the rattle of tin-ware, there were frequent and startling sounds, as of whispered conversation, singing, and subdued laughter—all perfect imitations of the human voice, but too low to enable me to detect the words used, if words they were. Still, however, none of these unusual sounds had entered the sick room. They followed the footsteps of Mrs. Green like a demon echo, but paused on the threshold of that room, as if debarred by a superior power from entering there.

I found Mr. Hayden was worse and sinking very fast. He had passed a bad night. Doubtful whether he would survive to see another morning, I left him, promising to call at evening and spend the night with him, resolved, in my secret thoughts, to be "in at the death." If there was to be a ghostly warning, I meant to hear it, and, if possible, to solve the strange enigma.

* * *

The day had been exceedingly cold and stormy, and the night had already set in, dark and dismal, with a fierce gale and a driving storm of rain and hail, when I again stood beside my patient. The moment I looked at him, I perceived unmistakable indications of the near approach of death upon his features. He was free from pain, his mind perfectly clear; but his life was ebbing away with every feeble breath, like the slow burning out of an exhausted lamp.

Meanwhile the storm rose to a tempest, and the gloom grew black as death in the wild night without. The wind swept in tremendous gusts through the adjoining forests, rattling the icy branches of the trees, and came wailing and shrieking through every crack and cranny of the building.

Within there was yet wilder commotion. All that had been said or sung, written or dreamed of ghostly visitations, was then and there enacted. There was the ringing of bells, moving of furniture, crash of dishes, whispers, howls, crying, laughter, whistling, heavy and light footsteps, and wild music, as if in very mockery of the infernal regions. All these sounds grew wilder with the rising gale, and toward midnight they were almost insufferable.

As for us three—the patient, Mrs. Green and myself—we were all as silent as death itself. Not a word passed our lips after 9 o'clock. As for the state of our minds, God only knows. Mine, in the wide world of thought and event which followed, forgot the past, save what I have recalled and penned, bit by bit, above. I remember only looking for the final catastrophe, which grew rapidly nearer, with a constant endeavor to concentrate all my faculties of mind and senses upon the phenomenon which I, at least, had begun to believe would herald the death of my patient.

As it grew closer upon 12 o'clock, (for upon the striking of that hour had my thoughts fixed themselves for the expected demonstration), my agitation became so great that it was with extreme difficulty I could control myself.

Nearer and nearer grew the fatal moment—for fatal I knew it would be, to the patient at least—and at last the seconds trembled on the brink of midnight; the clock began to strike —one—two—three! I counted the strokes of the hammer, which seemed as though they never would have done—ten —eleven—twelve! I drew my breath again. The last lingering echo of the final stroke had died away, and as yet there was no token of any presence save our own.

All was silent. The wind had lulled for a moment, and not a sound stirred the air within the house. The ghosts had fled.

I arose and approached the bedside. The patient was alive —drawing his breath very slowly—dying. The intervals between his gasps grew longer—then he ceased to breathe altogether—he was dead!

Mrs. Green was sitting in her place, her elbows resting on her knees, her face buried in her hands.

I closed the open mouth and pressed down the eyelids of the dead. Then I touched her on the shoulder.

"It is over," I whispered.

"Thank God!" was the fervent reply.

★ ★ ★ ★

Then we both started. There was a rustling of the bed-clothes! Mr. Hayden was sitting erect, his eyes wide open, his chest heaving in a mighty effort for one more inspiration of the blessed air. Before I could reach the bed he spoke:

"My God! she is coming!"

At the same instant the wind came back with a sudden and appalling gust and a wild shriek as it swept through the crevices of the building. There was a crash of the outer door—then a staggering and uncertain step in the outer room. It approached the sick-room—the latch lifted, the door swung open—and then—my God! what a spectacle!

I wonder, even now, that I dare describe it—think of it—remember it. I wonder I believed it then, or do now—that I did not go mad or drop down dead.

Through the open door there stepped a figure, not of Mrs. Hayden, not of her corpse, not of death, but a thousand times more horrible, a thing of corruption, decay, of worms and rottenness.

The features were nearly all gone, and the skull in places gleamed through, white and terrible. Her breast, abdomen and neck were eaten away, her limbs were putrid, green and inexpressibly loathsome.

And yet to those putrescent jaws there was born a voice—smothered, indeed, and strange, but distinct:

"Come William! they wait for you—I WAIT!"

I dared not turn my eyes from the intruder; I could not if I dared, though I heard a groan behind me and a fall.

Then it—the thing before me—sank down upon the floor in a heap, dark and loathsome—a heap of putrescence and dis-membered fragments.

I remember that I did not faint, that I did not cry out. How long I stood, transfixed, fascinated, I know not; but at last, with an effort and a prayer, I turned to the bed. Mr. Hayden had fallen upon the floor, face downward, stone dead.

I raised and replaced him; I composed his limbs, I closed his eyes, and tied up his chin; crossed his hands upon his breast and tied them there. Then I bore out the body of his sister, insensible, but not dead, into the pure air—out of that horror and stench into the storm and darkness—out of death into life again.

"County of Grand Traverse, Michigan, SS:

"Mrs. Joseph A. Green, being duly sworn, deposes and says, that the letter of Dr. John Morton, hereunto appended, which she has read, is strictly true, so far as it goes, though much of the history of what occurred at her brother's (the late Mr. Hayden) house is omitted.   MRS. JOSEPH A GREEN.

"Sworn to and subscribed before me, a Notary Public, in and for the County of Grand Traverse, and State of Michigan, on the 25th day of May, A. D. 1858.

"JAMES TAYLOR, N.P."

"County of Grand Traverse, Michigan, SS:

"James Hueson, being duly sworn, deposes and says that he, in company with George Green, Albert J. Baily and Henry K. Smead, on the 1st day of April last, in the afternoon of said day, did go to the house of William H. Hayden, then deceased, and that they found upon the floor of the room in which the body of the said deceased lay, and near the door of said room, the putrid remains of a human corpse—a female, as the deponent verily believes and avers; and that they carried away and buried the body of the said Hayden, deceased, and found the grave of the wife of said Hayden, deceased, in the month of August last, open at the head of said grave, and that said grave was empty, the body of the said wife of said Hayden, deceased, being gone from said grave; and that they returned to the said house wherein said Hayden died; and, after removing the furniture from said house, the deponent did, at the request of Mrs. Green, sister of said Hayden, deceased, and of Mr. Green, brother-in-law of said Hayden, deceased, set fire to said house, and that said house was thereby entirely consumed, with all that remained in said house, and burned to ashes. This I aver of my own knowledge."

"JAMES HUESON."

"We aver and solemnly swear that the above affidavit is strictly and solemnly true, of our own knowledge."

"H. K. SMEAD,
"GEORGE GREEN,
"A. J. BAILY."

"Sworn and subscribed before me, a Notary Public, in and for the County of Grand Traverse, State of Michigan, on the 25th day of May, A. D. 1858.

"JAMES TAYLOR,
Notary Public."

Lucy A. Randall

The Christmas Ghost

Lucy Ann Randall Comfort (1836-1914), *daughter of a county school superintendent in New York, was already in print at age thirteen and was widely published by the time this story appeared in* Frank Leslie's Illustrated Newspaper *on December 26, 1857. Stories where some living being, having no intention of portraying a ghost, is nonetheless perceived as one often end with a marriage to a lovely sleepwalker or a laugh about a braying animal outside: not so here.*

I T WAS THE DAY BEFORE CHRISTMAS—a bright, freezing day, with dazzling blue skies, and a sharp, cold wind, which spread a coating of glittering rime over the piled-up snowbanks on the roadside and the white fields and hills in the distance. The long shadows of evening were slowly creeping across the landscape, when a crowded stage-coach came lumbering up to the door of a quiet little village hotel in one of the central counties of Maine.

"Stanton, sir!" cried the driver, pulling up his steaming horses with a jerk. "You get out here, I believe!"

"Stanton already? It seems but a moment since we left Hillsboro," said a pale, weary-looking man, glancing around him with a bewildered air, as he slowly descended from the vehicle.

"Yes, I think we've done it in pretty good time," responded the driver, tossing the mailbags upon the piazza steps, and clipping off with his whip a bit of snow from the sprigs of cedar and holly with which his horses' heads were garnished. "Careful with the little girl there! All right!"

He cracked his whip in the resounding air, and once more the heavily-loaded stage rolled away across the frozen roads toward the fiery sunset, which was blazing behind the pine thickets in the far-off west.

"A strange couple that!" observed the red-faced and jovial passenger who sat beside the driver on the box. "No luggage but a basket, and they've been riding all day."

His face was tied up in furs and handkerchiefs, till nothing but the tip of his nose was visible; but there was a healthy, genial tone in his bluff voice, and a sort of character in the very bit of ivy twined round his hat, which had been snatched from some cottage porch in the day's progress.

"Well, it *is* strange, to say the least of it," remarked the driver, thoughtfully, as he leaned over the box to catch a last glimpse of the strangers, "for such a couple to be travelling together over the country. They look so foreign; too. And the child—a pretty, bright-eyed little thing she is—doesn't look fit to brace such a wind as this."

The stout passenger pulled his handkerchief close to his ears, as a piercing wind swept round a cluster of protecting woods; the driver buttoned his coat tighter, with a loud ejaculation to his horses, and the stage dashed on its way along the winding, snowy road.

Meanwhile, the pair who had so excited the curiosity of their fellow-travellers hurried along the village street. The man might have been about forty-five years of age. He was tall, pale and slender, with a brow seamed with premature wrinkles. The child, on the contrary, was a lovely little creature, with soft, earnest eyes and a sweet Italian face.

"Are you warm enough, Ninetta?" asked the man, feeling the slight form cling closer to his side, as a freezing blast shook the leafless trees above their heads.

"Yes, papa—O yes!" she answered, cheerfully. "But this is

not our home; the driver said it was Stanton, and I thought we were to go somewhere near Deepford."

"So we are," said the father, with a melancholy smile, in answer to her eager, upturned face. "But Deepford is, by itself, a lonely old place, and no stage route passes within six or seven miles of it."

"Six or seven miles!" repeated the child, sadly; and her large, lustrous eyes turned first to the long road that lay before them, and then to the crimson fire, in the western heaven.

"I know it's a long way, Nina," said the father, hopefully; "but we'll soon be there. I've walked this road as a boy many a time, and if you keep up a brave heart it will be no distance at all. I would have engaged a horse and carriage at Stanton but for this reason, pet, and a stern reason it is!"

He tried to smile as he held up a lank green purse, with only a small silver coin gleaming through its network.

"O, we'll walk," said little Nina, laughing. "It's Christmas Eve, you know, and all the good saints and spirits will be abroad to help us."

"Ah, you little Italian," said her father, pressing the tiny hand closer in his own, "your brain is full of old Gianetta's stories. Christmas Eve in America is not like the Christmas Eve of foreign countries; no crucifixes, no lights and decorations, no forms and ceremonies—only a time of great faith and hope, and a time, I trust, for the reconciliation of all old breaches and separations." He spoke the last words with a faint, uncertain voice and a deep sigh.

Nina was silent. Child as she was, she had already learned to respect her father's changing moods, and she knew from his tone that some vague fear or bitter memory was at his heart.

"Ninetta," he resumed in a moment, "you saw no such bright winter landscapes as this in Italy. How white the snow glitters on the slopes, and how blue the sky is! Do you see those pine trees that stand out so bravely among the bare oaks and beeches, and that blue-green cedar that towers by itself, like a hoary king?"

"It is beautiful, I know," she said softly, "but it is not like the orange groves and olive trees of *home*."

He said nothing, but bent down to smooth the raven hair from her white brow, and to draw the mantle closer around her slender throat, and they walked on in silence, each absorbed in thought. She was musing on the thousand legends and memories associated with the holy hours of Christmas Eve in that bright, imaginative clime where she was born, and already her vivid fancy had peopled the clear wintry sky with saints and angels innumerable. He was wrapped in thoughts of his youth, among whose familiar haunts his weary footsteps were now treading. It was on a Christmas Eve, twenty years ago, that he had left his home—left it in anger, with a hot flush on his cheek, and angry words upon his lip.

How well he remembered the hour in which he had been banished—the quiet, subdued exultation of his only brother; younger than himself by several years, but older far in the calendar of strong will and stealthy purpose. But what were his own boyish excesses and mad extravagance compared with the dull, ceaseless malice of that household enemy?

And he remembered, when he had pleaded to see his mother, only for an instant, to say farewell, that triumphant gleam in the cavernous eyes, the stern, relentless message that left no farther room for hope or fear, was delivered, as from his mother's own lip. God pardon him, but he could not forgive that brother, even now! And Rose, the fair New England maiden—was she dead, or had she, too, learned to hate his very name?

But all suspense would soon be ended—he was drawing nearer the old, old home, with every step, and he approached it, a worn, weary, disappointed man, who had dwelt for twenty years on a foreign shore, and during all that time had never once exchanged a word or message with his native land. Perhaps they were all dead; perhaps—but no! he could not bear to think that their hearts might be hardened still. He would trust to his mother's old love, and to the holy influence of Christmas Eve.

The sad, cold moonlight was penciling the dark outline of the little church of Deepford on the snow, when he toiled wearily past, carrying Ninetta in his arms. A mile yet—a long, cold mile!

There was a faint light gleaming through the stained glass window of the unpretending church, and the door stood ajar. The old man who had the charge of its decorations had been giving the finishing touch to the wreaths of princess-pine and ivy, and cedar boughs, which hung around the altar, and under the emblazoned glass, whose tints of amber and purple he remembered so well. Though it was twenty years since, he still recollected the old customs of Christmas Eve at Deepford.

He softly pushed the door open and looked in. No one was there; but a few sprays of red-berried holly, and a cluster or two of mistletoe, gathered from the old dead trees in the wood beyond, lay in the aisle, and one lamp was burning in a carved niche. As he turned away from the porch again, an old man came whistling along the road, swinging a lantern as he walked.

It was old Simon Giles, the sexton—looking just as he had been wont to look, only the hair was whiter, and the wrinkles deeper. Richard Chester forgot that he was an outcast and a wanderer; his heart leaped up at the sight of this weather-beaten old man—the first familiar face he had seen. The white icy radiance fell full upon his own haggard countenance, as he stood in the porch, and the instant the old man saw the worn features he dropped his lantern, and uttered a shrill cry, as if struck by mortal terror, and fled with wild speed along the road, leaving the wondering wayfarer alone in the winter night.

The curtain rises on another scene—the old-fashioned house at Deepford, where Richard Chester's boyhood had been passed. It stands in the midst of a wide and sloping lawn, whose descent is dotted by spreading cedars and evergreens. Without, there is the pure moonlight, and the black, sleeping shadows of motionless trees—within, the cheerful gleam of wax candles, and a merry fire, quivering through rich red draperies. A little group is gathered around the wide fireplace, where spires of dancing flame are stealing in and out, like serpents, through a massive pile of logs, and the red sparks are flying in miniature whirlwinds up the chimney. It is a large room, and though all is bright and warm just around the social circle, deep shadows linger in every angle of the apartment, and the dim canvas of the old family portraits is almost entirely in darkness. The moonlight streams upon the carpet opposite the large bow window, and now and then the rude cross on the walls, formed of ivy and holly, and the cedar boughs, above the mantel, stir softly as a door is shut or opened.

Mrs. Chester, bent with years and grief, was sitting musing by the hearth, with a subdued mist of tears in her gentle eyes, and, close at her side, reclined a pale and lovely lady, watching, with timid, frightened glance, the dark-browed man opposite. It was very much the gaze which the fascinated bird may be supposed to direct toward the baleful serpent. Joseph Chester, the man whom she regarded with such manifest dread and terror, stood leaning against the chimney-piece, with a heavy cloud on his dark brow. His sunken and glowing eyes were fixed intently on the fire, and there was not one tender or gentle line in all the wrinkles that furrowed his brow and lip.

"It is Christmas Eve," said the old lady, breaking a long silence, "and still it does not seem as if Christmas were so near. Twenty years to-night since Richard went away—eighteen since he died!"

At the mention of Richard's name, a thrill ran through the

slight frame of the younger lady, Joseph Chester's wife, but the next instant she glanced timidly up, and met the sinister eyes of her husband.

"These are strange memories, mother!" said Joseph, sternly.

"I cannot help it, Joseph; I have thought much of poor Richard lately. If I could only have seen him before he went away and told him that I loved and hoped for him still; but you would not allow it. If he could but have known that my poor husband forgave him on his deathbed!"

"Mother, this is folly!" interrupted Chester, almost fiercely.

"On Christmas Eves I think of him oftenest; at such times as this, when long-parted families meet once more, and happy household groups sit round their blazing fires, I cannot but remember my oldest-born, and wonder where his lonely grave is made."

Chester turned away impatiently, and walked towards the window, while Rose stole her hand softly into that of her mother-in-law, as if to express a silent, loving sympathy.

"What is that?" cried Mrs. Chester, starting from her chair a moment afterward, as a confused noise reached her ears from the servants' rooms.

Chester turned quickly, and in the same second old Simon Giles rushed in, pale and trembling, his hair standing upright, and his eyes distended wildly.

"Simon, what is the matter?" cried the old lady.

"Speak, you fool!" said Chester, sternly. "What do you mean by terrifying us in this manner?"

"I've seen his ghost! Mr. Joseph, as sure as I'm a living man, I've seen his ghost!" faltered old Giles, clinging to a chair for support.

"His ghost! Whose, you fool?" asked Chester, turning livid.

"Mr. Richard's! Your own brother's ghost."

Mrs. Chester's face was white as ashes, as she sank back, powerless, into her chair, still holding the chill, nerveless hand of Rose, who leaned, trembling, on her shoulder.

"Are you insane, man?" demanded Chester, in a deep and stifled voice, "or are you drunk?"

"Mr. Joseph, it stood there in the church porch, looking me full in the face. I had been over home to get the hammer and nails to fasten up a wreath of ivy that had fallen down, and when I returned, it was in the porch."

"*It* again. Simon Giles, do not trifle with me. Speak what you mean!"

"Your brother's ghost! The ghost of a man eighteen years dead!"

An awful silence fell on the group—you could almost hear the beatings of their hearts, while the fire snapped and crackled, and the old clock, speaking from amid its holly garlands, struck nine, with a hollow sound.

"Simon, you may go," said Chester, sternly; "and the next time you allow yourself to be overcome by liquor on such a night as this, you will lose your place."

"Mr. Joseph," began Giles, indignantly; but he quailed before the evil eye fixed fiercely on his, and withdrew, muttering to himself.

"Joseph, Joseph, what does this mean?" faltered Mrs. Chester, rising to her feet, as pale as death.

"Mother, do not let yourself be so disturbed. It is a foolish fancy of old Giles's. I tell you that Richard died in Rome eighteen years since."

But his firm hand quivered, nevertheless, and there was a cold, damp sweat oozing from his corrugated forehead.

Even as he spoke, a footstep echoed on the threshold, and Richard Chester, with the child clinging to his hand, stood before them—he whom they supposed had long slumbered, cold and stark, in his far-off grave. The mother advanced a step, trembling; what intuition told her that it was no ghost, but a living reality? and in another instant her favorite child was clasped to her heart.

"Mother, I have come back to you once more. You will not send me away again?"

"Never, never! How could you suppose it?"

"Joseph's word was my decree of exile."

"And Joseph told me you had been dead eighteen years—he saw you in your coffin when he was at Rome."

Richard Chester turned, with a burning forehead, to seek the villain who had usurped his patrimony, and blighted his life's most cherished hopes.

But Joseph was gone. Dizzy, faint and reeling he had crept from the room, when first the living contradiction to his skilfully laid plots had crossed the doorstone, and instinctively he sought his own apartment above.

"Where is that cunning drug?" he murmured, "for I need all my senses now, and the walls swim around me. To be taken to nerve the mind and clear the brain—yes, yes!"

He crept to a heavy oaken desk, and felt blindly for some secret spring. It was a dark apartment, illumined only by the fitful glow of a sea-coal fire, and rendered still more gloomy by its thick hangings, and the dark-veined wood of its furniture. The spring yielded to his touch, and he drew out a tiny rosewood box, filled with almost invisible phials, reposing in crimson satin nooks. He took a wine glass from the mantel, poured it half full of water, and shook a single drop from one of these phials into it. A dull purple hue ensanguined the clear element; he raised it to his lips, drained its contents, and the next instant fell dead.

They were subtle, deadly drugs; some for good and some for ill, but his eyes were dim, and his hand trembled, and he had mistaken the phial.

The dull, heavy fall roused the group below, they hurried up, and stood pale and silent around the corpse. In that hour they forgot all the wrongs of years, all the woes wrought by that pulseless brain, and only grief, and pity, and forgiveness stirred their hearts, while the mild stars of Christmas Eve looked in through the softly tinted medallions of the stained windows, and the wind moaned sadly through the leafless trees. The hour of retribution had come!

From top to bottom: *Nottingham Guardian* (England), Dec. 17, 1857; *Butte Daily Post*, Dec. 25, 1895; *Ottawa Citizen* (Canada), Dec. 23, 1898.

The Hermit of Iowa

The Frozen Husband

A Tale of Terror for Christmas Eve

"The Hermit of Iowa" was FRANK IBBERSON JERVIS (C.
*1823-1885), editor, journalist, poet, and portrait painter. This
story appeared in the* Quad City Times *on December 26,
1869. Iowa was a relatively young state (1848), and the* Times *a
young paper (1855), while the story presents an evil older than the
memory of the oldest citizen.*

[This tale is recommended for perusal late at night, in a lonely
house, by an unsnuffed candle, with the wind roaring round
the dwelling, the room door ajar into a dark hall-way, and the
windows rattling in the most supernatural manner.]

O UR WESTERN COUNTRY IS TOO YOUNG to have those
mysterious inhabitants which people the mountain
glens, sylvan glades, and pleasant meadows of olden lands.
—Ghosts, gnomes, kelpies, brownies, bogles, goblins, Pucks,
Robin Goodfellows, and the numerous tribes of fairies and
sprites have an objection to novelty, and only exist among the
ivy-mantled towers and moss-covered keeps of by-gone centuries. There, every river's bank is tenanted with spirits, and every
hillside with fairies, and the moonlight reveals to mortal eyes
their merry midnight gambols and harmless revels. In America, which was peopled after the world became round, and its
inhabitants philosophical, spiritual manifestations are confined

to table rappings and the playing of tricks in darkened rooms
and magnetic circles. It would be poetical, and to our thinking,
a charming fancy to unite the spiritual doctrines of to-day with
the fairy lore of by-gone times and marry Titania and Mab with
all their attendant elfs, to the post-mortem somethings of the
romantic disciples of etherial entities of the present day. The
tiny creature cradled in a lily cup, or dancing tight rope on the
idle gossamer thread which stretches across the woodland path-
way, would harmonize with the disembodied life particles now
tenanting the spirit.—Such weddings as these would be, at any
rate, more to our taste than the one we are about to chronicle.

Many years ago, when Rockingham was looking forward
to the time when it should eclipse the other river stations, and
become the capital of Iowa, there lived between that place
and Davenport a poor widow woman whose husband had
died after clearing, fencing and breaking up the land which is
now one of the most valuable farms in the neighborhood. In
those days land was plentiful and of little value, while labor
was scarce and rated high, and it was with much difficulty
that this widow woman managed to support herself and her
only child, a daughter, who, as she grew into womanhood,
developed a beauty but rarely seen and which was the magnet
to draw many of the young men from surrounding farms for
miles away to assist the lone widow in the cultivation of her
little farm. Did her land want plowing it was strange if one
had not a half day to spare. Was a load of dried prairie grass
required for her cattle, some one was returning empty by the
very spot, and all these little kindnesses ended in a sly flirta-
tion with the coquettish Clarinda. Not one of these anxious
swains, however, received encouragement, for Clarinda's glass
told her she was fair, and her beauty made her ambitious of a
future in those eastern cities of which she heard her mother,
who came from New York State, talk so much, and she, with
the vanity of misguided youth, looked forward to the advent
of a gentleman wooer from the outside world.

Their snug little farm-house was situated in a little hollow between two of the swelling bluffs at some distance from the river, and they heard and saw nothing of the world around them beyond the news which they gathered from the farmers' sons who were drawn to the cottage by the wonderful beauty of the daughter of the glen as she was poetically called. It was an autumnal evening, the Indian summer had tinged the surrounding woods with gold and vermillion, the great red sun was sinking to rest over the Black Hawk hills and tinging with his parting rays the placid Mississippi, which lay like a mirror beneath them, when a strange horseman rode up to their door. This was an event in their lives, and, as he drew his rein tight and halted at their gate, they with country politeness, hastened out to give him any information he might require. "He had," he said, "lost his way and wished to be directed to the adjacent village of Davenport." He was invited in and a rustic meal of corn bread and new milk was placed before him. He made a hearty meal and by his fascinating manners quite enraptured both the mother and daughter. After resting awhile he started on his journey, but his visits soon became frequent, and it was not long before he became the acknowledged lover of the young girl, and with every appearance of wealth and a generous disposition, he was not long in gaining the consent of the widow to a union with her daughter. Consent gained, a neighboring squire was called in and the knot was tied, neither mother nor daughter, however strange it may seem, having any idea beyond his constant visits and respectable appearance as to who or what he was. One peculiar circumstance, however, had not escaped the notice of curious observers, which was that he was invariably dressed in brown, in fact he was known, to those ignorant of his name, as "the brown man." His hair was brown, his eyes were brown, his boots were brown, he rode a brown horse, and was always attended by a brown dog. He had often talked of his place over the hills, and it had become to their imaginations quite a familiar spot, and when after the ceremony he made the bride's mother a present of a heavy purse of gold to answer present needs, and mounted his newly acquired wife on a pillion to take her to her new home, not a shadow crossed the widow's mind that all was not right. "Are you ready, darling," said he, as she rose from kissing her mother a fond farewell. "I am," said the bride. The horse snorted, the dog barked, and with a leap and a plunge they bounded on their way. After keeping the river road for some little distance, they passed into the woods, and, as dark night drew on, halted at the entrance of a log hut of the rudest construction. "Here is my home," said the brown man. "This your home," replied the bewildered girl. "Come in," said he, helping her to alight, "this is my residence." "What! a log hut, worse than mother's old frame," answered the proud young wife. As the door opened the bride looked round, and a shudder passed over her as she heard a horrible noise, and saw, or fancied she saw the horse and dog disappear. As her eye became accustomed to the uncertain light of a miserable dip placed in the rude window of the hovel, she saw the misery of all around. The bed in one corner was but a heap of straw with a filthy blanket, and a heavy table, a chest, two stools, a kettle and a pan or two formed the whole of the furniture.

Weary and worn out, tired of surmising and anxious for morning, she retired to sleep—only to be waked about midnight, by a gentle neighing, and a subdued bark, seemingly at the window. She feigned sleep,—her husband passed his hands over her face. She snored,—"I come," said he, and rising, left her. In half an hour, he was by her side again. He was cold as ice. The next night, the same. She pretended sleep—he rose —she waited—he returned cold—the morning came. On the third night she was determined to know the mystery. She seemed deeper asleep than ever. He passed a light before her eyes. Her heart trembled, but she remained quiet and firm. He seemed to hesitate. A voice at the door exclaimed in subdued accents, "You are long in coming. The earth is removed. Haste!

haste! the feast is waiting." "I'm coming," said the brown man. She rose and followed him,—he took a well-trodden path through the woods. The shadows of the trees concealed her, and she kept close upon him. He turned and looked round, she shrunk against a tree—he went on—the wood was cut away, and in the moonlight gleamed the deadly white of those upright mementoes which cannot be mistaken. With a sickening sensation, which she could not explain, she saw him enter the enclosure. The wind, hollowly howling through the tall trees, startled her.—She gained heart, however, and looked on through the picket fence. The brown man, the brown horse, and the brown dog, were there, by a yawning pit. The moonlight shone full on them and her. Looking down, towards her shadow on the earth, she started with horror to observe it move, although she was standing quite still. It waved its shadowy arms and seemed to beckon her back; it raised one hand and pointed homewards; then slowly rose and confronted her. She saw it in advance and quickly followed it; she had scarcely gained her bed when the door creaked and her husband was by her side. She started, pretending to be just awakened—"How cold you are love," she said. "Cold," replied he, "you are not very warm, I think." The next morning she plucked up heart and asked leave to go on a visit to her mother. "If you wish to see your mother I will bring her here," he answered looking strangely at her.

He departed and the young wife was left alone in that retired and lonely spot. She sat at the door and looked wistfully around. All nature seemed to sympathize with her grief, the skies lowered, a cold drizzling rain fell and beat upon her face. She heeded it not, a little bird twitted and chirped upon a stunted oak in front of the hut and as she looked at it she sung, sadly crooning to herself—

"The little birds were singing on every green tree,
And the song that they sung was sweet liberty."

Morning passed away, noon came, but she did not stir, the sun rose above the opposite bluffs, passed over head and sunk, latticing the west with bars of gold, but she heeded him not. A dull, cold melancholy possessed her as she waited for, yet trembled at the idea of her husband's return. Without twilight, as is usual in the early winter months, to those who live in wooded glens, night dropped down, and she reluctantly rose and entered the cabin. She could not work, she dared not sleep. She must think, and slowly and wearily the hours sped on till morning. Her husband came not until the second night, when, having again sought the interior of her comfortless dwelling, she saw the well known and long saved Sunday garments of her mother. "Oh, mother are you come," she cried, putting all the pent up feelings of her weary heart into the exclamation, as she rushed forwards to embrace her. She was stopped by the aged figure—"Hush! hush! my child!—I stepped in before the husband to know how you like him? Speak softly or he'll hear you—he's turning that devil of a brown mare loose in the bottoms."

"Oh! mother, mother! such a sad, sad story!"

"Quiet child—whisper! how does he treat you?"

"Cruelly, mother dear, that straw my bed, coarse my food —and—"

"Well?"

"And then at night—listen mother.—The first night I came, about twelve o'clock—"

"Ah! speak softly, darling."

"A bark and a neigh, came at the window, and he got up and went out and stayed away an hour, and when he returned he was quite frozen. He ate nothing the next day. The next night it was the same—the next day he never tasted food, and the third—"

"Ssh! ssh!"

"Well,—the third night, I thought I'd watch him. Mother, don't hold my hand so hard. He got up, and I rose after him—

oh don't laugh so strangely, mother, it's frightful—I followed him to the burying ground, on the other side of the bluffs—Mother, mother, you hurt my hand—I looked through the pickets—it was moonlight, clear as day, and I saw—"

"Well, darling—softly—what did you see?"

"My husband by a newly opened grave, and the horse—turn your head aside, mother, your breath is scorching hot—and the dog—and they were—they were—"

"Well?"

"Oh! you are not my mother!" shrieked the miserable girl, as the brown man flung off his disguise, and stood grinning with devilish malice in her fading eyes. A shriek rent the air, a stifled sob—a horrid gurgling sound, a shrill peal of demoniacal laughter, and all was still; the moon came from behind a rifted cloud and gazed peacefully upon the scene.

The next day there was dread and terror by the whole river side. The widow was found by some neighbors, who chanced to call, dead in her bed—five livid spots upon her neck betokened strangulation, but as nothing except her holiday attire was missing, her murder was evidently not for plunder. Search was made in the neighborhood for her daughter, and after many weary hours, a vacant log hut was found where the oldest settler never knew of the existence of even such a sign of civilization—it was charred and tenantless—a heap of mouldering straw in one corner, and some rusted iron pans still hanging to the dilapidated walls, were all that told of its ever being a human habitation. It was left in its solitude and still remains about a quarter of a mile from the river's bank, as you go through the little coppice hard by the deserted mineral spring. A curse seems to rest upon it, and around it, for throughout the year the trees are sickly, the grass withered, and not a bird will roost in any of the overhanging branches. When you take a moonlight sleigh ride, just turn up westward beyond where the little stream crosses the road, and you will come upon it, and if old wives' tales be true, should you chance to be there about midnight, you may see the shadowy forms of the brown man, and his demon mare and hound, and hear the piercing shriek, like the long wailing of a plover, echo through the trees. To mortal eyes a sight of any of the actors in this mysterious tragedy were never seen again in the flesh, and the deserted log cabin is known to all around as the home of the Frozen Husband—or the Brown Vampyre Fiend.

> "The maid was seen no more, but oft
>   Her ghost is known to glide,
> At midnight's silent, solemn hour
>   Along the river side."

DID YOU EVER SEE A GHOST?

Well, if You Did, Here's a Chance to Tell of It.

"The Evening World" Will Give a Gold Double Eagle for the Best Ghost Story.

Everybody May Enter the Lists, so Send in Your Experience.

It Will Be an Interesting Contest and in Keeping with the Christmas Holidays.

Did you ever see a ghost?

The Evening World has a hankering desire to see that ghost through your spectacles.

The ghost story must not be more than 200 words long, written on one side of the paper only, and addressed to the Ghost Editor.

Send on your ghost experiences! The contest is now open.

Evening World [N.Y.], December 23, 1889

Emma Frances Dawson

A Sworn Statement

EMMA FRANCES DAWSON (1839-1926) *wrote the following tale at the request of the editor of San Francisco's* The Wasp, *Ambrose Bierce, for the Christmas* 1881 *issue. Bierce had praised her as "head and shoulders above any writer on this coast with whose works I have acquaintance." Unusually, the story incorporates poetry and song as potential clues in the mystery faced by the protagonist.*

> This ae night, this ae night,
>   Every night and alle,
> Fire and sleet and candle-light,
>   And Christ receive thy saule.
> —*Lykewake Dirge.*

I FIRST MET MR. AUDENRIED through his advertising for a valet. I liked his appearance, and engaged with him at a lower salary than one of my experience and ability will usually work for. He was then living in a furnished house on Rincon Hill, whence he could see the bay. He sat for hours looking at it and writing verses. He had money, but was neither young nor strong, and seldom went out. He had been very handsome, was still fine-looking, with eyes that glowed with a lurid, internal fire.

There was one other person in the house, a quiet lady, yet one to be noticed and remembered. I pride myself on my discretion. It was nothing to me how many "Coralies" or

"Camilles" existed. It was long before I alluded to her, though I met her in the upper hall, on the stairs, and sometimes found her in the room with my master and myself, or just outside the door, standing near, as if waiting for me to go. After a while, I got the notion that she did not like me, and it made it unpleasant. After long thinking it over, for I did not want to leave, I gave a month's notice.

"Why is this, Wilkins?" says Mr. Audenried. "If it is a question of wages, stay on. I like your quiet ways," says he. That is just what he says.

"To tell the truth, sir," I says, "it's not my pay—it's the lady, sir."

"What!" says he.

So then I told of her air of watchful dislike, and how I was not used to being spied upon, and that it was needless my recommendations could all show. He turned quite pale, so white that I thought Heaven forgive me if I'd made trouble between them, for she looked sad enough anyway. He did not speak for a long while.

Then he muttered to himself: "*This* man, too!"

He made me tell him all over again. Then, after a pause, he says: "Find me another place, Wilkins, and help me move."

So I thought there was a quarrel. We did move from house to house, from street to street, from city to city, all through the State and to others near. Mr. Audenried never spoke of her, nor noticed her, but as soon as she came, as she always did come, he at once gave the order to start. He seemed to watch my face, and I fancied he knew in that way when she was about. I wondered what their story might be, and tried to make out from verses he wrote that time, but all I could get hold of were these:

PROPHETIC.

Unto the garden's bloom close set
Of lily, larkspur, violet,
Sweet jasmine, rose, and mignonette
    More beauty lending,
Fair Marguerite stands in the sun,
Plucks leaves from daisy, one by one,
While Faust, impatient, sees it done
    And waits the ending.

See! on the garden-wall behind,
Their happy shadows plain defined,
Bent heads and eager hand, outlined
    Like soft engraving;
And there athwart their fingers' pose
A shape whose presence neither knows.
Mephisto! 'T is his head that shows
    A cock's plume waving!

Sometimes we rested a few days or weeks, sometimes went on, day after day, without stopping, but she was my master's shadow; she followed us everywhere. I used to try and puzzle out what their secret was. If it had been love, it must now be hate, I told myself, seeing how they often met and passed without a word. He did not appear to even see her.

We had come back to San Francisco, and it was nearing Christmas-time when I was first seized with my queer spells. We had taken another furnished house, far out and high upon Washington street. I thought we had got rid of the woman; but coming home late one afternoon I found her in the window, while my master had been looking over his writing-desk. Before him lay withered flowers, a ribbon, a lady's glove, and a photograph with some look of this persistent woman, but younger and handsomer.

I felt uneasy. Mr. Audenried sat with head on his hand, lost in thought. When I spoke he did not hear nor notice me until I put the medicine he had sent for into the hand in his lap. Then he did not know it at first, though in giving the parcel I touched his hand. Something about him I could not describe kept me an instant motionless in that position.

A stupor came over me. The carved ivory hourglass we had filled with Arizona sand from before the Casa Grande, our bright, thick Moqui blanket on the lounge, our foreign fur rugs, our Japanese fans, bronzes, and china—the whole room came and went as to one who is sleepy yet tries to keep awake. Again and again it vanished, reappearing enlarged to twice, three times, its size. Then it was lost in a mist, from which rose a different scene.

The chandelier had changed to long lines of lights, the pictures to great mirrors, and arches with banners and streamers. Devices in evergreen showed that it was Christmas Eve. I was aware of a rush and whirl of dancers, waltz-music, flowers, gay colors, and the scent of a sandal-wood fan; but I saw plainly only one woman, young, gay, lovely, but with a faint likeness to some one I had seen who was older and wretched. I rubbed my eyes, and when I opened them at the sound of my master's voice, it was the room I knew, with all its familiar objects, and he and I were there alone.

One day I met our quiet lady coming from Mr. Audenried's study, and found him there in a fainting-fit. As I was helping him across the hall to his bedroom I had the second of my odd attacks.

A dullness and vague fear troubled me. Our many-branched antlers, our lacquered-work and carved cabinets and great Chinese lantern, the stained-glass skylight, the big vase of pampas-grass, the open doors and windows, the sunny yard, with callas and geraniums in bloom, all wavered before me, went and came and vanished.

I saw a room with flowered chintz in curtains and furniture-covers, a glowing anthracite fire, and Christmas wreaths hanging in long windows looking on frost-bound garden and river.

And the beautiful woman of the ball! Still young, but now
unhappy, looking at me in despair. Both arms outstretched
in an agony of entreaty, and tears rolling down her cheeks.
Terribly distressed by her woe, I gave a cry of pity just as Mr.
Audenried, gasping and falling on the bed, brought me back to
him, to myself, and to his room.

Putting away his things for the night I found these verses in
a woman's writing:

IN ABSENCE.

In my black night no moonshine nor star-glimmer
On my long, weary path that leads Nowhere
    I get no shimmer
Of that great glory our day knew.
I cannot think the world holds you;
It is not ours, this Land of Vague Despair—
    I scarce can breathe its air.

I am as one whom some sweet tune, down dropping,
Has left half-stunned by silence like a blow;
    Like one who, stopping
In drifting desert sands, looks back
Where sky slants down above his track,
To mark the tufted palm whose outlines show
    An oasis below;

Like one whom winter wind and rain are blinding,
And storm-tossed billows bear from land away,
    Who, no hope finding,
Should yield himself to bitter fate.
Can I do this! Ah, God! too late—
Have I not felt thy dear, warm lips convey
    Commands I must obey?

"Forget-me-not!" a kiss for every letter.
"Forget-me-not!" a kiss for every word.

> It could not better
> Have stamped itself upon my soul
> It passed beyond my own control.
> All thought, all circumstance are by it stirred,
>   Invisible, unheard.
>
> Though, like Francesca, ever falling, falling
> Through dizzy space to endless depths afar,
>   Thy kiss recalling
> Would charm me to forget my woe;
> Of Heaven or Hell I should not know,
> Nor as I passed see any blazing star,
>   Nor mark its rhythmic jar.
>
> If such remembrance only—moon-reflection
> On depths untried of my soul's unknown sea—
>   Mere recollection—
> Could hold me spellbound by its sway,
> What of your true kiss can I say?
> Ah! that is wholly speechless ecstasy,—
>   No words for that could be!

I thought it might be I had myself grown nervous about the quiet lady, to have these crazy fits after seeing her, and I dreaded to have her come again. But it was not my place to urge Mr. Audenried to move, and he seemed tired of changing.

One evening he had a severe attack of palpitation of the heart, and called me in great haste. I had been wondering what had put him in such a flutter, when that lady opened the door and glanced round the room as if she had forgotten something, but did not come in. Mr. Audenried was so ill that he had to sit up in bed and have me hold him firmly, my hands pressing his breast and his back.

Again that strange dread and drowsiness fell on me like a cloud. My master's pearl combs, brushes, crystal jewel-box, with its glittering contents, and a bunch of violets in a wine-glass on the bureau, his Japanese quilted silk dressing-gown thrown over a chair, embroidered slippers here, gay smoking-cap there, and a large lithograph of Modjeska, glimmered through a fog, came back, withdrew again.

The one high gas-burner became a full moon, the walls fell away; I stood out of doors in a summer night's dimness and stillness that make one feel lonely; grass, daisies, and buttercups underfoot, and overhead stars and endless space. The beautiful woman, worn and wild-looking, with flashing eyes, stood there in a threatening posture, calling down curses! I shrank in horror, though the vision lasted, as before, not more than a quarter of a second.

Mr. Audenried, wasted and wan, had grown so nervous that after this time he refused to be left alone, and above all, cautioned me to stay beside him on Christmas Eve.

"An unpleasant anniversary to me," he says.

The doctor advised him to change to a hotel, to have cheerful society. We moved to the Palace Hotel, and to divert his mind from its own horror Mr. Audenried gave a dinner-party in his rooms on Christmas Eve.

It was a wild night, just right for "Tam O'Shanter," which one of the gentlemen recited. The weather or my master's forced gayety made me gloomy. There was a raw Irish waiter to help, and once I went into the anteroom just in time to catch him about to season one of Mr. Audenried's private dishes from a bottle out of our Japanese cabinet. It was marked "Poison," but he could not read.

"What could possess you," I says, "to meddle with *that*?"

"Sure," he says, "the lady showed me which to take."

"The *lady*! What lady?" I says, trembling from head to foot.

"A dark lady," says he, "with a proud nose and mouth, and eyebrows in one long, heavy line."

I was horrified. I did not want to figure in a murder case. I liked Mr. Audenried too well to leave. I was too poor to lose a good place. I resolved to stay and protect him, but my heart beat faster. For my own safety I meant to say over the multiplication-table, and not get bewitched or entranced again. I told myself over and over, "She shall not outwit me."

The wind and rain beat against the windows, and I heard one of our guests singing "The Midnight Revellers:"

> "The first was shot by Carlist thieves
>   Three years ago in Spain;
> The second was drowned in Alicante,
>   While I alone remain.
> But friends I have, two glorious friends,
>   Two braver could not be;
> And every night when midnight tolls
>   They meet to laugh with me!"

As I took in some wine, a gentleman was saying: "Too wild a story for such a commonplace background as San Francisco."

"One must be either commonplace or sated with horrors to say that," says Mr. Audenried. "What city has more or stranger disappearances and assassinations? There have been murders and suicides at all the hotels. Other cities surpass it in age, but none in crime and mystery."

It was a lively party. A love-song from one of the gentlemen turned the talk on love affairs, and I went in just as Mr. Audenried was saying: "Aaron Burr relied wholly on the fascination of his touch. I believe in the magnetism of touch; that it cannot only impart disease but sensations. Holding a sleeper's hand while I read, by no willpower of mine he dreamed of scenes I saw in my mind."

Trained servant as I am, I disgraced myself then. I dropped and broke some of our own bubble-like glasses I was carrying. I was so unnerved by this explanation of my queer turns. It flashed upon me how they had only come when I was touching him. I had heard a former master, a learned German, talk about his countryman Mesmer, and I understood that what had appeared to me in my spells was what Mr. Audenried was thinking of!

I could scarcely recover myself for the rest of the company's stay. I recollect no more about it, except that somebody played the flute till it seemed as if a twilight breeze sighed for being pent in our four walls and longed to join its ruder brother-winds outside; and that Mr. Audenried read these verses of his:

RONDEL.

To-night, O friends! we meet "Kriss Kringle";
　　He comes, he comes when falls betwixt us
The chiming midnight-bells' soft klingle,
When, glad, we crowd round cheery ingle,
　　Or, lonely, grieve that joy has missed us;
　　Or, in cathedral gloom, pray Christus;
Or drain gay toasts where glasses jingle.
　　Though marshalled hosts of cares have tricked us,
In wine's Red Sea drown all and single—
　　　　"Christmas!"
　　Drown recollection that afflicts us—
Our bowls, like witches' caldrons, mingle
　　Too much of old Yule-tide that kissed us—
　　The bitter drink that Life has mixed us
Forget, and shout till rafters tingle—
　　　　"Christmas!"

The last guest had hardly gone when Mrs. Carnavon's card was brought up. This was an elderly lady we had met in our travels, who took an interest in Mr. Audenried's case, though a stranger. She came in, bright and chatty, and my master was so cheered up by it that he readily let me leave.

I did not want to go. I had not been drinking; I was well and in my right mind, but my whole skin seemed to draw up with a shiver and thrill as at some near terror. But he sent me to a druggist to have Mrs. Carnavon's vinaigrette refilled.

As I left the passage to our suite of rooms and turned into the long, lonesome hall, more dreary than ever in its vastness at this quiet, late hour, I saw a little way ahead our brunette stepping into the elevator. I fancied a mocking smile on her face as she looked back at me. I forgot the multiplication-table, whose fixed rules were to keep me in my senses. For the first time it struck me that she was the woman of my visions, grown older and sadder.

I hurried, but when I reached the door she had gone, and stout Mrs. Lisgar was coming up, like the change of figures in a pantomime. She was another mystery of mine; for her maid had told me Mrs. Lisgar and my master knew each other abroad, but were sworn foes now, neither of us knew why.

"I beg your pardon, Madam," I says; "did you see the lady who just went down? A handsome brunette, with eyebrows that join above a Roman nose, and a very short upper lip. Where did she go?"

Mrs. Lisgar swelled bigger and redder. "Has Mr. Audenried sent you to annoy me?" she says.

"Certainly not, Madam," says I. "But I saw her!—heavy, meeting eyebrows, scornful mouth, and—"

"Silence, sir!" she cried. "There was no one in the elevator. Don't you know you are speaking of my poor sister, dead for many years?"

In my confusion I gasped out at random: "Mrs. Carnavon is here. Do you know her?"·

Mrs. Lisgar says: "She was my sister's most intimate friend. But you are either drunk or crazy. I was with her when she died in Arizona last week."

An awful suspicion seized me; a cold sweat broke out on my brow. I had not lost sight of Mr. Audenried's door. I bowed to Mrs. Lisgar and tried to hurry back, but a numbness in every limb weighed me down till I seemed to move as slowly as the bells that were striking twelve.

As I drew near, I heard angry voices inside, then a fearful groan, which seemed to die off in the distance. But I found every room in our suite vacant, except for my figure, which I caught glimpses of at every turn, staring out of the great mirrors, ghastly, haggard, with bloodshot eyes, and a strained look about the mouth, madly straying among the lights and flowers, tables with remnants of the feast, and the disordered chairs, which after such a revel have a queer air of life of their own.

A long window in the parlor stood wide open. Chilled with fright, with I don't know what vague thought, I ran and looked out. Six stories from the street, nothing to be seen outside but the night and storm, neither on the lighted pavement far below, nor among drifting clouds overhead! Nothing but impenetrable darkness then and afterward over Mr. Audenried's fate.

This is all I can tell of the well-known strange disappearance of my unhappy master. It is the truth, the whole truth and nothing but the truth.

AN OLD-TIME CHRISTMAS AT THE Y.M.C.A.

There will be a yule-tide sociable for the members of the Y. M. C. A. in the parlors on Christmas night.

A very fine talker has been procured to tell ghost stories and to amuse the fellows.

It will be a great treat for the young men who are members and whose homes are too far away to reach for Christmas.

It will be a thoroughly enjoyable evening. A very unique menu has been provided and the room will be beautifully decorated with Christmas greens.

There will be a regular old-fashioned log fire in the grate and an old-time Christmas will prevail.

Mount Vernon Daily Argus, December 23, 1899

Anonymous

The Snow Flower of the Sierras

A Christmas Story

The following tale was printed in the December 26, 1884 Coop-erstown Courier *in the Territory of Dakota. It was a new paper* (1883) *in a new city* (1882), *in a new county* (1881); *North Dakota wouldn't become a state until* 1889. FREDERICK H. ADAMS (1851-1895), *an attorney originally from Vermont, became editor and owner of the* Courier *in May* 1884 *and may perhaps have authored this story.*

On the crest of the Sierra Nevada Range, amid eternal winter, there appears a gorgeous blood-red plant, massed with star-tling brilliancy against pallid banks of snow. In size and shape, the cloud-flower resembles a hyacinth, but the leaves and stem, as well as the blossoms, are of one vivid crimson hue. Unlike the Alpine flower, of hardy stem and straw-like texture, this plant is succulent and ruddy, but it is a phantom formed of ice and fire. Picked from its cold bed, it drips its life away in your hand, and in a few moments all the fire and color is gone in icy tears, and there remains only a wet, shapeless, colorless film.

The traveler up the Sierras, hears of the strange blossom from returning wayfarers, long before he reaches the heights where it blossoms. No care is able to transplant or even to carry to the lowlands the unique flower. On the altars of the upper air it is laid, where no other flower-shape is found, and he who would see it, must go to that shrine of icy splendor.

In early times, the fire-flower, as it was called, was counted miraculous by the pious few who, on missions of mercy, crossed the icy peaks. More than a hundred years ago, when English, Dutch and French formed a sparse border of civilization on our Eastern coast, the dark-eyed Spaniard entered America by its Western way, and marked his march along the Pacific slope not by forts, but churches, which with their shrines and altars yet stand in decaying grandeur amid gardens of olive and palm. From these outposts, guarded by the sacred cross, missionary fathers in the robes and sandals of the Franciscans, penetrated inland, carrying good will to the savages of the New World. It is said that one of those devoted brothers, seeing on the white summit of a mountain the red snow-flower of the Sierras, sprinkling the snowy field like drops of blood, fell on his knees in wondering adoration, and called the mountain "Sangre de Cristo," the Mount of the Blood of Christ. This brother died in the wilderness, and it is told that the crucifix which dropped from his lifeless hand was transformed into a marvel among the clouds. For, far lifted above mortal, or wing of bird, towers a great cross of snow against a mountain side known as the "Mount of the Holy Cross."

The most careless tourist feels a thrill of awe, when, from mid-air, appears the isolated "Mount of the Holy Cross." Long ago the splendors of Mount Sinai faded into the gray of the past; long ago the priceless drops of the Savior's blood were shed on Mount Calvary; yet on the wondrous stretches of our mountain ranges, red drops crimson the pale wastes, and, in splendor of diamonds and pearls, gleams the eternal snows in form of the blessed Cross, lifted up, that all, on height or lowland, can see the symbol of Divine and universal love.

In a cabin that had long been roofless and fireless, a mockery of comfort upon the windy summit of the range, there lived, once on a time, my guide told me, a maiden, dazzling and pure as the stars.

It was July when we stood there, but the snows that had

drifted over the hearth were unmelted, and the wind roared through the crevices with an angry grief. What the place must have been when winter buried it could scarcely be imagined.

The father of the beautiful girl whose home this had been, had perched his habitation on this crag, not altogether by chance, for in summer he acted as guide to tourists in the Yosemite, and in winter, on his snow shoes, carried mail and messages to scattered cabins and settlements. Silent Jack—so he was known—was a mystery, even among those hidden and mysterious men who find a refuge in the mountain gulches. He was a misanthrope, who had taken the youngest of his four children and fled, leaving their mother and her complainings and struck out, in vindictive sullenness, for the wilderness and peace. The child, he swore, should grow up in quiet, if nothing more. If from the glance of the little girl's dark eyes he turned in thought, sometimes to other dark eyes like them, which in his early manhood had been lode-stars of destiny; if the fond name, "father," brought to his remembrance other children who had lisped the same dear word, none knew. He mentioned his old life to no one. He spoke of his wife and children but once during the years of his stay on the mountain.

Silent Jack was not an unlettered or vicious man. He taught and cared for the child of his love with morose and pathetic devotion. He taught the little one of God—strange teacher of the word. The Bible was her spelling-book, her geography and story-book;—for the rest she had the grand solitude, the stars near by, and the blossoms in the snow-bank of her home. The miners and trappers of the slope called her, with instinctive homage of man to the beautifying and pure, the Snow Flower of the Sierras. She was to them the object of adoration, as the namesake flower, to the early devotees. Whispers of the divinity shrined in the mountain snows, floated downward along the paths of semi-civilization. Stories of a maiden somewhere, either in cloud, or snow, lithe, brilliant and innocent; strong as the mountain pine, blooming as the mountain flowers, pure as the mountain air, with eyes clear as dew-drops, and voice like the rich gurgling mountain brook.

Before the swarming tourists began pilgrimages Yosemite-ward the Snow Flower of the Sierras had brimmed her soul with its beauty. She had seen her pretty eyes looking up at her from Mirror Lake; South Dome had answered her, when she questioned; the Merced River had sung its story of mercy to her while yet she was a child.

At length the trail crossed the range near the cabin, and during the brief summer equestrians appeared on the summit, going down toward the valley. From her hidden post she saw the world's people pause, with full hearts and brimming eyes, on Inspiration Point, whence is taken the first look into Yose-mite. She saw, and understood.

But none who see the valley in summer time gain its full magnificence. One must live with it to grow into the vastness and solitude of its grandest grandeur. The mountain maiden, with the oxygen of the air flaming in her cheeks and lighting her eyes, skimmed on her snow shoes over billows treacherous as the waves of the sea, and was given ideal pictures.

For the solitary blooms the desert rose; for the solitary are upreared the mountain snows. The best of everything is seen in the company only of God. In solitude we are closed with the Most High, and, whether leaf thicket or ice cavern, it is the place of worship and joy. Therefore, the heart of the maiden was stirred deepest, when on a winter's day, alone in the vast white universe, she peered from Glacier Point, into the frozen crater of jewels. Then the valley shone in a white splendor that its summer worshippers can never see. Down the walls the falls hung dumb and motionless, suspended by an unseen hand, trailing miles of crushed jewels, opal and sapphire, and emerald. El Capital lifted his white plume among the army about him. The exquisite Bridal Veil swept in frosty tissue down the white-robed cliff. The Cathedral Spires rose crystal clear into the blue sky, and on Cloud's Rest, the white drifting nimbus of the sky caressed their sister snowdrifts of the peaks. The great pines of the valley were cones of amethyst; the very air was set with dazzling jewel points, and the pure solitudes pulsed with imprisoned sparks of heavenly fire.

An artist sketching the picturesque groups of mountaineers, heard of "the girl up yonder"—a girl whose daily haunts were where the clouds and silence wander, a maiden who was seated beside the moon, while the stars twinkled like fireflies about her.

In time he found her. Never flower before bloomed like this snowflower beneath his gaze.

Snows can not smother passion, or stars stir the pulses like the light in nearer eyes. To this ardent poetic soul, with its disregard of fitness, of constancy, or duty, or happiness beyond the present hour, the snowflower gave her life. He had found beauty, he worshipped it. The humble eye is satisfied forever with the shabby print of a Madonna on the wall, but new pictures replace the old on the easel of the artist. His search is always for beauty; having fixed one face upon the canvas his eye roves for a brighter cheek and sunnier hair.

But, for the time, she was his angel. Disregarding the world, society, friends; forgetting education, style, culture—all that he would at another time remember—he took her from the heights where she had been the companion of nature, to show her to a groveling, putrid world.

Alas! Snowflower of the Sierras! Alas, that fatal name—that pure and fatal name—flower of the snows!

Did Fate christen thee, child of the upper air? Hast never seen the beautiful sunflower drained of its rosy beauty, by ice-dripping tears? Dost thou not know that the plant of the clouds has never been transplanted to lower fields?

The father talked wildly to the wayfarers who came now and then to lift his latch-string for a night's shelter by the cabin fire. He repeated, in wretchedness, that retribution had over-taken him. As cruelly as he had fled from the wife of his youth, his girl had gone from him. Not all his love or care could prevent her from giving the blow which fate had reserved for him. Muttering, or silent and glowering, the weeks and months found him, until at last he disappeared from his home and was lost forever to human view.

This is the story the guide told me as we stood by the fireless hearth of that deserted home.

She died, poor girl—died of a broken heart.

For those who dwell in lowlands, the roses bloom; for creeping things there are the mosses and the violets. Each plane in life has its own corresponding, recompensing loveli-ness. Let him who lives in rose-thickets be content, nor seek to pluck the blossoms of the crags; nor he who roams the snows think to keep in its freshness the rose that nature left in warmer climes.

She died, so the story runs, on Christmas Eve. Many years ago at Christmas time, in the dazzling radiance of a moonlight night, wanderers on the snow slopes saw a phantom gliding on the pearly snowshoes over the glittering peaks. She was shrouded in white, and out of her pale face her eyes gleamed like midnight stars. From mountain to mountain she wan-dered, and her hands were full of blood-red blossoms, that she kissed with lips as cold as they.

Every year since her earth life ended the dead girl revisits her early home. On those fields of snow, fit for an angel's feet, before the Christmas morn breaks in the East, this unforgetting spirit walks on high. Sometimes she is seen muffled in clouds; sometimes the blossoms in her hands make ruddy patches in the wintry sky. Her voice is heard in the wailing songs of the restless winds, and the fall of her snowshoes echoes like silver sleet down the mountain side.

That the Divine Jesus, whose birthday we celebrate, brings holy thoughts to men by devious means is not unlike. Whatever makes men lift their eyes raises the soul; whether the sweep of wings that startled the shepherds, or the dying color on the distant cloud, turns the face upward to the gaze of God.

Lo, not unmeet is it that at the time when, of old, the angel-heralded Christ-child came, all along the sides of the solemn Sierras, the lowly, the lonely, the wretched, the wicked, gaze upward, for the form of the pure maiden, who loves and haunts the snow-range of the air.

Children are told to be good that they may see the beautiful lady who was taken from her home on high, treated so cruelly, and killed by wicked men. And at midnight, along the western peaks, eyes dim, patient or bleared look upward into the lonely night for the sweet spirit form of the "Snow Flower of the Sierras."

THE GHOSTS WERE THERE.

AN ENTHUSIASTIC SCRIBE WRITES AND DESCRIBES A GHOST PARTY.

At the residence of Dr. Judson Davie, at "Old Spring Hill," on the evening of Dec. 30th, a Christmas entertainment was given in the shape of a Ghost Party, which was one long to be associated with the jollities and gayities of a merry Christmas. Although the night was a bitter cold one there were twenty couples present and all were in high praise of the pleasure of the occasion. The house was beautifully decorated with evergreen and flowers while the young ladies were indeed a palm of love-liness. Of course the boys—. At ten o'clock an elegant repast was served when all were unmasked and some fellows had their best girl and some didn't, while a young Eufaulian found to his surprise he had Mr. Robert Alston. In a very few minutes the young gentleman paid his respects to Dr. and Mrs. D., saying he was quite sick and departed for home. After satisfying the inner-man there was lots of music, banjo and guitar duets. Miss Annie Davie's piano solo deserves special mention. No one but a musician both by nature and training can handle the keys as she does. Dr. and Mrs. Davie entertain in an elegant manner and certainly know how to please the young people.   GHOST.

Eufaula Daily Times (Alabama), January 5, 1893

Julian Hawthorne

The Devil's Christmas

Salem, Massachusetts-born JULIAN HAWTHORNE (1846-
1934) *was the son of author Nathaniel Hawthorne. Satan had
long haunted American Christmases, from his appearance in
Spanish colonial performances of "Los Pastores," to Cotton
Mather's belief that devils would have a "merry meeting" with
women guilty of witchcraft on that day, and through newspapers'
Christmas poems of the* 18th *century that would mention him
in ways similar to the carols "God Rest Ye Merry Gentlemen"
and "O Come, O Come, Emmanuel." In this story, the text
of which is taken from the Christmas Day,* 1885 *issue of the*
Norfolk Virginian, *the title character mirrors the appearance
of those around him, in this case as a man of high society—not
unlike how he would appear in Marie Corelli's* The Sorrows
of Satan (1895).

A BOUT THE MIDDLE OF DECEMBER, I received a card
from Mrs. Farasay inviting me to attend the Christmas
celebrations at her home on the 24th of December; and at
the bottom of the card were written the words "To meet the
Prince." Though it did not occur to me at the moment who
this prince was—whether English, French, Russian or African
—I was confident, from the well known reputation of the
hostess, that he would surely be a personage well worth meeting. Mrs. Farasay entertains only the best people and has never
been known to make a social mistake. Indeed, had I enjoyed
the distinction of being her only guest, I should have been cer-

tain of meeting all the purest aristocratic element of society, concentrated, as it were, in her single affluent personality.

It is needless to add, however, that I was not called upon to pay her the above tribute of appreciation. When I arrived at her superb mansion on the avenue, I found it already thronged with an assemblage of beauty, celebrity and fashion such as it has seldom been my lot to encounter. The rooms were beautifully decorated. The staircase, a broad and gradual ascent from the great entrance hall, was so embanked and canopied with flowers that one seemed to be climbing a floral mountain. The languorous perfume of these myriad sweet blossoms was translated, as it were, into audible harmony by the strains of music which rose and fell and found their way everywhere, though their source was ever hidden. The cornices of the reception rooms were traced out with English holly, and drooping festoons of mistletoe depended from each lofty doorway, and seemed to impart a brighter tint of beauty to the cheeks and lips of the fair women and maidens who passed beneath, and to kindle a more ardent sparkle in the eyes of the gallant cavaliers who attended them. Ah, what warm and glowing reminiscences do those cool green leaves and pale white berries conjure up! Upon the walls crosses were designed in the undying verdure of the pine, and in the dining hall a huge Christmas tree extended its level boughs at the head of the table, lustrous with the soft light of a thousand aromatic tapers and sparkling with the gold and color of innumerable bonbonnieres and costly sweetmeats. And everywhere, thronging yet not crowding, were the splendor and the delicacy of the silk and lace of ladies' dresses and the gleam of jewels on their white necks and lovely arms, and the murmur of voices and tinkle of light laughter, forming an undertone to the music of the unseen instruments. The whole sumptuous scene was an epitome of the triumphs of civilization, refinement and of that mastery of mortal conditions which is called wealth. It causes the complaint of misery and the squalor of poverty to seem like a gross and grotesque illusion, foisted upon our senses by the deception of some delirious dream. It was the stately and tacit refutation of the shrieks of self styled reformers and the blatant arguments of anarchists; for when and where has human nature ever risen, or can it ever rise, to a greater height of power and felicity than was represented here?

In the midst of these agreeable reflections I found myself face to face with my hostess, who stood like a queen worthy to reign over such an empire. Mrs. Farasay's position at the head of the best society is so assured that one fancies she must have occupied it ever since society began; and yet, such is the youthful loveliness of her appearance, that a person meeting her for the first time would imagine her to be a star that had just begun to illuminate the social firmament. In this respect she might be said to represent society itself, whose charm is out of all relation with the passage of stars, and will appear to our great grandchildren no less seductive than it did to our great grandparents. But I do not know that I can more fully express my sense of Mrs. Farasay's merit than by saying that she was better fitted than any other woman there to appear beside the figure who stood at her right hand and shared with her the homage of the assembly. I recognized the Prince as soon as I set eyes on him; although, among the many points in which he is remarkable, in none is he more so than in the difference of his aspect at different times. He is never out of keeping with the group in which, for the time being, he finds himself; or, rather, he seems to sum up in himself the predominant characteristics of his immediate associates, to show the pure type of which they are the more or less complete illustrations. And never in my experience had I found his Highness more thoroughly himself, more royally at home, than he was here. I attribute this chameleon-like quality (as it might be termed) less to any deliberate intention on his part than to that exquisite involuntary sympathy which is fundamental in his nature. He enters so cordially into the life and interests of those who surround him as to render himself the mirror of their ruling traits. Of course, however, the distinction and authority which are innate in him make it impossible, under whatever disguise, to mistake him for another, and I allude to this peculiarity of his merely as affording an additional explanation of the extraordinary popularity he has always enjoyed among the elite of this world.

"I see you need no introduction to our guest of the evening," said my hostess, when I had offered my compliments. "Indeed, I tell the Prince that even his own principality can scarcely contain friends more intelligently loyal than many who have assembled to do him honor here."

"The season and the place are alike congenial to me," observed his Highness graciously. "The season of Christmas and the social center of the American Republic. It is impossible, when I contemplate a scene like this, not to feel that I have not lived altogether in vain!"

I was both surprised and touched by this avowal, which exemplified the generous nobility of the royal nature. For surely, the land of civil and religious liberty and the great anniversary of Christendom might not, at the first blush, be thought conducive to the moral tranquillity of a person of the Prince's supposed views. At this moment I caught sight of Father Ecks, a divine of extreme orthodox tendencies, who was standing at Mrs. Farasay's left. He was reputed to be her religious adviser, and was an old and valued friend of my own. I approached him and grasped his hand. "You remind me of the apple of gold in the picture of silver," I remarked.

"We are all gold together," he returned, laughing pleasantly.

"How is business?" I asked.

"The scene before you is a more eloquent answer to that question than I could give," was his answer. "Positively, I feel at times as if my office were little more than a sinecure! It is the realization of my ideal—the church and the world reflecting each other so closely as to be practically indistinguishable. Whether as a man, a priest or a Christian I am equally content."

"Is it the church or the world which has made the greater advance?" I inquired.

"They are becoming more and more merged in each other. There never was any radical quarrel between them; mutual misunderstandings have been at the bottom of all their differences. The increasing light of intelligence, penetrating the dark caverns of error and ignorance, have shown or are showing the superficiality of all disagreements. Believe me, my dear sir, the day is not far distant—it is even now at hand—when the religious enthusiast and the so-called devotee of fashion shall breathe one creed and follow one ideal."

"How blessed a consummation!" I exclaimed fervently. "And is it true, then, that the arch enemy of human perfection is forever conquered?"

"A word in your ear!" replied the father, beckoning me to his side. "Our only real enemy has been a prejudice of the imagination, which distorts friendship into the likeness of hostility. The assurance of peace lies in the fact that he whom we thought our foe is in reality our ally. It is not a question of victory but of reconciliation. If I might indulge in a paradox I would say that we have been fighting the air all this while, for the Prince of the powers of the air has never been at heart opposed to us."

"I comprehend; evil is undeveloped good, or good is undeveloped evil, or both. But, though I am prepared for the widest tolerance on the part of his Highness, here, I must confess that I was a little surprised to find him joining so amiably in our celebration of this particular day, of all others. It seems an instance of magnanimity almost excessive."

"Ah! did you but know him as I do, you would marvel no longer!" returned the good father, piously. "But I will not presume to interpret him. Possibly an occasion may present itself for him to define his position in his own words."

The tale of guests was by this time complete, and the melodious notes of a silver trumpet, echoing through the splendid rooms, apprised us that dancing was about to begin. Mrs. Farasay gave her hand to the Prince to lead the first figure. In receiving it the clasp of his Highness' glove caught in the delicate chain which held his eyeglass, and it dropped to the ground. He did not notice the accident; but I picked the eyeglass up, and was about to restore it to him when he moved out of my reach, and I was obliged to defer the execution of my purpose to another opportunity. Meanwhile, not being myself a dancer, I stepped aside into the deep embrasure of one of the windows.

The curtain happened to be drawn aside, and the snow-covered street was visible. The last carriage had departed, and the stately thoroughfare extended, silent and deserted, before me. The light of electric lamps shone down upon it with a frigid and ghastly brilliancy, which made the stars, twinkling in the sky overhead, seem more distant and unattainable than ever. Presently the stooping and decrepit form of an old woman appeared, coming slowly and with difficulty along the sidewalk. She wore a dingy cloak, which was evidently an incomplete protection against the piercing chill of the Winter night, while her head was bare, save for the gray locks which fluttered disorderly in the breeze. When she arrived opposite the window from which I was gazing down at her, she stopped, and, raising her head, stared earnestly up at the great edifice. Her features, thus revealed, were worn and aged, and bore the marks of deep suffering and anguish; but there was something about them which, for a moment, strangely recalled to my mind another face, beautiful, calm, alluring, young, which was as widely known and celebrated in the highest circles of the city as that of this old hag was ignored and despised. The resemblance, far-fetched and doubtless imaginary though it was, perplexed and offended me, seeming, as it did, to imply some human connection, however slight, between our gracious hostess and this miserable vagabond; and it was with a feeling almost of personal irritation that I turned away, and appeased my fretted sensibilities with the gorgeous spectacle of loveliness and luxury which filled the noble dancing saloon from brim to brim.

The rhythmical movement of the swaying groups, keeping time to the rich melody of flute, violin and horn; the flash of diamond and the sweep of silken trains; the mellow light and fragrant warmth illuminating and vivifying all, soon drove from my memory the haggard specter of the street. I marked where, conspicuous and eminent above all the rest, the hostess and her Prince led the revels; and I realized, with inward satisfaction, that happiness and prosperity are the only true life; want and misery are but a negation and a shadow. Thus musing, and toying with the Prince's eyeglass, which I still held in my hand, it chanced that, in pure absent mindedness, I raised it to my eyes.

No sooner was it fixed in its place than the voluptuous scene before me underwent—or seemed to undergo—a monstrous transformation. The rose-embowered hall assumed the appearance of a savage glade in the mid heart of a wild and shaggy forest. The subtle music changed to the crazy moan of the winds and the long howl of beasts of prey. And the guests, one and all, instead of the graceful bearing and comely presence of a moment before, put on the aspect of a mad crew of grisly creatures, frantically jigging to an infernal tune that was beaten out by the quick throbbings of their own evil hearts. Round and round, forward and backward, they whirled and flew, mowing and gibbering in ghastly merriment, and all making obeisance, as they passed, to the fearful Prince and Princess of the carnival. But from these last, after one glance, I was fain to turn away my eyes, or the spectacle would have blasted them. Language of human beings cannot portray the horror investing the figures of those two. And yet—such was the hideous spell of his Highness' eyeglasses—that pair aped

the gestures and reproduced, as in loathsome parody, the linea-
ments of the dainty lady and the royal guest in whose honor
we were gathered together!

With a groan I staggered back against the window, clasping
my hands over my face. As I did so the eyeglasses dropped from
my eyes.

"Well, well! here is a singular proceeding," exclaimed the
voice of my friend, Father Ecks, laughing good humoredly.
"To think of a man like you taking a nap, of all times and
places in the world, at such a time and place as this! Wake
up, my dear friend, and be one of us again. Here is the Prince
asking for you; and, by the way, do you happen to have seen
his eyeglasses?"

Shrinkingly I raised my head and stared about me. The terrible vision of the witch's Sabbath had vanished. Here again
were the swelling music, the flowers, the perfume and the
splendid company. Had I indeed been dreaming? It must be
so.

"It must have been the fragrance of the roses," I muttered,
trying to recover myself. "I am peculiarly susceptible to
odors."

"Nothing more probable—and here are the eyeglasses,"
added the amiable father, picking them up. "Come, they are
going to the dining hall, and the Prince particularly desires
that you should sit next to him."

So saying, he began to thread his way through the courteous throng, and I followed him, my brain still haunted by tan-
gled reminiscences of my hateful dream. Even the sanctified
figure of good Father Ecks himself unaccountably brought
to my memory one of the most active and diabolical of the
infernal crew. But—down with such thoughts! They were
an outrage on good breeding and an insult to common sense.
Was Mrs. Farasay's home a haunted forest? Were the friendly
and fashionable faces I saw around me those of witches and
demons? With a laugh at my own absurdity, I put to flight my

weaknesses and took my place beside the Prince with an air of confidence and composure.

It so chanced that his Highness was, at that moment, just on the point of rising to respond to the toast of "The Guest of the Evening."

"My friends," he began, lifting himself to the height of his commanding figure and embracing in a glance the eager array of upturned faces, "that we are friends, with all that friendship implies, is due in no small measure to the historic episode whose chiefest festival we celebrate to-night. Into the history of the last two thousand years I will not enter here. It is a history of suffering and of error, but also of solid and steady progress. The causes which have wrought toward the present consummation have been often misconceived and perverted and their issue thereby delayed; but they were potent still and they have at last triumphed over adverse conditions. The consciousness of having been, to the extent of my humble capacity, instrumental in this result is to me the crowning satisfaction of my career. In Christianity, little as your forefathers may have suspected it, I recognized my opportunity, and I may add without egotism that it was an opportunity which I have not failed to cultivate. The horizon has seemed dark at times; there have been seasons when hope appeared naught but folly; but throughout all, my friends, I have held fast to my faith in man. I have never surrendered my conviction that his instincts were more potent and persistent than his reasonings; that what he was would finally prevail over what he could be taught. Man—vilely as he has been misrepresented, cruelly as he has been misled—man has in him an innate sense of respectability which nothing can entirely extirpate. It has brought him safely though all his vicissitudes and has culminated in the brilliant gathering which surrounds this hospitable board to-night. You are truly the elect, and every secret pulsation of your hearts that convinces you of your moral and mental superiority, and of the assured distinction of your future destiny, is a direct aid and encouragement to me in my constant effort toward human emancipation. Other struggles, other reverses may perhaps yet lie before me, but, if ever my purpose falters or my courage quails, I shall remember you as I behold you now, and gather fresh strength and heart from the recollection."

As he said the last words his Highness put on his eyeglasses, which Father Ecks had a minute before slipped into his hand. Recalling (as I could not help doing) the sinister effect which these same glasses had apparently produced upon my own vision, I looked with some interest to discover whether the Prince were similarly affected; but the happy serenity of his expression and the kindly manner in which he bowed his acknowledgements of the applause resounded through the room at the conclusion of his little speech, persuaded me that my odd experience, whatever else its origin might be, was clearly not to be charged to the royal spectacles. No doubt Father Ecks was right, and I had merely fallen asleep and had an ugly dream.

The interest aroused by the Prince's remarks had prevented most of the guests from observing—what had, nevertheless, not escaped my own notice—that Mrs. Farasay had been summoned from the room almost at the opening of his harangue. A servant, with a troubled expression on his features, had made his way to her side and whispered something in her ear that had caused her to start and change color, and also to slip from the table as quietly as she might. Her absence now began to be noted; but the Prince, with thoughtful tact, gave the conversation an entertaining and anecdotal turn, and speedily we were all laughing and chatting, in temporary forgetfulness of her unexplained departure.

This happy state of things was suddenly disturbed, however, by a loud shriek from one of the ladies, and immediately afterward she fainted, amid the greatest commotion. Upon examination a great clot of blood was found upon her otherwise immaculate bosom. While we were speculating as to how it got there I happened to glance up toward one of the chandeliers which depended from the ceilings and was startled to observe a thin red stream trickling down it and falling from its lowest pendant to the floor. A wild panic and confusion ensued upon this discovery and a rush was made for the doors, causing a jam, in which, I fear, many persons were injured. Thus unexpectedly was the graceful harmony of a moment before changed into frantic riot and disorder. The table, with its golden salvers and crystal goblets, was overturned; the gigantic Christmas tree toppled to the ground and at once became a mass of flames; the festoons of flowers were torn from the walls, and, almost in less time than it takes to tell it, the whole superb house, so lately the shrine of luxury and refinement, was a howling pit of destruction, filled with maddened and struggling shapes and choked with smoke and fire.

Of all the fair company, the Prince and Father Ecks alone retained their self possession. The former exchanged a glance with the latter, and they hastened up stairs, whither I, impelled by an awful fascination, followed them. Arrived at the floor above, they turned to the right, and the Prince threw open a door leading into Mrs. Farasay's bedroom. He and the father entered, but I paused upon the threshold.

Mrs. Farasay was standing beside the body of an aged woman, who was stretched on the ground dead, with a knife buried in her heart. Her gray hair, her ragged black cloak and the contour of her haggard and bloodless features told me at a glance who she was; nor was it possible, in that moment of lurid enlightenment, to doubt her relationship to the murderess who hovered over her. As the Prince entered, Mrs. Farasay raised her eyes, and they met his in a glare of terror and despair.

"Come, there is no time to lose!" said he, in a harsh voice of command. "My carriage is waiting for you. Come!"

"Oh, my mother!" said she, in a sighing voice, and then she laughed.

The Prince wrapped his dark cloak around her, caught her up in his arms and was gone, and Father Ecks went with him. They seemed to vanish in smoke, and then I heard the rumble of wheels. But when I myself reached the open air there was no trace of them to be seen, and the church bells were ringing in the Christmas morn.

BOY SANTA CLAUS DYING

———

Schoolmates See Lad a Mass of Flames at Christmas Celebration—Mother Is Burned.

HUNTINGTON, IND., Dec. 22. (Spl.)—"I won't play Santa Claus any more," were the last words of Fred Falck, 8, as he lost consciousness, while the flames of a blazing Santa Claus outfit were still burning over his body in the Central School Building late yesterday, during the annual Christmas exercises of the school.

The lad, dressed in a suit of white cotton, was distributing presents from a Christmas tree to his fellow-schoolmates, when the cotton became ignited from a lighted candle.

Before the fire could be extinguished the boy was fatally burned, and death is expected.

The mother was a guest and assisted in smothering the fire, herself sustaining severe burns.

Kentucky Post, December 26, 1906

Thomas Wentworth Higginson

Harlakenden's Christmas

THOMAS WENTWORTH HIGGINSON (1823-1911) *was an abolitionist, women's rights activist, financial backer of John Brown, leader of the 1st South Carolina Volunteers black regiment during the Civil War, and correspondent of, and co-editor for, Emily Dickinson. The ghost ship of the poem was the* Countess Augusta *and was in fact wrecked in* 1738.

[One of the best known traditions of our Atlantic coast is that of the "Palatine Light," popularly associated with the wreck, off Block Island in 1720, of a ship bearing emigrants from the German Palatinates. The light is reported as appearing at irregular intervals for more than a century, and was last seen in 1832. Its appearance is minutely described by an eye witness, a resident physician, who saw it December 20, 1810. See Sheffield's "Block Island," p. 42.]

R OGER HARLAKENDEN climbed the hill
Where no other fishermen dared to go;
The east wind was blowing, bitter and chill,
   Sheer was the cliff and the footing slow;
Handgrip on rock and knee on the sod,
At last on the headland's height he trod.

In the days of the pirates three footpaths led
   To that dizzy cliff; but now there was none
      Save for the fox, the goat and the bird.

One path o'er the seaweeds green and red;
    From high-water mark to the cave-mouth, one;
      And thence o'er the Pirate's hill, the third.

Roger Harlakenden threw him down,
    Breathless at last, on the thin, dry grass:
He could see his dory that glistened brown,
    He could see the men and the women pass
Tending the fish-flakes, from door to door,
And then he looked off to the ocean floor.

Like a land-locked haven in sight of the sea
    The life of the twelvemonth past was spread;
    Peaceful contentment of heart and head
Since the Lord had found him, from sin set free.
Yet sometimes the thought of his wilder years
    Rushed back upon him, teeming with ill.
Wicked joys and delicious fears;
    And then he climbed to the Pirate's hill.

Was it worth the strength of a man like him
    To dwell by the bay, with a calm sweet wife,
No stir in the blood, no peril of limb,
    No wild, fierce joy of the coming strife?
Just to clean the boat and to haul the seines,
    To cook the fish by the drift wood fire,
To play with his boy through the autumn rains
    And on Sunday sing with his wife in the choir?

Straight from the far horizon's line
The east wind blew; the smell of the brine
    Banished the months of weary peace
    And bade this desolate torpor cease;
It was almost sunset; there was the sea!
Only a night's hard pull, and he

With his dory made fast to a whale-ship side
Could rock once more on the ocean wide.

What to him the fare of the men?
The ruder the better. He held his own
    Still with the roughest. God! how he longed
    To be once more where the sailors thronged
Or the old-time wreckers might shout again
    On some cruel isle of the middle zone.

See! with the sunset came once more
    The Palatine Light, the ship on fire,
    Each generation, son and sire,
Had watched it gleam, since the current bore
    The fated ship to a merciless wreck
    With the crew in sight on the blazing deck.

There was the phantom now; the flame
    Climbed stay and halyard to pennon-staff:
There was neither pity nor joy nor shame
    In Roger Harlakenden's bitter laugh.
"Let it burn!" he said. "Let the ocean roar!
    I have looked on burning ships before.

"I will watch that light with a steadfast eye
    From this moment out, till the sun goes down,
If it lasts till the last red sunbeam, I
    Will be quit this night of the cursed town;"
Then he tried to think of his wife and child,
But his lips grew stern, and the wind was wild.

Suddenly met him the startled face
Of a boy who had climbed to that dizzy place,
    Half-triumphant and yet half-scared,
    But daring whatever his father dared.

The fisherman trembled, but made no sign.
   Terror next in that young voice rang:—
   "Father!" it cried. Harlakenden sprang—
Out went the Light of the Palatine.

He clasped the child in his strong embrace,
He thrust back the curls from the rosy face,
   Then faded the last bright beam of day,
A shadow fell on the ocean swells,
   And soft from the mainland dim and gray
Came the sweet fair sound of the Christmas bells.
   Never since then the horizon line
   Has gleamed with the wraith of the Palatine.

SANTA CLAUS SHOT DEAD.

Farmer Made Up for Kris Kringle is Killed by a Neighbor.

BOONEVILLE, Ind., Dec. 22.—Peter Smith, a farm laborer working near by the home of Frank Jaco at Paradise, this county, went to the latter's house last evening and Jaco, hearing the dogs bark, opened the door. He saw a man at the gate, and, receiving no reply to questions, stepped back into the house and got his gun. When he again opened the door he saw no one. Later a rap came to the back door, when Jaco, followed by a Mr. Hewins, opened the door and saw what he supposed was a masked man. Again receiving no reply to his questioning Jaco struck the man, partly turning sideways at the same time. Hewins grasped the gun and fired over Jaco's shoulder, striking Smith in the breast and shoulder, killing him almost instantly. The statement in explanation of his conduct was he was acting as Santa Claus.

Pantagraph [Bloomington, Ind.], December 24, 1894

F. H. Brunell

The Ghostly Christmas Gift

A Story of This Land and That

FRANK H. BRUNELL (c.1852-1933) *was founder of the groundbreaking horse racing newspaper the* Daily Racing Form, *a sportswriter, and secretary of an early baseball players' union and league. This story appeared in a paper for which he had also served as sports editor, the* Cleveland Plain Dealer *of December 25, 1887, and delivers on its narrator's belief that ghosts should not be commonplace.*

S OME TALES ARE BEST NOT TOLD. Until today, with an assignment to contribute to the CHRISTMAS PLAIN DEALER staring me very hard in the face, I had held this idea of the story that I am going to tell. But in sketching the past, real and imaginative, for an incident out of which a tale and my task could be accomplished, I hit on this—the strangest story that I ever heard connected with mortal man. It didn't happen to me, for which I am glad. But I knew the man whose life was wound in with its weird incidents, whose soul was warped by the mysterious visitations taken, as he firmly believed, as penance for a revengeful act, and whose death was dramatic to a degree of mysterious atrocity.

It is perhaps one of the oddities of literature in its connection with humanity that Christmas is essentially a season of ghosts. And it has always seemed an oddity to me that there should be such a lack of oddity about the typical ghost—if that is the right term and a ghost can be typical. There doesn't seem to be any particular reason why ghosts should be so commonplace. Very few of the literary and reminiscent specters with which I have been acquainted—I am glad that the connection has been no closer—have been dull, thin and melancholy wraiths without light or mellowness, and certainly lacking anything that could be galvanized and called humor. There have been fat ghosts and jolly ghosts, if there have been any ghosts at all, and some shades or lights—there is no reason why a spirit should be libeled as a shade—that have returned their earthly smiles. At least there should be if there are not, and considering the fact—which is unquestioned if we admit the other fact of ghostly existence—that ghosts stay out late o' night and are light of foot, jollity and variety must lurk within their airy breasts. If ever I run against a spirit, and am not too startled to use my faculties, I shall, for the good of literature and verbal tales of the future, draw it out, note the peculiarity of the spectral mind and peer through its conversation for a piece of fancy or a flash of humor. But perhaps it will be as well for a literary illusionist—and to the man or woman of imagination all is possible—to paint or pen a ghostly Hood or a spectral Harte better than natural acquaintance with such a ghost would serve to establish it in the records. And this notion seems most eyeable when I consider the power of such a creation and the possible weakness of the actual creation. After all both would be airy and neither could be put under the set and austere eye of the microscope or dissected by the logical and exposing examination of your materialistic investigator. And at the present stage of the human game a fanciful pretty is of more account than a home fact.

But this is not telling my story. Having never seen a spirit myself and holding no energetic desire to see one, I can but say that I believed the story that John Fleming told me, because I believed in John Fleming. Faults he had. What man has not? But he was built on very fine mental and physical lines, and if I am deceived it was only because he too was the victim of a morbid fever that gripped his life away, and because there were unmistakeable evidences—to me—of the influences that wrought his ruin. We were entirely different. My life had been in the town, where civilization asserts itself and claims supremacy. Of course such a habitation forces itself into the humanity it holds and surrounds. But John had been a wanderer from his youth, had seen the four corners of the world, and profited by what he had seen. I had known him as a young man when my school days were beginning; later, as the brawny and bronzed lion of our small town when I was on the brink of college, and he resting restlessly between jaunts to the other end of the world. In his youth Fleming had been a little wild and the stories connected with him had made him the bane of the mothers of the beauties of the town and the idol of their daughters. But as far as M—— was concerned nothing was seen of Fleming's wildness. I started for college and John for Liverpool via New York on the same day, and he shook hands with me most heartily as father and I left the train when our station was reached, promising to hunt me up when he came back, "If I ever do," as he said with a ringing laugh. I finished my college work and began the more serious business that followed, but didn't see John Fleming again for ten years. One fall evening as I sat at my desk, hard at work, a tall and spare man with bronzed and lined face and thick black hair, mustache and beard, in which the gray was coming fast, strode into my room and holding out his hand, said—"How are you, my boy?" I should have known the eyes if I had not seen them, and the voice had I not heard it, in fifty years. It was John Fleming, but a different John Fleming from the athletic man I had left at the little railroad station in New York state ten years before. We shook hands heartily, he telling me how he had come from M—— to see me when he found out where I was from mother. He inquired about my life and plans and left me to finish my work, I having agreed to dine and talk over old and new times next day.

When he had gone to his hotel I could not help thinking—
to the great damage of my copy for the next day's paper—how
much John Fleming had changed and aged and thinned. These
thoughts were renewed to the damage of my sleep when I
reached home. The man seemed well but there was a settled
look of melancholy in his eyes and a corresponding ring in
his voice that made me wonder more than I wondered over
anything within my recollection, "What had changed John
Fleming?" But I slept the question into submission, rose at
noon and hurried to John Fleming's hotel for dinner, thinking
perhaps that I should find him more cheerful of eye and voice
and that continued travel might have temporarily depressed
him. But the man I met had the same melancholy aspect and
his manner sank deeper into me as I talked with him before
dinner. There was evidently a pall of some kind on John Fleming. We lingered over dessert and the old days and characters at
M——. As we left the table John said: "Finish your work and
come up tonight." I told him that I couldn't get away from the
office until midnight. "No matter," he said, "come then. I shall
be up."

I "ground out" the usual amount of "copy" and left the
office at 11:30, going straight to Fleming's room. He was up
and writing as though supplying the insatiable genius of "The
Daily Necromancer," always hungry for copy.

As I entered he threw down his pen and said: "My dear
fellow, I am glad you are here. That Star had nearly frozen me
to desperation," pointing to a peculiarly bright and twinkling
star that shone through the window as if asking for admission.
And as I looked at the star I was struck with the fact that it
alone illuminated space. Not another ray or spot of light stood
out of the dark sky. And the Star was very near, very bright and
very nervous. But for the melancholy in John Fleming's voice
I should have been inclined to laugh at its peculiar appearance.
There was humor in it and in me, but mine was checked by the
interest and curiosity I felt in John Fleming's depression. But

the Star compelled attention, and after fifteen minutes' silent smoking and eye fencing with it I acknowledged its strange attraction and slashed the curtain between it and my eyes. "I should be glad if you could shut the cursed thing out," said Fleming as the curtain fell down and, wondering at such a remark, I glanced at the window covering and started as I saw the jagged edges of the star in deep red outline in the curtain's center. As I started John said with more intensity than I had ever associated with his voice, "Ah! you see it, too. That kills the hallucination theory and proves your interest in me."

All this was puzzling to me, and my blood ran colder than was its wont. The Star and Fleming were evidently old acquaintances, and the peculiar outline on the curtain and the stillness of the room affected me more than anything ever had affected me up to that time. At last Fleming, who had been smoking viciously at a big, strong cigar and blowing huge clouds at the Star's outline, as though to cloud it out of view, said:

"The cursed thing! And so it affects you, too?"

I said that it did and peculiarly.

"But not guiltily," said John.

I started. Guiltily? Was it the shadow or symbol of a crime and, if so, who was the victim? Surely not John Fleming!

And I pondered in silence with the desire but without the energy to ask the question. And the Star twinkled malevolently on. I had become sure by this time that in its twinkling there was spite, because of a constant and jerky movement. Human spite and malevolence is so thrown out, and it has always been my experience to find them more energetic than any kind attribute. My ruminations were cut short by John Fleming's sharp question:

"You do not see the Face?"

"What face?" I asked him.

He gave no answer, but the Star's outline danced diabolically.

At last Fleming roused himself and, with a defiant glance and shake of his fist at the outline on the curtain, and before which menace the outline seemed to wabble and fade, said: "I may as well tell you the story of my life and of that devilish Star and the more devilish Face behind. Could you see the face it would aid in substantiating my story. But you know me well enough to know that I will tell you the truth. Beside this, men make confessions to ease their souls, or minds, or what you will. And there is no ease in adding to the weight we carry. I have carried my weight for nine years, and for the life I took at that time my own is gradually going out."

I shivered as Fleming said this. He laid his hand upon my arm and continued: "Hear me out. My act was heady and full of revenge, but no assassination. It had men's approval but never my own. You know how I have wandered all my life and remember the day, now ten years ago, that I shook hands with you and your dead father at E——, N.Y. I went straight to New York, from thence to Liverpool and sailed from that town without a week's delay for Melbourne, Victoria. A party of us was to organize and equip an expedition for the western Australian pearl fishing grounds, with headquarters at Perth at the head of the Swan river. The expedition started with four vessels and ten of us sharing in them, crews, divers and apparatus. But a storm knocked us all to pieces before we rounded Point d'Entrecasteaux, and of the ten bosses and forty sailors and divers but six and eighteen reached what is now Albany. The rest went down with the fishing boats. By a lucky grab I had managed to save one of the partners from drowning. I had never seen him until he had joined us at Melbourne and told me that his name was George Wilson. He was a Californian, strong, alert and evidently a man who had seen and acted a great deal. I took to the man after grabbing him from the hungry southern Pacific and he seemed to take to me. The sailors soon found work on the upgoing pearl fishing boats, fortunate enough to have escaped the gale and four of

the partners decided to go up and renew their fortunes at the
pearl oyster banks. For myself I had had enough of pearls and
so, I found, had Wilson. At least he asked me to join him and
return to America. He showed me charts of a strip of country
in South America where there was gold enough, he said, to
make a score of men as rich as Monte Cristo. Would I go? Yes,
if I continued to think as well of the trip as I then did. But why
hadn't he gone before? He said that he had only had the chart
a month. It had been given to him by an American miner who
had died of Queensland fever in a Sydney hospital, and after
he had invested all his money in the pearl fishing expedition.
It would take £500 to equip and put us on the Columbian
ground, where the gold was. I had the money, was satisfied
with the explanation, and we hurried to Sydney and took the
first Pacific steamer for San Francisco. We landed there in June,
and after nine days, spent in fitting ourselves out, I supplying
the cash, we took a trading steamer for Buenaventura, United
States of Colombia, and after a week's lounging and outfitting
started anew and over the Andes, choosing the fertile passes for
a route to Santa Fe de Bogota. Another rest and another start,
southeasterly, over the Llanos de St. Juan and across the river
into the strip of land five hundred miles long and three hundred miles wide, southeast of the Columbian and northwest
of the Brazilian line, then claimed by both countries and given
over to the desperadoes of each or those of any land that chose
to wander so far from civilization. We met plenty of hunters of
gold, such as we were, on the road, and had to watch our riding
and pack mules very closely. Twenty days out from Bogota
we began to consult Wilson's chart and found ourselves within
a few miles of our gold ground. We found the valley and old
river bed that were set down as our chief guides about the time
that we ran across as motley a group of prospectors as was ever
gathered. There was half a score in the party and it was led
by a Chilean desperado. Such men in such callings are rare in
South America. The fellow, Juan Comigo, as he was called,

demanded that we join his band and tell our business. Wilson
was nervously furious and, had I not held him in, would have
made a fighting dash for it. But I explained to the brigand that
we were engineers, employed by the Colombian government
to make maps of the debatable ground for diplomatic use,
assured him that we had no taste for a life on the plains with
its horse and cattle stealing forays, much as it might be to our
interest to join the band of such a genius as Juan Comigo. He
was sinister but let us go unwillingly. An hour out we found
that spies were on our tracks and they dogged us for five days,
during which I made hundreds of imaginary calculations in
my voluminous notebook, used a large compass and line, for
alleged measurements, all the while pretending not to see the
spies and ordering Wilson not to notice them. At the end of the
fourth day Comigo's dogs withdrew, and at the end of the fifth
we stopped our mummery, and after riding ten leagues as fast
as our animals could carry us, found a cave and lay in hiding for
a week. Then we cautiously retraced our steps and were soon
within the marks of our chart, with Comigo and his coyotes
away. Three days later, in the partially concealed depression
of the valley, evidently an old stream bed, we found enough
gold in nuggets to found a monarchy or corrupt the world. It
was pure metal, in rugged and partially shining lumps, from an
ounce to several pounds in weight.

"In two days we had divided the necessities in our pack
mule's burden between us, cached the rest, and loaded the
spare animal and our own with between four and five hundred pounds of the yellow nuggets most exposed to view. On
the night of December 24 we were within three days' ride of
Bogota and in a wild and arid plain. It was Wilson's turn to
guard and mine to sleep. At midnight I was wakened by a shrill
neigh. I glanced toward the fire, saw the pack mule saddled and
Wilson in the act of mounting his own riding animal and with
the bridle of my own in his hand. In a second I saw that he was
about to desert me with the gold and seizing my rifle I drew

a bead on him and shot him through the back as he prepared to jump into the saddle. He never spoke a word or moved a muscle after I reached him. The shot was a killing one. Upon the blanket in which I was rolled I found a note which jeeringly bade me goodby and told me that I had served his purpose well. I buried him in the valley, divided the load of gold between the two mules and pushed on to Bogota and thence to Buenaventura. At the latter place I boxed the gold and shipped it with myself to San Francisco, where I turned it into cash. It yielded $18,000.

"So much for the story of my relations with Wilson and the manner of his death. He richly deserved what he got, though I would rather have lost my own life in the Colombian plains than taken his. But I shot him on the impulse of the moment. The $18,000 grew and multiplied in California and I am rich. That does not interest you.

"The strange part of my story remains to be told. Since the day I killed Wilson his spirit and its symbol, that devilish Star" —and as he spoke the Star leaped as if in laughter and grew redder—"has attended me. It has come between me and those I loved and is ever present. I have never rested in its baneful presence, and each Christmas day I find upon my table a lump of gold in the form of a star, in which Wilson's features are impressed. See them!"

And John Fleming went to a cabinet and took from a case therein nine shining and rough pieces of gold, each in the form of a star and each with the features of a man sunken in them. Each of the nine was an exact duplicate of the other. I could not resist a shudder as I saw them, and a strange thrill or concussion, as from a current of electricity, passed through me as I lifted one from the drawer. And the shadow of the symbolic Star leaped and laughed on the curtain as though in malice at my terror. John Fleming buried his face in his hands and raised it as I put my hand on his shoulder and said that he was the victim of a trick.

"Oh, no! You do not see that horrible face beyond," said he, with a shudder. "It is not for other eyes than mine. The Star is visible; the Face is not."

I ran to the window and dashed up the curtain. There hung the Star in the dark sky, yet out of it, and it was the only light on that sky's front. It danced at me and threw its bloody glare on the wall. But no face was visible. I drew the curtain down again, preferring the shadow to the Star itself. I was impressed against my will as to its supernatural origin, but turned up the lamps and called for more light so as to drown it. The servant saw nothing and Fleming told me that only those he loved ever saw the Star, and none but himself the Face. I bade him good night and went home to think, but not to sleep.

I had hardly got to bed when I was summoned by a message from P——, the night clerk at Fleming's hotel. Something was wrong with Mr. Fleming. I hurried on my clothes and ran to the hotel and upstairs to John Fleming's room. He sat at the table where I had left him—dead. In his hand was a pistol, and through his temple a bullet. The Star's reflection still danced on the curtain and its origin was still shining bloodily in front of the sky. I seemed to see the thin outline of a receding face also as I lifted the curtain, but do not know whether it was the recollection of the visage on the gold stars still hanging on me. And then the Star faded out and from that day to this I have never seen it. On the table before which all that was left of John Fleming sat were two letters. One was addressed to me. It charged me to see that his belongings went to his sister, and that $18,000 was paid to the local hospitals. He left me his watch and ring and the nine golden stars. I went to the cabinet to see them. Their case was there but they had gone. The ghostly Christmas gifts from the malevolent spirit which controlled the Face and the Star and marking the Christmas tragedy upon the Colombian plains had been taken back to that land from this.

Luke Sharp

The Blizzard

Tragedy of the Man Who Interviewed His Own Skeleton

Humorist ROBERT BARR, JR. (1850-1912) *reportedly adopted his* nom de plume *"Luke Sharp" from a Toronto area undertaker's sign. A Canadian, he was nonetheless a regular contributor to the* Detroit Free Press, *in which this story appeared in the December 9, 1888 issue. Barr was a friend of Arthur Conan Doyle, and the first to parody him with "Detective Stories Gone Wrong, or, The Adventures of Sherlaw Kombs," again in the* Detroit Free Press, *in 1892. At the time he was writing, no reader would have had the narrator's experience of seeing his own bones, apart from a nasty break; X-rays would not be invented until 1895.*

I. THE APPARITION.

JOHN BRENT WAS ENGAGED in the unromantic occupation of mixing mortar with a hoe. He was not accustomed to such work, but a man who sets out to carve a fortune for himself on the plains of Dakota has to do many things that he has not been accustomed to do, or let them go undone. The stuff he was mixing could hardly be called mortar in the plasterer's sense of the term, for lime and many of the other necessary components were lacking. The mixture was merely mud, but the pioneers thought it would do for the purpose. As Brent worked at the mud, his partner, George Wentworth, was in the bush near by cutting sticks with which, in conjunction with the mud, they intended to build the chimney of the cabin they had just completed.

The bending over was very tiring, and John straightened himself up with a sigh, to rest for a moment. An astonishing sight met his eyes. So astonishing was it that he rubbed the moisture from them and looked again. A skeleton sat on a stump looking at him, if the eyeless sockets can be said to look, and on the fallen log beside the stump sat a second skeleton with its skull resting in its bony hands, an attitude that reminded him oddly of his friend Wentworth.

"Hello," cried Brent, when he had somewhat recovered from his surprise. "Who are you?"

"I am your own skeleton, John," answered the apparition, "don't you know me?"

"Can't say that I ever had the pleasure of seeing you before," replied John; then, feeling the bone of his arm, he continued: "And now that I do see you I don't believe in you. My skeleton is in its place all right enough."

"Well, perhaps I am hardly justified in saying that I am your actual skeleton. But you know queer things happen on the plains. Perhaps you have seen a mirage since you came out? Yes. Well, I am what you may call a mirage of your real skeleton. Understand?"

"Yes, I think I do. But this is so unusual, don't you know, that I hardly—say, would you have any objection to my calling my friend Wentworth?"

"*I* haven't. Perhaps his own skeleton here would like to have a talk with him," then, turning to the other specter, the first said: "Say, George, how is that? Do you want to see your—"

The other skeleton, without looking up, merely shook his skull in a solemn way, and then the first turned to John and said;

"No, he doesn't seem to care about having your friend here. He's a very reticent fellow, George is, and don't like a crowd."

"Yes, I know he is."

"I mean his skeleton. I could hardly get him to come at all."

"Well, is there anything particular that you wanted to say to me? I presume you did not take all this trouble for nothing."

"No. I wanted to know if you realized what you were mixing with that mortar?"

"I know there are a good many things that ought to be in it that are not in it. We can't get any lime out here, you know."

"Do you know what you *are* mixing in place of lime?"

"Yes. Sand and water and all the clay I can get, which isn't much. I don't know of anything else."

"Well, there *is* something else, and a very important ingredient, too. You are mixing your own life with that mud."

"How can that be!" cried the young man. At that moment he heard his partner approaching.

"George," he shouted, "do you see anything on that stump?"

Wentworth looked with astonishment at his partner and then at the stump.

"I see the stump," he said.

As John himself looked at the stump he noticed that the two figures had become very dim, and as he gazed they entirely disappeared.

"You're sure you noticed nothing?"

"Nothing unusual. What's the matter with you, John? Not going to have a return of the fever, I hope."

"I don't know. Hope not. I think my head's not quite all right yet." Then he told his comrade what he thought he had seen.

"The ghost wasn't far wrong," said Wentworth as he seated himself on the log from which his spectre had just disappeared.

"The warning, I imagine, was allegorical. We *are* mixing our lives up with that mud and building it into the shanty and wasting it on these plains."

"Don't do that, George," cried his companion sharply.

"What? Don't my sentiments suit you?"

"I don't mean the sentiments, but the attitude. Don't sit with your head in your hands. That's exactly the way your skeleton sat. Keep your head up whatever trouble comes. And about the sentiments, as you call them. What's the use of them?"

"What's the use of anything, for that matter?"

"There you go again. Who wanted to come out here? I'm sure I was not wild for it. It was your idea. 'Far from the madding crowd,' and all that sort of thing. Now I'm sure we're far enough, if that's any consolation. And yet you are not satisfied. Keep up your head; I insist on that."

"That wasn't in the articles of agreement, John."

"Well, it's in from now on. But now that we *are* here, what's the matter with this sort of life? It's what you expected, isn't it?"

"I suppose so."

"You can't expect Piccadilly out here, you know. If you yearn for the limitless plain, you can't have the limited Piccadilly, too."

"Oh, I don't know. William Black had 'Green Pastures *and* Piccadilly.' We've got the green pastures—miles of them. Perhaps we shall have our Piccadilly when we make our fortunes at sheep raising."

"Well, this sort of talk will not build the chimney. Do you think you have sticks enough?"

"Yes."

"All right. Let's combine 'em."

And they did. The sticks were laid in the form of a hollow square and plastered inside and out with the mud.

II. THE BLIZZARD.

When John Brent came breathlessly into the shanty a fierce blast of bitter cold swept into the room with him. It pushed vigorously at the door as he struggled to close it and then rattled its frail frame work against the stout bar that John put up to keep it shut.

Brent threw his overcoat and wraps in a corner and came to the huge fire that was roaring in the open chimney. "Good gracious!" he cried; "what a Christmas eve this is. Fifteen degrees below zero at sunset and Lord knows what now. Heavens and earth, George, sit up and don't keep your head in your hands that way. Don't you know it makes me nervous. I believe you do it purposely to make me low-spirited."

Wentworth looked up wearily, but said nothing.

"I don't believe," continued John, "that there will be one of our sheep alive in the morning. Certainly not if this cold continues. I've done all I can for them, but nobody can stand it out there more than a few minutes at a time."

"Don't trouble about the sheep," said Wentworth dejectedly; "we shall be more than lucky if we come out of this alive ourselves. Indeed, I don't expect that we shall."

"Oh, trust you for taking a lively view of things. If you have one merit more than another, George, it is a talent for cheerfulness under all circumstances."

"We shall never get out of this alive, John. It is getting colder all the time. I am freezing here in spite of the big fire. It would actually be a pleasure to be burned to death."

"Nonsense. This sort of weather can't last long."

"It doesn't need to."

"We have a week's firewood piled up here and more outside. We'll live through it all right. Next Christmas we shall be in London, you bet your life."

"We have bet our lives now and we have lost."

Brent did not answer him. He looked with dismay at his friend. Wentworth sat with his chin in his hands, gazing at the roaring fire, and it seemed to Brent that the light of madness was in his eyes. All that day he had made no effort to help with the necessary work of the place and Brent had uncomplainingly done everything that was required.

Suddenly Wentworth started up and seized a blazing brand from the fire. With it burning, he started for the door.

"What are you going to do?" cried his comrade.

"I'm going to see how the thermometer stands."

"I wouldn't open the door if I were you."

"You mind your own business, will you?" shouted Wentworth, facing around, with the blazing brand in his hand, and glaring at him with a look that chilled Brent more than the extreme cold. John said nothing, but stepped aside and let him pass. Wentworth, after a moment's pause, flung down the bar and the door flew open. The wind, cutting like a razor, roared into the room and made even the strong fire seem a mockery.

Wentworth held the red brand up against the little thermometer that hung on the outside, and Brent, looking over his shoulder, was appalled to see that it stood at 42° below zero. Wentworth swayed from side to side and seemed unable to read the figures. At last the brand fell from his hand and he staggered into the room. Brent picked up the burning stick, and, flinging it into the fire, closed the door again.

Wentworth resumed his old attitude before the fire, shivering now and then. Brent put more wood on and then sat down.

"How cold was it, John?" asked Wentworth mildly. He had apparently forgotten all about his rough remark.

"About 40 below."

"So much as that? And they told us that when it was twenty below all wind stopped. Great heavens! how they do lie about this cursed country."

After a few minutes' silence Wentworth suddenly sprang to his feet.

"What was that, John," he cried nervously. "Did you notice that?"

"Notice what?"

"Something was thrown down the chimney on the fire."

"Nonsense," said Brent. "You had better go to bed."

"There it is again."

As he spoke a chunk fell into the center of the fire, then another and another.

Brent's ruddy face paled as he realized what it was. The useless mud with which the chimney was built was crumbling with the heat and falling away, leaving the dry sticks bare to the flames. Before he could think of what it was best to do an ominous, sullen roar came down the chimney.

Wentworth jumped toward the door and threw it open. He laughed wildly and called to his dazed partner:

"Look, John, look."

The landscape outside was lit up with the red glare of the burning shanty. The sight roused John from his stupor.

"Come, George," he cried, "let's get out what we can. You take the clothing and I'll carry out some provisions. This shanty won't last ten minutes."

"Of course it won't. You leave if you want to. This is *my* spot."

"George, this is no time for nonsense. Help me out with the things."

"All right; here goes."

He flung the clothing indiscriminately out of the shanty, and then, without a word of warning, sprang on his partner and seized him by the throat.

"Out of this, you cowardly hound," he yelled. "Out with the rest of the dunnage. This fire is for *me*. Out with you."

The superhuman strength of the madman was something Brent was utterly unable to cope with. He was flung in a heap on the pile of clothing, and before he could rise to his feet Wentworth was inside again and had the door barred.

The roof was now one mass of flames. Brent seized a piece
of wood and tried to batter in the door, but he could make
no headway, and although the fire burned his face, the terrible blizzard benumbed his arms and made his efforts useless.
Every time he struck the door there was a yell of laughter
from within that sounded above the roar of the flames and the
blizzard. At last there was a crash and the roof fell in. Brent
stood back with a groan of anguish and looked helplessly at the
bonfire, from which there now came no human sound. He sat
down on the stump and gazed hopelessly at the burning logs
as they fell one by one into the mass of flames. Gradually all
sense of discomfort from the bitter cold left him. A soothed
and pleasant feeling came over him. The flames seemed to
grow dimmer and dimmer. Even the sense of regret and grief
left him.

"John," said a voice at his side.

Brent turned around and saw sitting on the log beside him
the second spectre that he had beheld with wonder in the
summer. This time, however, it did not seem to surprise him.

"Well, what is it?"

"John, I acted with unpardonable rudeness to-night; but
you know I was not in my right mind, or I never would have
done so."

"I knew that. Anyhow it doesn't matter now."

"No, it doesn't. Strange, isn't it. Such opposite elements.
You by frost; I by fire. John, a merry Christmas to you. Do you
see the light breaking in the east?"

Brent did not answer.

"Come," said the spectre, "you are ready now. Let us go."

Louis Glass

Warned by the Wire

The story may be indebted to Charles Dickens' 1866 "The Signal-Man," but its environment of railroad telegraphy was drawn right from the life of its author. LOUIS GLASS (1845-1924) *was not known as a writer, but had himself been a telegraph operator, mining superintendent, manager of both the Pacific States and the Sunset Telephone and Telegraph companies as well as manager of the Pacific Phonograph Company, and was co-inventor of the nickel-in-the-slot phonograph—a forerunner of the jukebox. The tale reprinted below first appeared as the first of a page full of stories under the heading "Ghosts by the Glare of the Coals" in the* San Francisco Call *on December 25, 1895.*

I HAVE IN MIND an incident of my life that has been a great mystery to me—a mystery simply because it has never been explained, even to the smallest extent.

Back in the '60s, when railroad building was new on this coast, I was a telegraph operator for a small road running between two of the mountain towns in this State. In constructing the line I was utilized as a traveling operator, my duties being to remain with the construction force and handle the wire running to headquarters. My instrument was of that variety used for light telegraphy, and could be easily transported from place to place, batteries and all.

The division superintendent and myself occupied bunks arranged for us in a small, red boxcar that had been fitted up with a few conveniences and so arranged that while on the road we would be able to enjoy a few of the comforts of civilization.

We generally retired about 8 o'clock being fagged with the day's work, and as a rule our slumbers were undisturbed until daybreak. The night I have in mind, which was the beginning of this mystery, was cool, and being worn out with the labor of the day I went to my couch prepared for a good rest. No sooner had I touched the pillow than I was lost in slumber. Just how long I slept I do not know, nor am I able to recall the hour of my awakening. But I certainly was aroused by the ticking of my instrument, a most unusual procedure after sunset. It seemed to be running wild but the sound of it fully restored me to wakefulness. I listened attentively and my practiced ear caught the words as they came to me clearly and with great regularity.

Could it be possible that I was yet asleep? I got up and walked over to the little shell upon which rested the key. No, I was not asleep. Everything was too clear to me and the ominous click ticked out the following sentence:

"Spike-driver Catton will be killed in the new cut tomorrow at 10:30."

I was appalled and bewildered at this intelligence, and sat down to think it out. There was no use for me to attribute it to supernatural influence. I did not believe in such things. Finally I went back to bed, with the conviction that some one had hoaxed me from the other end. Calmly and without mental discomfort I rolled over and went to sleep again. In the morning the matter was almost forgotten and the gang of men went out to work as was the daily custom. I saw Catton pass my door with the spikehammer on his back, but merely recalled the message of the night before for an instant. As he passed from view I forgot all about it and turned to my key.

I had been working a few hours, and in order to stretch myself a little got up and stepped off the car for the purpose of taking a walk up to the cut to see how things were getting on.

As I turned the curve which brought the section men into view a dull, rumbling sound struck my ears and looking up I saw to my horror about twenty tons of rock fall away from the main bank and come crashing down over Catton, the spike-driver.

In an instant I knew it was all up with him, and when we recovered his remains they were crushed out of all semblance to a human being.

Imagine my feelings when I recalled that message of the previous night, and the indifference with which I had received it. Was I responsible for Catton's death? The thought disturbed me greatly, but after looking at the matter from every conceivable point of view, I came to the conclusion that I was not. Catton was a marked man and he met his fate.

I confess, however, that I was not as regular in my slumbers after that, and I would awaken with a start at the slightest suggestion of a tick from my instrument. The strain of anticipation was awful.

Catton was insured, and the widow received over $3000. One day I saw her, and as she seemed more contented with the money than with her lamented husband, I gradually got over brooding about the affair. It took me six weeks though, and I am sure it told upon me. After a time I let it pass out of my mind altogether, as my head was filled with the business of getting the road to the next town.

Fate, however, did not intend that I should be free from misery, and the next visitation came to me under quite different circumstances. It was late in the afternoon and I was getting away my daily report. When I sent thirty and closed the key my receiver straightway ticked back:

"Tie-walker Hopkins will fall in a culvert at 5:25 and break his legs."

This time I acted instantly, and, manning a handcar with eight men, I urged them to backtrack with all possible speed. It was 5:20 when we got under way and there were two miles to cover. Never was a handcar sent along the rails like that one.

The minutes seemed to glide away with wonderful rapidity, but, as I feared, we were too late. As the car swung into the canyon I saw Hopkins throw up both hands and stumble into a culvert. Our speed was so rapid that it was impossible to stop the car as we passed over him, as he lay on the rocks beneath groaning with pain. It took us but a moment to get to his assistance, but both legs were broken and he was helpless.

It was no use to grieve over this accident. I had taken every possible precaution to avert the disaster, but without success.

I gave as a reason for my hasty manning of the handcar that I wanted to see the unfortunate man on some track business, and that I forgot to give him the order in my excitement at seeing him injured. I feared to convey my knowledge to any one, and would doubtless refrain from it to-day were it not for the fact of the incidents being so far back in my history.

We gave Hopkins every comfort, and after he had been fixed up to be sent back to the other end of the line I went straight to my car and tore the receiver from its fastenings, vowing that I would no longer have such a damnable prophet at my elbow. I fixed another instrument where the first had been, and from that time on I received no more messages while working on the new line. When we got it through to the adjoining town I packed my valise and started for San Francisco, and, moved by some invisible power, I placed the old receiver in the depths of my bag, as I considered it a curiosity.

To this day I am thankful that I took it with me as I consider it my savior. Its third message and the one that made me swear never to let it get out of my possession came to me in Stockton, although the instrument was connected with no live wires. I had packed it in its customary corner of my grip and was just bidding the clerk good-by. As I walked out of the door toward the train I heard something ticking in my grip. I listened perfectly dumfounded and heard repeated several times:

"Do not go to-day."

Was this another warning that disaster awaited me, and perhaps others? Certainly, I would yet have time to stop the train if I made haste. No, on second thought I would not do that. People would call me a crank. I would return to the hotel and wait for results.

Following my thoughts I slowly walked back and informed the clerk that I had concluded to stay a little longer. On the following morning I eagerly sought the daily papers, and as I expected that train was ditched and the man who occupied the berth directly over the one I had engaged had his back broken and is a cripple for life.

When my time comes that instrument will tell me the day and the hour.

SANTA CLAUS SHOT DEAD.

—

Tragic End of a Christmas Party in Mississippi—Noted Instructor Killed.

JACKSON, Miss., Dec. 25.—Prof. L. W. Saunders, a deaf mute, and for many years a teacher in the State Deaf and Dumb Asylum, was shot and killed last night, by his nephew, C. R. Young. Prof. Saunders was to act as Santa Claus at the Christmas tree gotten up for the amusement of the deaf and dumb children in the institute, and called at Mr. Young's house in his Santa Claus garb.

He knocked at the door and Mr. Young, the only occupant, demanded, "Who is there?" a time or two and receiving no reply, fired through the door at which he supposed was a burglar. Prof. Saunders dropped inside the hall and died in two minutes. The ball passed through his body. The professor was a brother of Capt. R. L. Saunders, World's Fair Commissioner from this State, and was highly respected. Mr. Young is crazed with grief.

Fall River Daily Herald [Mississippi], December 26, 1895

H. C. Dodge

Poor Jack

HERWICK C. DODGE (1847-1922) *was the nephew of Mary Mapes Dodge, a woman best known as the founder and editor (1873-1905) of the children's journal* St. Nicholas *and author of* Hans Brinker, or, The Silver Skates. *Though he never had a book of his own, he wrote hundreds of poems for newspapers and was particularly known for his shape poems. Most of what he wrote was funny or sentimental, or at times didactic or political; this poem's demonic toy from 1892 was an exception.*

I am Jack in the Box. If
you press on the locks I
jump out and do all the rest.
I'm owned by a boy who takes wonderful joy in making you practice the test. From a stocking that hung
by the chimney I sprung. St.
Nick put me " in it," they say;
so if I am bad, or my looks
make you mad, it isn't my
fault, anyway. The girls
big and small don't like me at
all, and scream when I show
them my face; the babies, oh,
dear, get spasms of fear and
yell when I pop from my
case. For giving such shocks
I am squeezed in my box to squat in
the dark without air. Now, how
would you feel if you had
such a deal? I guess you my
anger would share. Of all

the queer jokes that are played by
some folks I think I'm the poorest
about. It's tough on my pride in
my prison to hide, and yet I'm
ashamed to come out. Some time
I'll get square with my owner. I'll
scare the little boy when he's abed.
In spite of his cries I'll shoot out my
eyes and bite him until he is dead.

Pierre-Barthélemy Gheusi

Christmas Wolves

PIERRE-BARTHÉLEMY GHEUSI (1865-1943) *was French, and this story first appeared as "Le Loups de Noël" in* Figaro Illustré, *January* 1897. *Its first appearance in English was in* The International [*Chicago*], *December* 1897, *and it was later reprinted in the May* 1940 *issue of* Weird Tales *as "The Red Gibbet." The translator, credited only as H. Twitchell on this and numerous French stories and books, was Hannah Stackpole Perret-Gentil Twitchell* (1851-1942), *of Wisconsin.*

TOWARD THE CLOSE OF DAY the snow ceased falling; the wind suddenly veered into the north, and its gusts cut like blows from a switch. Night fell; the silver light of the winter moon flooded the sky, lit up the ermine helmets of the Vabre and of Baffignac, and was reflected from the ice covered rocks of the gorge which hung over the raging Agout.

Just as the door of a wayside inn opened with a great rattling of chains, and the landlady stepped out on the threshold, a horseman came in sight around a turn in the road, his powerful horse snorting with terror, and stopped in front of the door of the rustic inn. The woman hastily summoned the hostler, while the traveller, dismounting, exclaimed roughly:

"Hallo! here is Joue-en-Fleur! Wine and a fire, my good woman! Tell the boy to give my horse a bountiful supper, and see if he is wounded in the flank."

"Holy mother!" cried Thiébaude; "how you look, seigneur! Your corselet and sleeves and even the knot on your sword hilt are dyed with blood and dirt!"

"May Astaroth choke every beast of them!" shouted Amalric. "They have ruined my best doublet. And I was dressed for the midnight mass and feast at the château of the Sire de Ferrières! I look more horrible than the Vabre butcher, the terror of all the hogs in the country!"

Angry and crestfallen at the same time, the reister laid his heavy gun on the table, and sat down before the roaring fire, a genuine Christmas fire. Half a dozen carousers, sitting at a table at one end of the room, resumed their interrupted game of cards, whispering timidly to each other; they seemed to stand in awe of the new comer. When his steaming wine was set before him Amalric, of his own accord, related his misadventures to the hostess, who served him with timid deference.

"It is a bright night, to be sure, on account of the moon. But what a road, *ventre de lézard!* chasms, torrents, precipices, snow drifts, and in the ravines all the wolves in Cevennes, more stubborn and relentless than the Calvinists! When I left Vabre they contented themselves with following me, watching for a misstep on the part of my horse. But near Therondel I had to slacken up a little, for it would have been mortal to gallop fast. Then a famished creature leaped on Argant's back and I had trouble in getting him off; had to use my dagger! But look at the *tourteaux* on my doublet! From a distance, one would take me for Guillaume de Montpellier's herald!"

Some of the players, leaving their game, which lagged for the want of oaths and uproarious mirth, had drawn near the fireside. One of them even ventured to raise his voice and question the formidable reister.

"Monseigneur, do you think it would be imprudent to go to Albignier to-night?"

"You would certainly never reach the end of your journey, whether you went on foot or on horseback. Stay here, if you value your rustic hides; Joue-en-Fleur will say your midnight mass for you."

"Is your lordship not going to order a battue soon for all these famished beasts?"

"The first one will be called before the Epiphany; all the wolf hunters of the neighborhood will be summoned."

"But if monseigneur would condescend to put himself at the head of our *rabatteurs* to-morrow . . ."

"Silence, knave! I hunt with you! See those cowardly faces, Joue-en-Fleur!" exclaimed Amalric with insulting contempt. "Is there a man here who could pass the Red Gibbet at night without dying with fear?"

A thrill of terror passed over the audience; heads dropped; no one replied.

"The Red Gibbet?" said the hostess crossing herself; "but it is . . ."

"Occupied? I know that very well! It was about a week ago—wasn't it?—that we hung the old witch of la Balme? That old hag who howled every one's fortune at him, and who practised witchcraft."

"L'Armassière?" asked Joue-en-Fleur, crossing herself again, and glancing furtively toward the door, which had just opened and closed noiselessly behind the king's officer.

"Exactly! At this season she will keep fresh for a long time; she will serve as a scarecrow on the Ferrières road. Yesterday Argant shied and nearly threw me into the Agout under the old hag's hooked nose."

"Seigneur captain," said a trembling voice, "I will go to the Red Gibbet!"

The reister started in surprise, and turned fiercely upon the speaker; he was a youth, almost a child, whose large, dark eyes shone out from his pale face with an expression of perfect fearlessness. "Here is a cub of a dangerous sort! Is he a habitual visitor here, Mistress Thiébaude?"

"No, monseigneur."

"Who is his master? Does any one here know him?"

"We took him in to-night for the first time," stammered

Thiébaude, under the compelling influence of the boy's magnetic glance. "We never saw him before."

"Come here, my bold fellow. Where do you hail from?"

"From the forest of Montagnole."

"But before that?"

"From the caves of Anglés."

"Where did you get that hang-dog look? Have you been poaching a little on our lands?"

"I have no other trade, captain." At this unexpected reply, so quietly made, a stupor fell upon all in the room; Amalric himself was disarmed by the boy's audacity.

"*Ventre-Mahon!*" he growled, half laughing and half angry; "you shall enter my service. My war page let himself get hung at La Salvetat. Do you want his place? But braggart, will you really go to the Red Gibbet to-night?"

"I will."

"Alone?"

"Alone."

"How shall I know it?"

"I will await you there, since you are to pass that way in an hour."

"The wolves will leave nothing of you but your carcass."

"You might lend me your gun."

"So you know how to handle that plaything, do you? Let me see you shoulder it, you rascal."

The vagabond smiled confidently; with the dexterity of an old soldier he grasped the heavy weapon; to the officer's surprise he rapidly unloaded it, then reloaded it, all the accessories being so manifestly familiar that Amalric could not help showing his admiration.

"If you shoot the gun as well as you load it," he exclaimed, "it would not be pleasant to be your target! At forty paces you must be able to blow the kernel out of a nut, or the brains out of a trespasser."

"Easily, monseigneur."

"And at the first shot you can bring down the most nimble game, I'll wager."

"Dozens of your hares would bear witness to that, monseigneur," replied the young poacher, strangely bent on a provocation as impudent as it was uncalled for. This was the master-stroke. The drinkers exchanged glances of consternation and terror at the furious expression on the face of the Seigneur de Vabre.

"Serpent!" he shouted. "You shall join the old woman on the Red Gibbet, with a cravat of hemp just like hers!" He rose and stood threateningly over the boy, who made no effort to avoid the soldier's raised fist. Amalric paused in astonishment at this defiance. "Why do you confess that to me, you robber?" he asked at length, pleased at such courage. "I like brave hearts; you suit me perfectly. Here is the gun; wait for me out there. If the wolves press you too hard climb up on the crossbar of the gallows; the old woman will keep you company. I'll warrant that she'll not be talkative, but if her presence annoys you, send her into the Agout with a kick!"

The boy became livid; his lips trembled, and his eyes fairly blazed. He grasped the gun offered him, and without a word slipped out into the clear, frosty night.

"By Hercules!" cried Amalric, "there is a man for you, you cowards! That is what I call having a heart in one's breast and blood in one's veins."

One of the peasants now ventured a reply which alarmed the adventurous cavalier. "To be sure, seigneur! But there is also a Spanish musket which you will probably never again see on your gun rack."

"What do you mean? Do you think that that rascal . . . ?"

"It was a clever way for him to get firearms. At any rate, the gun is in good hands, as your wild boars will know to their cost a dozen times before Epiphany."

Convinced of his credulity, Amalric swore like a pagan. But where could he go to search for the robber? He drank his warm wine, and no one dared risk exasperating him further. When he was well warmed he wrapped his dark cloak about him, leaped into his saddle and rode away in the moonlight. Reassured by his departure, the other guests resumed their carousing, while Thiébaude anxiously listened for sounds outside, as if she were expecting something to happen.

Amalric rode along at a good pace over the snow already hardened by the intense cold. The moon shone brightly in the pale sky. The roaring and rushing of water rang out in the stillness of the frosty air as the Agout flowed rapidly along. The mournful, continuous howling of wolves, repeated by the echoes of the mountain, sounded like a lament over the buried landscape. Argant, who had not recovered from the hurt received from the Therondel wolf, shied at every isolated bush and every dark turn in the road. Guided by a hand of iron, he fairly flew along the dangerous declivities bordering the precipices.

Being unarmed Amalric anxiously scanned the dark hedges among which the road wound about on the mountain side. To reassure himself he whistled the strains of an old Venetian march, not without a multitude of false notes, however. His horse, growing more and more excited, would certainly have broken the neck of the musician if the latter had persisted in his efforts.

To repress the impatience which devoured him, the captain next evoked the images of the two ladies he was soon to meet; one was a beautiful blonde of the Flemish type, the other a charming brunette. With these two noble dames he was to take communion this Christmas Eve, and afterward feast at the board of the opulent d'Azais de Ferrières, the greatest baron in the country. With soldierly stupidity he repeated to himself the gallant remarks which he intended to address to these beauties; he had learned them for the purpose from the Senechal de Castres, who made pretensions to being a wit and who was much better equipped with platitudes than with ideas.

In spite of his application, Amalric could with difficulty recall the vision of the two profiles. In their place all his misdeeds—hangings without trials, rapines and violences—rose before him like so many ghosts. To his summary way of dealing with offenders—freed as he was from all control, by the isolation of his estate and the troubles of the epoch—the gallows which dotted the highways for leagues around bore witness.

Recently the sorceress of la Balme had predicted that he would hang from the last gibbet he had constructed on the Ferrières road, and he had summarily hung her to the tree, without any fear of her supernatural prowess.

He certainly would not die by hanging, he, the brave soldier whose glance alone terrorized the mountaineers of the region. But he was not so sure that some fine winter's night, during one of his frequent expeditions, always for a wicked purpose, an ambuscade of exasperated peasants would not leave his lifeless body by the wayside. And what a sinister night the present one was; how thoughtlessly he had allowed himself to be disarmed by a poacher, a mere child at that! A thrill of fear passed over him. As he rode around a turn in the road the Red Gibbet loomed up before him.

An exclamation escaped the reister's lips as he recognized the vagabond of Luzières perched on the ghostly tree, the moonlight reflecting from the shining metal of the gun he held in his hands! He had not for a moment thought the boy would keep his word; the surprise he felt was mingled with joy at the thought of not being alone in the icy waste.

"So you are here!" he exclaimed. "A brute of a peasant back there took you for a thief; you might shoot him, for practice at large animals. Well, it is settled then. You are to be my page and the first *arquebusier* of my company. Has my musket been of use to you in keeping off the wolves?"

"Not yet, monseigneur," replied the boy trembling, with cold, doubtless.

"Were there no beasts on the road?"

"There were many, monseigneur, with eyes like blazing furnaces. They followed me without daring to touch me; I walked along singing at the top of my voice, and beating the measure with the click of the musket."

"An excellent way to keep the bullies at bay; a shot would have been better, however."

"I saved that for a better enterprise."

"What?"

"You shall see, monseigneur."

"You must have been cold on your picturesque perch; you should have warmed yourself up by giving the brutes a taste of saltpetre and lead."

The boy now descended and walked slowly toward the captain. "I could not hit the wolf I wanted to kill."

"Which one was it?" questioned Amalric, and he looked around expecting to see the blazing eyes of some beast.

"A very large one, which I do not want to miss," replied the strange boy.

A gust of wind cut the captain's face so sharply that he swore a great oath and exclaimed: "Jump on behind and we will go. I will take you to Ferrières since you are henceforth to be in my service; if I leave you here, nothing will be left of you by to-morrow. If the old he wolf you have your eye on comes near I give you permission to dispatch him at once."

"Let him die then!" exclaimed Amalric's page, taking sudden aim at his master. A sharp detonation broke the silence of the night. The reister, struck in the heart, fell heavily in the snow.

The boy grasped Argant's bridle and fastened it securely to a strong root. With granite firmness he climbed up to the gibbet. Leaning out over the gulf he uncoiled a rope which was wound around his waist, and tried to fasten it to the body hanging there, and draw it toward him. As he worked he murmured:

"You have been avenged, grandmother, and you shall be buried in consecrated ground. I told Thiébaude this night that you would be avenged before the dawn!"

But even as he spoke the body of the woman which had been exposed so long to the cold and storm dropped to pieces, and, falling from rock to rock, at last disappeared in the tumultuous waters of the Agout.

At that moment a bell rang out not far away; its clear music resounded through the still air like a prayer winging its flight above. Other bronze voices replied in the distance celebrating that Nativity which promises to the humble blessings to be realized, and to the wicked a chastisement for their iniquities. The vagabond, leaning over the gulf, made the august sign of redemption; then descending he went up to the body of the soldier, which was already stiff, and regarded it with a look of bitter hatred.

Approaching howls warned him to hasten with his task. He dragged the body to the gibbet, and, by means of a slipknot, drew it up to the beam lately occupied by the other corpse. It swayed to and fro in a sort of funereal dance in the moonlight; the gibbet creaked, and a pack of hungry wolves rushed out from the hedges, attracted by the scent of blood.

Crazed with terror, Argant kicked vigorously at his agile foes. One of them had already sprung into the saddle and was about to close his jaws on the charger's neck, but swinging the heavy musket around, the boy broke the beast's back with a terrific blow; then springing upon the horse he gave his life into the keeping of the terrified animal's instinct. The noble creature sped away like an arrow toward Luzières, followed by a pack of howling wolves; the captain's body swayed in the moonlight, while the silvery bells at Fernières sent their joyous Christmas peals down through the echoing valley.

Henry Beaugrand

The Werwolves

Our next story first appeared in English in The Century *magazine of October 1898 and was later collected in 1900's* La Chasse Galerie, and Other Canadian Storie*s by* HONORÉ BEAUGRAND (1848-1906). *In 1913 the story was loosely adapted by an American company into the first werewolf film and released by Universal Film, which as Universal Pictures would produce horror film classics* Werewolf of London (1935) *and* The Wolf Man (1941). *The* Werewolf (1913) *is unfortunately one of the approximately 70% of American silent films that are considered lost.*

A MOTLEY AND PICTURESQUE-LOOKING CROWD had gathered within the walls of Fort Richelieu to attend the annual distribution of powder and lead, to take part in the winter drills and target practice, and to join in the Christmas festivities, that would last until the fast-approaching New Year.

Coureurs des bois from the Western country, scouts, hunters, trappers, militiamen, and habitants from the surrounding settlements, Indian warriors from the neighbouring tribe of friendly Abenakis, were all placed under the military instruction of the company of regular marine infantry that garrisoned the fort constructed in 1665, by M. de Saurel, at the mouth of the Richelieu River, where it flows into the waters of the St. Lawrence, forty-five miles below Montreal.

It was on Christmas eve of the year 1706, and the dreaded Iroquois were committing depredations in the surrounding country, burning farm-houses, stealing cattle and horses, and killing every man, woman, and child whom they could not carry away to their own villages to torture at the stake.

The Richelieu River was the natural highway to the Iroquois country during the open season, but now that its waters were ice-bound, it was hard to tell whence the attacks from those terrible savages could be expected.

The distribution of arms and ammunition having been made, under the joint supervision of the notary royal and the commandant of the fort, the men had retired to the barracks, where they were drinking, singing, and telling stories.

Tales of the most extraordinary adventures were being unfolded by some of the hunters, who were vying with one another in their attempts at relating some unheard-of and fantastic incidents that would create a sensation among their superstitious and wonder-loving comrades.

A sharp lookout was kept outside on the bastions, where four sentries were pacing up and down, repeating every half-hour the familiar watch-cry:

"Sentinelles! prenez garde à vous!"

Old Sergeant Bellehumeur of the regulars, who had seen forty years of service in Canada, and who had come over with the regiment of Carignan-Salières, was quietly sitting in a corner of the guard-room, smoking his Indian calumet, and watching over and keeping order among the men who were inclined to become boisterous over the oft-repeated libations.

One of the men, who had accompanied La Salle in his first expedition in search of the mouths of the Mississippi, was in the act of reciting his adventures with the hostile tribes that they had met in that far-off country, when the crack of a musket was heard from the outside, through the battlements. A second report immediately followed the first one, and the cry, "Aux armes!" was soon heard, with two more shots following close on each other.

The four sentries had evidently fired their muskets at some

enemy or enemies, and the guard tumbled out in a hurry, followed by all the men, who had seized their arms, ready for an emergency.

The officer on duty was already on the spot when Sergeant Bellehumeur arrived to inquire into the cause of all this turmoil.

The sentry who had fired the first shot declared excitedly that all at once, on turning round on his beat, he had seen a party of red devils dancing around a bush fire, a couple of hundred yards away, right across the river from the fort, on the point covered with tall pine-trees. He had fired his musket in their direction, more with the intention of giving alarm than in the hope of hitting any of them at that distance.

The second, third, and fourth shots had been successively fired by the other sentries, who had not seen anything of the Indians, but who had joined in the firing with the idea of calling the guard to the spot, and scaring away the enemy who might be prowling around.

"But where are the Indians now?" inquired the officer, who had climbed on the parapet, "and where is the fire of which you speak?"

"They seem to have disappeared as by enchantment, sir," answered the soldier, in astonishment; "but they were there a few moments ago, when I fired my musket at them."

"Well, we will see"; and, turning to Bellehumeur: "Sergeant, take ten men with you, and proceed over there cautiously, to see whether you can discover any signs of the presence of Indians on the point. Meanwhile, see to it that the guard is kept under arms until your return, to prevent any surprise."

Bellehumeur did as he was ordered, picking ten of his best men to accompany him. The gate of the fort was opened, and the drawbridge was lowered to give passage to the party, who proceeded to cross the river, over the ice, marching at first in Indian file. When nearing the opposite shore, near the edge of the wood, the men were seen to scatter, and to advance carefully, taking advantage of every tree to protect themselves against a possible ambush.

The night was a bright one, and any dark object could be plainly seen on the white snow, in the clearing that surrounded the fort.

The men disappeared for a short time, but were soon seen again, coming back in the same order and by the same route.

"Nothing, sir," said the sergeant, in saluting the officer. "Not a sign of fire of any kind, and not a single Indian track, in the snow, over the point."

"Well, that is curious, I declare! Had the sentry been drinking, sergeant, before going on post?"

"No more than the rest of the men, sir; and I could see no sign of liquor on him when the relief was sent out, an hour ago."

"Well, the man must be a fool or a poltroon to raise such an alarm without any cause whatever. See that he is immediately relieved from his post, sergeant, and have him confined in the guard-house until he appears before the commandant in the morning."

The sentry was duly relieved, and calm was restored among the garrison. The men went back to their quarters, and the conversation naturally fell on the peculiar circumstances that had just taken place.

II.

An old weather-beaten trapper who had just returned from the Great Lakes volunteered the remark that, for his part, he was not so very sure that the sentry had not acted in perfect good faith, and had not been deceived by a band of *loups-garous*—werwolves—who came and went, appeared and disappeared, just as they pleased, under the protection of old Nick himself.

"I have seen them more than once in my travels," continued

the trapper; "and only last year I had occasion to fire at just such a band of miscreants, up on the Ottawa River, above the portage of the Grandes-Chaudières."

"Tell us about it!" chimed in the crowd of superstitious adventurers, whose credulous curiosity was instantly awakened by the promise of a story that would appeal to their love of the supernatural.

And every one gathered about the old trapper, who was evidently proud to have the occasion to recite his exploits before as distinguished an assemblage of dare-devils as one could find anywhere, from Quebec to Michilimackinac.

"We had left Lachine, twenty-four of us, in three war-canoes, bound for the Illinois country, by way of the Ottawa River and the Upper Lakes; and in four days we had reached the portage of the Grandes-Chaudières, where we rested for one day to renew our stock of meat, which was getting exhausted. Along with one of my companions, I had followed some deer-tracks, which led us several miles up the river, and we soon succeeded in killing a splendid animal. We divided the meat so as to make it easier for us to carry, and it was getting on toward nightfall when we began to retrace our steps in the direction of the camp. Darkness overtook us on the way, and as we were heavily burdened, we had stopped to rest and to smoke a pipe in a clump of maple trees on the edge of the river. All at once, and without warning of any kind, we saw a bright fire of balsam boughs burning on a small island in the middle of the river. Ten or twelve renegades, half human and half beasts, with heads and tails like wolves, arms, legs, and bodies like men, and eyes glaring like burning coals, were dancing around the fire and barking a sort of outlandish chant that was now and then changed to peals of infernal laughter. We could also vaguely perceive, lying on the ground, the body of a human being that two of the imps were engaged in cutting up, probably getting it ready for the horrible meal that the miscreants would make when the dance would be over. Although we were sitting in the shadow of the trees, partly concealed by the underbrush, we were at once discovered by the dancers, who beckoned to us to go and join them in their disgusting feast. That is the way they entrap unwary hunters for their bloody sacrifices. Our first impulse was to fly toward the woods; but we soon realized that we had to deal with loups-garous; and as we had both been to confession and taken holy communion before embarking at Lachine, we knew we had nothing to fear from them. White loups-garous are bad enough at any time, and you all know that only those who have remained seven years without performing their Easter duties are liable to be changed into wolves, condemned to prowl about at night until they are delivered by some Christian drawing blood from them by inflicting a wound on their forehead in the form of a cross. But we had to deal with Indian renegades, who had accepted the sacraments only in mockery, and who had never since performed any of the duties commanded by the Church. They are the worst loups-garous that one can meet, because they are constantly intent on capturing some misguided Christian, to drink his blood and to eat his flesh in their horrible *fricots*. Had we been in possession of holy water to sprinkle at them, or of a four-leaved clover to make wadding for our muskets, we might have exterminated the whole crowd, after having cut crosses on the lead of our bullets. But we were powerless to interfere with them, knowing full well that ordinary ammunition was useless, and that bullets would flatten out on their tough and impenetrable hides. Wolves at night, those devils would assume again, during the day, the appearance of ordinary Indians; but their hide is only turned inside out, with the hair growing inward. We were about to proceed on our way to the camp, leaving the loups-garous to continue their witchcraft unmolested, when a thought struck me that we might at least try to give them a couple of parting shots. We both withdrew the bullets from our muskets, cut crosses on them with our hunting-knives, placed them back in the barrels, along with two *dizaines* [a score] of beads from the blessed rosary which I carried in my pocket. That would surely make the renegades sick, if it did not kill them outright.

"We took good aim, and fired together. Such unearthly howling and yelling I have never heard before or since. Whether we killed any of them I could not say; but the fire instantly disappeared, and the island was left in darkness, while the howls grew fainter and fainter as the loups-garous seemed to be scampering in the distance. We returned to camp, where our companions were beginning to be anxious about our safety.

We found that one man, a hard character who bragged of his misdeeds, had disappeared during the day, and when we left on the following morning he had not yet returned to camp, neither did we ever hear of him afterward. In paddling up the river in our canoes, we passed close to the island where we had seen the loups-garous the night before. We landed, and searched around for some time; but we could find no traces of fire, or any signs of the passage of werwolves or of any other animals. I knew that it would turn out just so, because it is a well-known fact that those accursed brutes never leave any tracks behind them. My opinion was then, and has never changed to this day, that the man who strayed from our camp, and never returned, was captured by the loups-garous, and was being eaten up by them when we disturbed their horrible feast."

"Well, is that all?" inquired Sergeant Bellehumeur, with an ill-concealed contempt.

"Yes, that is all; but is it not enough to make one think that the sentry who has just been confined in the guard-house by the lieutenant for causing a false alarm has been deceived by a band of loups-garous who were picnicking on the point, and who disappeared in a twinkle when they found out that they were discovered?"

III.

A murmur of assent greeted these last remarks of the speaker, and a number of *coureurs des bois* were ready to corroborate the absolute likelihood of his story by relating some of their own experiences with the loups-garous.

One of them, however, in his dislike for anything connected with military discipline, ventured to add some offensive remarks for the young officer who had ordered the sentry to be placed in confinement.

"Halte-là!" growled the sergeant. "The first one who dares insinuate anything contrary to discipline, or show a want of respect for any of our officers, will be placed in the dungeon without further ado. Tell as many stories as you please, but as long as you are under my orders you will have to remember that you are not roaming at large in the wilderness, and that you are here in one of the forts of his Majesty the King of France."

This had the effect of producing an immediate silence, and the sergeant continued:

"I am not ready to gainsay the truthfulness of the story that has just been told, because I am myself inclined to believe in loups-garous, although I have never met one face to face; but I will not suffer any one to speak disrespectfully of my superior officers. I will, however, if you desire it, tell you the experience of one of my old *copains*, now dead and gone these many years, with a female loup-garou, who lived in the Iroquois village of Caughnawaga, near Montreal."

At the unanimous request of the crowd, the sergeant went on:

"Baptiste Tranchemontagne was a corporal with me, in the company of M. de Saurel, in the old regiment of Carignan-Salières. We had come from France together, and he and I made a pair in everything connected with the service, having fought side by side in many an encounter with the redskins. The poor fellow fell into the hands of the Iroquois at Cataracoui, and he was tortured at the stake in the village of the Mohawks. He died like a man, smiling when they tore the flesh from his body with red-hot tongs, and spitting in the faces of his tormentors when they approached him to cut off his lips and to pull out his eyes. May God have mercy on his brave soul!"

And the sergeant devoutly crossed himself.

"Baptiste, in one of our expeditions on the south shore of Lake Ontario, had made the acquaintance of a young Indian maiden who was known as *La-linotte-qui-chante* among the warriors of her tribe. An intimacy sprang up between Baptiste and the young squaw, and they were married, Indian fashion, without much ceremony, the father's consent having been obtained by the gift of an old musket. The girl followed us back, and joined the tribe that had settled at Caughnawaga, under the protection of the guns of Fort St. Louis, opposite Lachine, where our company was stationed for nearly a whole year. Everything went well as long as we remained at Fort St. Louis, although, Indian-like, the young squaw was fearfully jealous of Baptiste, and at times would threaten him with acts of direful vengeance if he ever became unfaithful to her.

"One day our command was ordered to Fort St. Frédéric, on Lake Champlain, and our captain gave the strictest order that no camp-follower of any kind, men, women, or children, should be allowed to accompany us in the expedition. We started in the middle of the night, and Baptiste hurriedly said good-by to his Indian wife, telling her that he would return to see her in a short time. The squaw answered sulkily that she would follow him anywhere, and that, in spite of the captain or any one else, she would reach the fort before we did. We knew the Indian character too well to doubt that she would do as she promised, and when we marched over the draw-bridge of Fort St. Frédéric, five days afterward, we were not too much astonished to see, among the throng of Indians who had gathered to see us arrive, the face of Baptiste's squaw, half concealed under her blanket. Baptiste was slightly annoyed at her presence, because he feared that the officers might think that, contrary to orders, he had encouraged her to follow the company. But we had no time to reflect on the situation before our company was ordered to embark in canoes, to proceed at once to Lake St. Sacrament (now Lake George). Baptiste did not even have the chance to speak to his squaw before we got under way, with three more companies of our regiment, under the command of Colonel de Ramezay. We were away for three months, engaged in an expedition against the Mohawks; and we gave the red devils such a thrashing that they pleaded for peace, and we returned victorious to enjoy a few weeks of well-earned repose in the garrison of Montreal. Baptiste had lost sight of La-linotte-qui-chante, and he supposed that she had either returned to her tribe or else formed new ties with some of the trappers who regularly visited the forts to sell their furs and squander the proceeds in riotous living.

"The Indians having buried the tomahawk, there came a period of peace, when the governor-general at Quebec offered a grant of land to any soldier who would quit the regular service, and a dowry of eighty pistoles in money to any woman, provided that they got married and settled in the country. I never had any taste for wedded life or for the career of a *pékin*, but Baptiste was not slow in casting his eyes upon a pretty girl who lived at Laprairie, across the river from Montreal. He told me confidentially that he had made up his mind to leave the service and to profit by the liberal offers of the government. I attempted to dissuade him from his project, because I hated to part with my best friend; but he was smitten, and I had to make up my mind to bow to the inevitable when strange and unexpected occurrences soon took place that upset all his plans. One day, when we were both lounging about the market-place, Baptiste suddenly found himself face to face with La-linotte-qui-chante, whom he had last seen some six months before at Fort

St. Frédéric. To say that he felt embarrassed would be putting it very mildly; but he assumed a bold countenance, and spoke words of welcome that were received with apparent indifference by the Indian girl. She had returned to Caughnawaga, where she was now living, and she had come to Montreal with some Indian hunters who had brought their furs to market. She spoke not a word, but looked reproachfully at her old lover with her piercing black eyes, and disappeared in the crowd. Baptiste was seriously annoyed at this unexpected meeting, but as the girl had left without uttering any reproaches, he took it for granted that she had become reconciled to the idea of a final separation between them. My chum had applied for his discharge, and was to be married on the coming Easter Monday, and, as a matter of course, I was to act as his best man—his *garçon d'honneur*. Preparations were being made for the wedding, and there was hardly a day that Baptiste did not cross over the river to go and see his fiancée. Ten days before the date appointed for the ceremony, Baptiste returned one night in great trouble. His intended had been taken ill, seriously ill, with a violent fever, and no one at Laprairie seemed to understand the nature of her sickness. He would ask the post surgeon to go and see her in the morning. And besides, on leaving Laprairie, that very night, he had met La-linotte-qui-chante at the cross-road that led to Caughnawaga. No words had been exchanged between them, but her presence there at such a time was sufficient to give him food for presages of no pleasant nature. Accompanied by the surgeon, he repaired to Laprairie on the following morning, and he was horrified to learn that his fiancée had been stricken down with the smallpox, that was then raging among our Indian allies encamped about Fort St. Louis. Baptiste insisted at once that he should nurse his sweetheart through her dangerous illness, and the doctor returned to Montreal after having prescribed the necessary treatment. It was useless, however, for five days later my friend returned to Montreal with the sad news that his fiancée was dead. The poor fellow, in despair, reenlisted at once in our company, and declared that he would end his life in the ranks. He then took me aside and related to me the following incidents that occurred on the night before the death of his betrothed. During the day he had been astonished, on entering the large family living-room, to find La-linotte-qui-chante sitting by the fireplace, as the Indians are wont to do, coming and going oftentime without asking permission of any kind from the inmates, and ever without speaking a single word. Suspicious of her presence at such a place and under such circumstances, he immediately went to her and asked her what she was doing there.

" 'I have come to offer you help in your trouble and con-solation in your sorrow. The white maiden whom you love so much will be dead before morning, if I do not come to the rescue. I will go back to Caughnawaga, and ask for a potion that will cure her from our medicine-man. Meet me to-night, at twelve o'clock, at the first turn of the road, among the pine-trees on the riverside.'

"And before Baptiste could answer she had left the house, going in the direction of the Indian village.

"Although he did not half like the mysterious ways of the squaw, Baptiste said to himself that no harm could come of trying the decoction as a last resort, because the dreadful dis-ease had made such progress that it was evident that his sweet-heart was likely to die at any moment.

"Shortly before midnight Baptiste took his musket and went out to the rendezvous. He had been waiting for some time, and was getting impatient, when he heard a noise behind him, and in turning round perceived a pair of eyes glaring at him from a small distance in the underbrush. It could not be the squaw, and he supposed that it was some wild animal prowling about, probably a bear, a wolf, or a wild-cat. He instinctively shouldered his musket, and although he could not take a good aim in the dark, he fired, missing the beast, who sprang at him with a terrible growl.

"It was a wolf of enormous size, and for the first time Baptiste thought of a loup-garou. He was too well accustomed to danger to lose his presence of mind, and throwing his empty musket in the snow, he seized his hunting-knife, and made a lunge at the beast; but the blade bent on the hide of the animal as if it had been thrust into the side of sole-leather. Baptiste now bethought himself of the only way of getting at the wolf, by drawing its blood in cutting a cross in its forehead. The wolf seemed to realize the fact, and fought at paw's length with its powerful claws, tearing Baptiste's flesh into shreds, and trying to strike at his face so as to blind him, if possible, while keeping its own head out of the reach of the gleaming knife. The fight had lasted for some time, and Baptiste was getting exhausted, when by an adroit stroke of his weapon, always as sharp as a razor, he completely cut off one of the fore paws of the animal, who uttered a terrible yell resembling the scream of a woman, and fled through the woods, where it disappeared in an instant.

"Baptiste now understood the situation in a moment. La-linotte-qui-chante, who had been baptized and duly received in our holy religion, having afterward relapsed into idolatry, had been turned into a loup-garou, condemned to roam by night, while keeping her usual appearance during the day. Jealousy and revenge had induced her to attack her former lover, hoping to take him unawares, and to kill him in the woods, while his new love was lying on her death-bed, a victim to the terrible scourge that the squaw had brought to the house. Baptiste learned that La-linotte-qui-chante had been a frequent visitor for some time past, having succeeded in ingratiating herself with the poor dead girl, undoubtedly bringing to her the germ of the disease that was raging at the Indian village. Such was the savage revenge of the young squaw to punish the faithlessness of Baptiste to his former vows of love and affection. It was also learned afterward that a human arm, evidently that of an Indian woman, had been found in the snow by some children who had strayed in the woods, at the very spot where the fight had taken place between Baptiste and the loup-garou. It was undoubtedly the fore paw of the wolf, which had resumed its former shape as the arm of the renegade squaw.

"I have already told you," continued Sergeant Belle-humeur, "that poor Baptiste was later on taken prisoner by the Iroquois at Cataracoui, and that he was burned at the stake by the Mohawks. One of the prisoners who escaped from the red-skins, and returned to Montreal, told me that he had remarked a one-armed squaw, who seemed to take special pleasure in inventing the most abominable devices to add to the sufferings of poor Baptiste. It was she who pulled out his tongue by the root, and who crushed in his skull with a tomahawk when he fainted from pain and loss of blood.

"Now," summed up the sergeant, so as to cut short any more story-telling, "this is a real loup-garou story that I can vouch for, and that I would not permit any one to gainsay; and I now would call your attention to the fact that I will order the couvre-feu to be sounded, and that I shall expect every one of you to be snoring at the bugle-call, so as to observe the rules of this garrison.

"Lights out! And silence in the barracks!"

Paul Laurence Dunbar

The Haunted Oak

This poem by PAUL LAURENCE DUNBAR (1872–1906) *was first published in the Christmas number of the* Century *Magazine, December 1900, and was recited by him with other works at the Fifteenth Street Presbyterian Church in Washington, D.C. on December 16, 1901. In* The Century *the last two stanzas were cut; they first appeared in his 1903 collection* Lyrics of Love and Laughter. *In a year like 2020, during which slavery has been described as "a necessary evil" and a "blessing," the voices and the silences of "The Haunted Oak" seem as raw and necessary as ever.*

P RAY why are you so bare, so bare,
  O, bough of the old oak-tree;
And why, when I go through the shade you throw,
    Runs a shudder over me?

My leaves were green as the best, I trow,
    And sap ran free in my veins,
But I saw in the moonlight dim and weird
    A guiltless victim's pains.

I bent me down to hear his sigh;
    I shook with his gurgling moan;
And I trembled sore when they rode away
    And left him here alone.

They'd charged him with the old, old crime,
    And set him fast in jail;
Oh, why does the dog howl all night long,
    And why does the night wind wail?

He prayed his prayer and he swore his oath,
    And he raised his hand to the sky;
But the beat of hoofs smote on his ear,
    And the steady tread drew nigh.

Who is it rides by night, by night,
    Over the moonlit road?
And what is the spur that keeps the pace,
    What is the galling goad?

And now they beat at the prison door,
    "Ho, keeper, do not stay!
We are friends of him whom you hold within,
    And we fain would take him away

"From those who ride fast on our heels
    With mind to do him wrong;
They have no care for his innocence,
    And the rope they bear is strong."

They have fooled the jailer with lying words,
    They have fooled the man with lies;
The bolts unbar, the locks are drawn,
    And the great door open flies.

Now they have taken him from the jail,
    And hard and fast they ride,
And the leader laughs low down in his throat,
    As they halt my trunk beside.

Oh, the judge, he wore a mask of black,
    And the doctor one of white,
And the minister, with his oldest son,
    Was curiously bedight.

O, foolish man, why weep you now?
    'Tis but a little space,
And the time will come when these shall dread
    The memory of your face.

I feel the rope against my bark,
    And the weight of him in my grain,
I feel in the throe of his final woe
    The touch of my own last pain.

And nevermore shall leaves come forth
    On a bough that bears the ban.
I am burned with dread, I am dried and dead,
    From the curse of a guiltless man.

And ever the judge rides by, rides by,
    And goes to hunt the deer,
And ever another rides his soul
    In the guise of a mortal fear.

And ever the man, he rides me hard,
    And never a night stays he;
For I feel his curse as a haunted bough,
    On the trunk of a haunted tree.

Anonymous

The Anarchist's Christmas

This poem was credited to the Minneapolis Journal *by the* Passaic Daily News, *December 20, 1901. Most anarchists were not bomb throwers, but the 1886 Haymarket Square Riot in Chicago, attempted assassination of industrialist Henry Clay Frick in 1892 during the Homestead Steel strike, and the September 1901 assassination of President William McKinley made a deep impression, made deeper by yellow journalism. The murderous, punitive character recalls earlier depictions of St. Nicholas bearing both gifts and a switch, reuniting in one the benevolent Santa Claus with his dangerous companions like Krampus.*

'Twas the night before Christmas,
    The anarchist's house
Was dark, and the anarch
    Was still as a mouse,

A sheet-iron bombshell
    Was fixed up with care,
In hopes that St. Nicholas
    Soon would be there.

But St. Nick was crafty,
    He knew what would come,
So down the brick chimney
    He dropped a large bomb.

He had told Mrs. Santa
    He thought that he must
Give this anarch the joy
    Of a great Christmas "bust".

So this capsule exploded
    And blew up the place,
Bringing smiles of good cheer
    To the anarchist's face.

GRIM TRAGEDY ENDS BELSNICKLING PARTY.

—

NEW BLOOMFIELD, Pa., Jan. 2.—Word has been received here that last evening, while a party of boys were out belsnickling going from house to house in Buffalo township, one of the party had a revolver.

After the boys left the home of Isaiah Stephens, the revolver was accidentally discharged, the ball striking James Finton, Jr., son of A. R. Finton, in the forehead, killing him instantly.

Philadelphia Inquirer, January 3, 1900

—

SAD CASUALTY.—We are pained to learn that a little son of J. B. Taplin, of this place, about 7 years of age, was so badly burned on Christmas morning, as to cause his death a day or two afterwards. The little fellow had arisen before day, to see what magic Santa Claus had been working for him, and accidentally set fire to his nightclothes with the candle. His screams brought his terrified parents to his relief; but too late to save him.

Portage Sentinel, January 12, 1853

Hezekiah Butterworth

Camel Bells, or, The Haunted Sentry Box of San Cristobal

A Christmas Tale of Porto Rico

Rhode Islander HEZEKIAH BUTTERWORTH (1839-1905)
traveled widely, something that was reflected in his books and
poems. Puerto Rico was invaded by the United States during
the Spanish-American War, and ceded to the U.S. by Spain
upon the war's conclusion in August 1898. *American military*
governance followed, then civil government in 1900. *The story*
was published in the St. Louis Globe-Democrat *of December*
20, 1903.

A STORY WHICH WAS CALLED "The Haunted Sentry Box"
was related for many years on the palmy island of Porto
Rico as a supernatural event that could not be refuted, or
explained, as a ghost story with evidence.

A local poet of the island, whom it was my pleasure to meet,
broke the illusion by writing a legend which would have done
credit to Washington Irving, in which he illustrated how the
story might have been true without being supernatural.

The original story was that sentries were carried away
bodily from the sentry box of San Cristobal by an invisible
power, and were never seen again.

So it came to pass that when one questioned the appearance of spiritual powers in human affairs, he was answered

with caution: "Remember the Haunted Sentry Box of San Cristobal," just as a century ago Boston people used to remind usurers of "the devil and Tom Walker." People recalled these legends as often as the night storms shut out the stars.

Strangely enough, after the advent of the American flag, and the coming of the American soldier and teacher, a new form of superstition spread over the island. It followed the Hebrew thought that people were helped by spirits invisible. It was really a revival of poetic thought in the balmy palm island. Lecturers told pleasant ghost stories and crowds followed them, under a common leader of much eloquence, and were glad to forget the terrible old legends. These stories were much like that of Abraham's servant, who, angel-led and guarded, went out to find a suitable wife for Isaac. Some doubted these attractive tales. Such were usually silenced by some creole, who said: "But these tales are no more wonderful than those of the 'Haunted Sentry Box,' which no one ever doubted."

My curiosity was aroused to investigate this story of the susceptible creoles that "no one could doubt," and so I was led into a series of events that to my mind pictured much of Porto Rico's curious history, as well as the subtleties of psychic life.

In October, 1900, the Spanish flag fell from the palace of San Juan, and on the 18th of that month the United States colors rose over the city of San Juan and floated free in the cerulean air on the yellow seawalls of the halls of state and the castles. The Porto Ricans welcomed the flag; with them it was the "consent of the governed." It was something like fulfilling the prophecies of their great legend of Ponce de Leon and the fountain of youth. The news of the changed flags sped through the islands over the Spanish road, to the sugar and tobacco farms, and to the huts in the Sierra.

In the events that immediately followed some very strange and mysterious people began to make their appearance in the streets of San Juan. These people had been hiding in the mountain woods. They moved about the city like strangers in a strange land.

There came one man more mysterious than the rest. He could play upon a curious instrument; they called him a borinqueno. He announced himself simply as Miquel, and said that he was nearly 90 years of age, and that he had once lived in San Juan. In walking he threw one leg before the other in a curious way, and a young negro said to me one day, on the cool side of the street:

"There goes the scattered man."

He was shrunken and withered; his face was the color of leather, and his hands and arms seemed to be mummified, and one of his legs to be partly useless.

People stopped in the streets to look at him, and came to call him "the dried-up man." To me the word "scattered" described him.

I learned something of him, in several ways.

He used to inquire for certain people who seemed to be no longer remembered. His singular appearance and odd questions at last attracted the notice of one of the police. The latter shadowed him, and followed him to a Dominican church, to which he used to resort. In this church are the remains of Ponce de Leon, the founder of Porto Rico.

The old man used to enter the church under the rent made by Sampson's shell, kneel by the altar, beneath which are the remains of Ponce de Leon, cross himself and lose himself in prayer. Sunlight filled the plaza, and the trade winds blew without, but he seemed to find peace in the shadow of the altar.

One day he remained on his knees so long that a young priest touched him on the shoulder.

The old man started. His eyes gleamed furtively from his withered face.

"Pardon me," he said, "I have been back, living in the past. I

am just coming to myself. I'm in a new world now. I am looking for something. I see—it is time for me to go."

He went out past the grim statue of Ponce in the plaza
and sat down on the sea wall. The United States war vessels
were lying in the harbor, their flags floating rose-like in the
descending sun.

The great yellow fortresses rose near and the opaline waves
off the Caribbean broke in fountains of foam as always on the
coral reefs in the clear distance. The great fans of the cocoanut
palm waved along the sands, like a green stretch of sea, and
here and there above them towered the tops of royal palms like
emerald minarets in the amber air.

A policeman followed the scattered man and asked him
where he had lived.

"In the tamarinds, outside of Guyama," he said, which
conveyed little meaning. The tamarind trees in that part of the
country darkened the air like castles of green.

"What brings you here?" asked the policeman.

The old man seemed dazed, as one with two lives.

"I am looking for something, for one that I lost; that was
many years ago. One will look for a heart long, a heart that one
loved, when one comes back from wanderings."

He turned his head from one side to the other, as though it
were swinging. He suddenly said:

"I wanted to hear the camel bells."

Many years before, when the dons here were in their glory,
Christmas was celebrated on Epiphany, or Twelfth night,
in a very picturesque and curious way. It was believed that
three camels bearing the Three Orient Kings entered the city
bearing gifts to the children. Their bells tinkled as they passed
through the stone-paved streets. The children could hear them
and the tinkling filled them with delight.

"She was a little girl then," said he, "and I used to leave presents on the doorstep for her, and she thought that the camels
brought them from Araby. I would give red gold, if I had it,

for one day out of the past, when she was mine. How I did love my own little girl!"

Was this the dream of a mind wandering, or came the mental picture from some heart memory?

"Why did you not come back before?" asked the officer.

" 'Fore heaven, now, do not be hard on me and press me to answer that. I never did harm to any mortal—there never was blood on my hands. I never robbed or defrauded anybody."

He moved away, ambling, looking behind.

From the sea walls, he hobbled to the graveyard and visited the awful place where human bones were piled up in heaps in the burning sun.

That Porto Rican graveyard! I seem to see it now! There were graves to let there. After a body had been interred there a certain number of years, it was taken up and cast into a common heap of human bones!

The green sea dashed near this great heap of bones, throwing its fierce, white, glittering spray into the light of the sun. Near the place in the distance rose the coral reefs, those white walls of the sea, around which dashed fountains of upheaved waters, more grand than ever were those of Versailles or St. Cloud.

Not far away a yellow sentry box projected into the sea from the castle of San Cristobal. It was of that sentry-box the Porto Rican tale of supernatural power was told that "could not be doubted."

The old man went to the shadows of the prospecting sentry-box of San Cristobal.

"Haunted sentry-box," he said. "Ah-ha-yes, haunted. Men carried off by the pirate spirits—ah-ha-yes, in nights of storm. Yes, yes, in the black nights of storm. I can see the storm blacken; I can hear the waves dash and hear the hear the sentry turning, and turning. I can hear the guard cry 'Alerta!' high up on the wall. It all comes over me now."

He hobbled over the hard rocks and the shingles, where

waves were dashing, and sat down under the black-yellow turret that the decaying castle seemed to be lifting out to sea.

The policeman there appeared to him again.

"Old man, were you ever here before?" he asked in Spanish.

"The castle wears a familiar look to me," said old Miquel. "There used to be a little village out there; I mind the songs that they sang there, at the merrymakings. The huts and cabins are gone now. That was a generation ago."

"You said that you were looking for some one," said the policeman. "Now, I am not following you because I suspect you of being a criminal. A policeman can tell a criminal by the tones of his voice and from the expressions of his face that give away the soul. Whom have you lost?"

The old man looked up and said:

> The worlds above are great,
> And that one heart was small,
> But if I had a thousand worlds,
> For that I'd give them all.

"Age has unsettled your brain, I fear," said the policeman. "You are harmless, I see. I have nothing against you—I wish you well, but there is something mysterious about you that it is my right to know."

"I have wandered much among the mountains," said the old man. "It cooled my brain—the fire here." He pointed to his forehead. "You do pity me, don't you? I am an old man."

He hobbled away to the esplanade, looked up to the flag of the American Union, which seemed blooming in the sunset like a tropic cactus. He stumbled down the walls and disappeared amid the crowds in the twinkling lights of the plaza.

Queer characters, as I said, were to be seen in Porto Rico at this time, but there was something about that man of mystery that held my thought—a lonely light in his eye, a wistful look on his face, that seemed to say "If it could only be."

Christmas day had passed and it was near Epiphany, the fes-

tival night of the festival. I met him again on the semicircling
sea wall and I could not help approaching him. A friar passed
by bearing gifts that had been made to some religious house
for children.

"Gifts?" said I.

"Gifts, yes, gifts. There will be no gifts for me. My day is
gone by. It will never come again. But something is coming
—I can feel it—but I know not how."

"What would you have?" asked I.

"What gift?"

"Yes, my friend."

"I would feel her heart beat on my own again. I sacrificed
all for that. One heartbeat from out the past—I would have
a gift that money can not buy. Only love can make a Christmas happy. One kiss from out the past from a true heart—her
heart—would be more to me than the gold mountains of
Peru! You see I have never ceased to be a child. One kiss from
the dead would make me happy, but Ponce never found the
fountain of youth. The withered stalk never blooms again.
One kiss from her lips out of the past would be more than a
star to me."

His mind seemed to wander.

"Haunted sentry box," said he, wandering. "Ho, ho, spirit
of pirates! Alerta!"

He looked up as though a sentinel on the fortress wall had
called out to him.

There was to be merry-making on the twelfth night at the
barracks of some United States soldiers in San Cristobal. As
the so-called "Haunted Sentry Box," with its terrible legends,
was a part of the sea wall of the stupendous fortress, an officer
who had been made the American master of ceremonies asked
a Porto Rican, who was associated with the Atheneum, to
secure a native story-teller for the festival, and said: "Let him
tell the tale of the Haunted Sentry Box"; he added, "and get

some one to come with him and play the 'Borinquen' in the old-time way."

"I know of an old Spanish lady, a donna, who might tell the story," said the literary Porto Rican. "Donna Ellenda. She can sing the 'Borinquen.' She knew something of the second sentry that was carried away."

"Secure her if you can. What will we have to pay her?"

"Nothing. She would resent the offer of money for entertainment on the twelfth night."

"There is a dried-up old fellow that comes here every day," said the master of ceremonies, "possibly a state criminal of Spanish days. One day he looked down to the sentry box and said, 'I remember that tower and its secret passages in the years that are gone.' The words 'secret passages' interested me, and the tone in which he uttered the words seemed to indicate something peculiar. If he comes here again I will invite him to the entertainment, and will ask him what he knows about the fortress. He can play the 'Borinquen' on the queerest instrument I ever saw."

A day after I saw old Miquel sitting in the sun on the sea wall. I went to him unpretendingly. I was drawn to him, I know not how—I felt that he carried some deep secret in life, not intentionally criminal, and I was curious about it. I always like to study things that make life clear.

"My friend," I said, "that is the statue of old Ponce. He never found the fountain of youth."

"He may have done so—farther on."

He looked at me intently, and there was light beautiful in his face.

"Señor," he said, "I believe in things unseen—in helpers invisible, and in compensations for all that we suffer. I had a daughter once—and we used to listen for the camel's bells at Christmastide. She was the heart of my heart, the life of my life. Her mother died, and I, being a soldier, was called upon to give her up to another mother for her own good. I said to myself, 'How did the star know how to guide the camels? The same power will guide me—there are powers that know all that we suffer. In this world, or in some other, we shall hear the camel bells. There are helpers invisible that know their own. Faith finds its way to truth, and somehow the Christmas star is true.'"

I was greatly surprised at the hidden heart of this wayside philosopher, and I was struck with the thought as to what was the mind that guided the star of the magi over the desert sands.

I shall ever recall that Christmas tide. The old Spanish music of organ and bells floated over the palms, amid the incense of the golden altars. The churches thronged and offerings were made in floral scented airs. The joy of the nativity contin-ued eleven days, and was to end with many festivities on the twelfth night, among which was the American merrymaking among the American soldiers in San Cristobal.

That night came glorious, a tropic harmony of clear silver splendors under the moon and stars. The cocoanut palms and royal palms glistened as the moon, like a night sun of burnished gold, lifted herself from the dusky purple of the sea. Night is a glory in Porto Rico.

The "old" woman, Ellenda, came to the American assem-bly. She was apparently a creole who had been beautiful. She was middle-aged—they call such women "old" in Porto Rico. She was gaily dressed, and glittered with spangles and bright sashes. She brought with her a guitar, which was ornamented with sea pearl, and streamed with bright ribbons, and seemed as light as air.

The house where the merrymaking was to be held belonged to the medical department, and its verandas overlooked the wonderful harbor with winding ways amid the cocoanut palms.

The American soldiers had arrived early in the evening, and engaged in the light-hearted, jovial talk that the always sunny Porto Rican climate inspires.

"You are to have something new to-night, I hear," said an American soldier to the master of ceremonies, as the two stood on the veranda looking out on fading palms across the narrows of the sea.

"Yes; a Porto Rican dance."

"No, not that; but a ghost story with evidence; I used to read tales of the pirates of the sea, but this concerns the pirates of the air."

Forms dressed in white were moving hither and thither in the dusky gold of the plaza. A carriage stopped before the heavy veranda.

The coming of this woman, Donna Ellenda, suddenly broke in upon the merry ripples of talk. There was something about her that awakened an awesome curiosity and the house, which had seemed all in motion, now, as it were, stood still.

Her garments tinkled as she moved, at times nervously, about the room. She bent her dark eyes on the guitar, tuned the instrument, and then uplifted her silent face as if wondering. An assembly of American soldiers was new to her. The world here had changed.

The commander of the fortress approached her in the silence, hat in hand:

"The 'Borinquen,' if you please, Donna Ellenda. It would please our men if you would so honor us with the native song."

She simply said, "Señor," bowing.

She sang the "Borinquen" to the accompaniment of her guitar, the latter like music woven of air.

Just as she began to sing old Miquel came tottering into the gay inclosure, with his odd instrument under his arm. At the sound of the "Borinquen" he stopped as though turning into stone.

"I seem to hear the camel bells," said he, referring to the old custom of mock camels bearing gifts at Epiphany.

He drew a long breath and stood wavering.

"There are helpers invisible," said he, "and they sometimes

help true hearts to find each other. One kiss from her lips and I could die, it would so fill me with joy. I imagine I see her now, in that old woman. I fancy I can hear the camel bells in the street, as I heard them when I carried her in my arms."

He seemed to see something that others did not see in Donna Ellenda.

The master of ceremonies, hat in hand, was standing near the door, welcoming the guests as they came, and, with the true American heart, he extended his hand to the odd visitor. As he did so, he saw the old man stare at Donna Ellenda, he saw him shake, and his tan-colored cheek turned almost white, as if leperous.

"What is it, comerado?" said the master, familiarly. "What surprises you? You must have heard the 'Borinquen' before. Why the tremor, my friend?"

The latter swung one leg before the other, and his leather-like lips opened.

"I do not know, but I do know that which thou dost not know. I know the secret of the story that she is about to tell. I know the heart of it all. I know! I know! I have prayed for this hour—I prayed for it in the old church. The hour that we have prayed for comes to us. There comes to me a strange joy. Old Miquel, old Miquel, that thou should'st ever have lived to see this hour!" He addressed himself in these last words.

He turned almost as rigid as a man of clay, as the master said:

"Donna Ellenda, will you favor us with the old story of the sentry box? It will be new to the American boys."

She leaned lightly over her guitar, and said in florid English:

"It hangs still out there now, on the air, the sentry box. The moonlight is on it, the waves flash under it on the storm-eaten rock, but so lightly that we can not hear it. It was not so on the night of my story. I mean the second story.

"The events that I am about to relate happened in this very house, on the night that I was married."

She lifted her eyes.

"This room is trimmed with palm fans. It was so then."

Old Miquel lifted his arms, as if about to rush forward. The master of ceremonies laid his hand on his shoulder and said:

"Comerado!"

New guests were crowding into the room and the donna paused, her black eyes roving over the green palm branches.

"Why did you lift your hands so?" asked the master of Miquel.

"I do not know, general, but I do know that which thou canst not know. The past is coming again."

Above him hung the flags of the states—the flag of emancipation—on a wall covered with palms. The flag of the pine lands had here found the palm lands' decorations, and the stars and roses of the flag bloom beautifully on an escutcheon of palms. Its presence as a festival emblem here was one that could be felt, like the light of a new world of life, light and hope. It gladdened the atmosphere.

There was silence again. Without a white, glistening moonlight covered the yellow walls and terraces. In Porto Rico the night sky seems high and the stars hang low.

The master rapped for silence.

"In this very room, it happened," she continued. "The place had lovely gardens then, as it has now. Lovely, but those roses are gone; those are new ones over in the garden.

"There are hours that live again. That hour will never leave me; not that I was a bride, but that I saw life's mystery then.

"I would have been a happy bride that night but for one heartache; that was caused by the absence of my father from the wedding. I loved my father."

Old Miquel shook again, and his mouth opened. Blood came into his face as from hidden fountains.

"I was born at Porto Rico in the palmy days of the island," she continued, with a fixed look, "when it was the favorite possession of Spain. Like Cuba, which Spain then believed to be the 'ever-faithful isle,' Porto Rico was dear to the heart of Spain. The exiles from South America after the revolutions led by Simon Bolivar found refuge here, and were true to the crown. Spain loved Porto Rico; beautiful, beautiful Porto Rico!

"My mother died soon after my birth. A donna, who had lost her own child, came to my father, who was a soldier, and asked his leave to adopt me, but said that he, my father, must be as a stranger to me in the future. My father was so weighed down with misfortune that he reluctantly consented, and I rarely saw him after that day, but the moments when I did see him lived in my life. I loved my father." Her lips trembled.

"My heart went out to him as I grew older, and lived in his. He haunted me like a dream of the kinship of love. He followed the fortunes of the army, being stationed here and there, now in Morro castle here, now at fortifications at the Spanish ports. I loved him; how I loved him!

"I knew him and he knew me, yet when we met by chance we did not speak. He looked at me, that was all. He was only one remove from a common soldier. I can see that look now, the father was in it; his heart.

"There was a sadness in his face that settled itself in my mind. Every time I met that look my love for him grew. I was loved in the house of the don, but I hungered and thirsted for natural affection, for the kin touch.

"I had everything by the way of luxury that a girl could have, yet lived amid famine of heart. What would I have given to have thrown myself into my father's arms! It was my dream to do so.

"I used to stand on the wide veranda facing the sea when the army passed by on public parades and festival days, and I would cry out in the shadow that cooled the burning air: 'I am all alone in the world. I want my father!' Ah, those are deep waters—alone!

"In my girlhood an event happened that startled San Juan and caused the creoles to shrink up and shiver. A sentinel disappeared under such circumstances that the men of the garrison said that he had been taken away from his sentry box bodily by an evil spirit, a pirate spirit of the sea. There were places among the islands, like Blue Beard's castle, at St. Thomas, where the spirits of pirates were thought to dwell, and these pirates of the air were said to go forth on stormy nights and to continue their old iniquities in decoying ships, in hurling merchantmen against the breakers, and carrying away good people bodily; where, no one imagined—the people could only say of such victims, 'They never came back again,' or 'They came on black nights and went away in the darkness.' I do not understand such things.

"The sentry who had been thus carried away had been stationed in the sentry box of San Cristobal that projects like an arm out in the sea, close by. The waves roll under it, and the storms toss up to it their spray in foam. At low tide, the box looks like a swallow's nest at a distance, yellow and dark, and reflecting the intense rays of the sun. Go out and see it in the morning. It is now there as then, over the other side of the wall, only the secret passage is walled up now.

"People did not dare to walk by the place nights after that event occurred. They ran. The boatmen in the moonlight avoided it, and slanted their oars toward the open sea. Go out and see it in the morning," she repeated, shutting her eyes and slowly turning her head.

"On the night that the sentinel disappeared the watchman on the walls had cried 'Alerta?' and the answer 'Alerta!' had come back from the man in the sentry box. Thrice this had occurred. Then a storm arose. Such a storm! The cloud settled down on the sea like a sea from the sky. The phosphorescent coral reefs disappeared in the rising tide. The moon hid; there was blackness; then a wind that shook the mountains, and swept the tops from the royal palms; then thunder that seemed to come out of the earth, with lightnings so vivid as to be almost blinding! The world seemed to be breaking up.

"At that time there were some houses covered with palms near the sentry box, inhabited by fishermen. These toilers of the coast stood in their doors, as the wind might blow down their frail houses, and cried out as the thunder seemed to sift the earth and upheave the sea.

"As these fishermen were standing there, uncertain as to the fate of the hour, a vivid, death-dealing lightning flash revealed a sight that made them fall to the earth in terror. They saw a man hanging in the air, between the sentry box and foaming waters. Ten or more people saw it, and bore witness to it; there could have been no mistake.

"A cry rang out from the high walls.

"'Alerta?' It was the sentinel.

"There was no answer. What had become of the sentry?

"'It was the sentry that we saw in the air,' said the fishermen. 'The pirates of the air have carried him away!'

"They ran in the darkness into the town and told their tale at the doors of Casa Blanca. Their story became, as you know, a saint's warning, a Christmas legend. But so many people saw it and bore witness to it, there could have been no mistake. The sentry was never seen again.

"Years passed after that first story.

"Now, let me tell you my own story of the second sentry who disappeared."

She spoke English well, but used vivid and intense idioms.

"Twelfth night—the night on which I was married—was celebrated in unwonted splendor that year at San Juan. There were green mangers in the churches, guardian angels of silver and gold in dusky places, music that seemed to fall from the arches, victor angels everywhere over the supreme cradle. The altars blazed. Crowned kings, as masques, came into the churches and chancels with censers in incense, bearing gold, spices and nard. Everywhere were music, odors and stars.

"The populace in white robes filled the streets; old people, families, lovers, children.

"I stood in yonder door that night, a waiting bride—yonder door——"

As she looked toward "yonder door" her voice changed. Her eyes darted and then became fixed. Presently she shook her head, absently, and said:

"Oh, it was nothing!" words which the guests did not understand.

She continued, but casting her eyes on the floor.

"I stood in the open door that night of my wedding. The western sky over the harbor was yellow—like ashes of gold. I can see it now. It was so to-night.

"Everything changed.

"Suddenly a black wing seemed to sweep over the sky, putting out the stars. There were mutterings of thunder, like falling mountains. The trade winds swelled and gathered power, like giants of the air.

"I stepped forth a bride, at that dark hour, my heart beating.

"The marriage rites began. I recall my vanity as I passed before the glass before the astrals. People called me the 'beautiful creole,' and I thought myself beautiful. These withered fingers were not my hands as then. These gray locks are not the tresses that fell over my neck that burned with pearls then. The light has half gone out of these eyes. Señorita Ellenda of old is gone.

"How happy I would have been on that night, but for one thing—the absence of my father!

"There was music of guitars, the forming of a marriage circle, a priest arose prepared to do his office, and my bridegroom whispered to me:

" 'The storm is passing; it is a good omen; Ellenda, you look beautiful, as if angel-guided!'

" 'And you will always be good to me?' I asked, trembling. I did not doubt his heart, but was compelled to say something for relief from excitement.

" 'Always, always, my lovely bride.'

"And he kept his word.

"It was a moment of expectation. My heart seemed to suffocate me with happiness, for the tone of his words was sincere. All faces became transfigured, so deep were the joys of all hearts in mine. I was a happy bride but for that one thing. I longed for that parental look again to bless me at that hour. I turned toward the window; a star was in the sky where the cloud had been.

"The priest bent over in silence. I cast my eyes toward the window, yonder window, again, when I saw something there that thrilled me and made me live, as it were, a life in a moment!

"What was it, you ask?

"It was the face of my father! That look again—that look from out the family blood—out of the stream of life—out of the heart of hearts!

"Master of ceremonies, whatever may happen in life, we can not be divorced from our own. The heart comes back to itself again, to its own again.

"That face—it was the face of him who had given me life. Was it real? Was it a face made by some soul impression? There are such things as soul impressions, so I think. Master, do you not favor me?

"It was pressed against the pane, that face. How beautiful, how wonderful, it looked! Then a living thought came to me, as to one in a vivid dream. I asked, 'Does your father still love you?'

"Was my father dead? He could not be there. He might be one of the soldiers in the new garrison of San Cristobal for aught I could know. He had once been stationed in the garrison and new allotments were making by the military guards now. Wherever he might be, he would not have sought me, would he, unless I had sent for him?

"I trembled, and the bridegroom noticed my agitation.

"'Ellenda?' he said.

" 'Yours, siempre.' Tears had come to my relief. Then a pang smote me. If my father were living, why had I not sought to invite him to my wedding? I stood thinking, when—

"Saints! What was that?

"There arose a cry outside in the yard—a wild cry.

"The wedding guests listened.

" 'The pirates! The pirates have carried away the sentry!' shouted the strange voices. 'Another one has gone!'

"The cry was repeated.

"The medical men of the garrison were at this house. These street people were seeking them.

" 'Another sentry gone!' The people joined in the cry.

"The shouting men rushed in. They were fishermen from the shore of the sentry box. The priest raised his hand.

"There was silence.

" 'What have you to say?' asked the priest, presently, of the fishermen.

" 'The pirates of the air have carried away a sentry again,' said one, gasping. 'We heard the watchman cry "Alerta!" but the sentry did not answer. Then came a flash and we saw the sentry hanging in the air. This makes the other story true; there are pirates in the air. This sentry went as the other did, only——'

" 'Only what?' I asked, unable to repress my desire to know all.

" 'Only this man walked about in the air. Then came a second flash of lightning, and he still was there. We all saw him. His hands were lifted, as if upheld by some unknown or holding-on power. He remained there for a time between the box and the sea. There came a third flash of lightning, and he was still there. Then he was carried away—or was gone.'

" 'Silence,' said the priest. 'That can not be. That is the old story—such things can not be.'

"The ceremony went on. I sank down as soon as it was over.

"But——

"The sentry had disappeared from the box that night like the other. The officers searched the place, but the sentry was not to be found. A strange impression came over me; it was that the sentry who had that night disappeared was my father.

"San Juan trembled as the story ran through the streets on the next morning.

"On the morning after the wedding I sailed for Spain, and remained there for twenty years. Then my good husband died and I came back to my old home, but in all those years have I carried my father's memory in my heart."

The master of ceremonies stepped into the middle of the room.

"We have had to-night," he said, "a ghost story, with evidence, one that could not have been otherwise than true, as a most astute court of law would say. Let us give a 'Chautauqua salute' to Donna Ellenda!"

Donna Ellenda had probably never heard of a "Chautauqua salute," but the soldiers knew the meaning. White handkerchiefs fluttered in the air, under the palm decorations.

"I am glad," said the commandant of the castle, "to have heard one story of invisible influences of which there can be no refutation."

Without the castle it was a gay night. There may have been no mock camels in the fluttering streets, but the great stars shone bright on the winding harbor, and the palms glistened in the silver over sea.

Little bells were tinkling near the windows, recalling the camels of old with their gold and nard, and of the Star that should arise in Jacob.

Old Miquel stepped into the open space in front of Donna Ellenda and lifted his hands.

"Ellenda, did you ever see this look before?"

She fell back.

Faces pressed forward.

"Ellenda, I was the man in the sentry box that night; it was my face that was pressed against the pane; it was my form that the fishermen saw by the lightning flash dangling on a chain in the air!"

An unusual light filled her face; a radiance that came from the soul.

Then her face clouded.

"Father, my father; you was not a deserter!"

The room was still; so was the air without, save the "camel bells."

"No, no, Ellenda. Honor is a star, and my star of life shines clear, save that I left my post just to see you in life; one great hour. I went back, but the wind had blown the rope that I had left hanging down to lift myself up to the box again, over the box. For me to have gone back after that would have been death. I fled to the tamarind trees. I should not have left my post, and I stopped and prayed on the rope in midair as the lightnings flashed around me."

Miquel hobbles forward, but with a strange, new life in his movements, and father and daughter meet in each other's arms under the flag.

Outside the band is playing, up high on the yellow walls, in the white moon, "My Country, 'Tis of Thee!"

The men catch the air and take it up, and Donna Ellenda plays once more the "Borinquen," after which the two creoles go out into the night.

I stood on the veranda. The moon was hanging over the sinuous harbor, the tamarind tree castelled mountains, and great purple sea.

"So that ghost story with evidence may not have been true," said I to the master of ceremonies. "If the second sentry reappeared, may not the first have disappeared in the same way?"

He shrugged his shoulders and said, "Quien sabe?" and then added, absently, in a subconscious way:

"But, somehow, the Christmas Star is true."

And the children were going home, tinkling, tinkling —"camel bells."

HORRIBLE SEQUEL TO A GHOST STORY.

As Christmas approaches it may be well to call attention to the terrible consequences which, according to the *Indianapolis Journal*, ensued the other day in that city from an hour's amusement in telling ghost stories. A number of young ladies, patients of the Surgical Institute, were assembled in one of the rooms of the establishment, at a late hour in the evening, and whiled away their time by relating to each other stories of apparitions, hobgoblins, ghosts &c. Either intentionally or by accident the gas was suddenly turned off, and, in the climax of a vivid story, one of the young ladies imprudently threw her shawl over the head of a trembling companion seated next to her. There was a little rustle and a short stifled scream. When a light was obtained the melancholy fact was revealed that the poor girl was mad. She has remained so ever since, and very slight hopes are entertained of her recovery. Considerable risk, indeed, attends the reading aloud of the average Christmas ghost story. Strong must be the nerve of any one who can bear unmoved the first few lines of one of these thrilling narratives knowing that he is expected to sit through the remainder. If not stricken with idiocy at the beginning of the tale, he generally becomes more or less stupefied before the climax is reached, and his distressing condition has become patent to all.

Cambridge Independent Press [U.K.], December 4, 1875

Anonymous

The Ravings

A poem from the Arctic Eagle *of December 25, 1903 by a member of its crew during a North Pole expedition led by Anthony Fiala (1869-1950) of Brooklyn. The newspaper was initially printed on board the ship* America, *then on Prince Rudolph Island when the ship was crushed in pack ice. "The Ravings" was reprinted in the* Brooklyn Eagle *of September 10, 1905, from which paper the type had been borrowed. Fiala observed that he'd "thought that a newspaper, issued from time to time, might help to liven the men up and keep them cheerful."*

(With Apologies to Edgar Allan)

ONCE, in Arctic night most dreary,
    While the ship's crew rested—weary
Of the task of building sledges
    That had been built once before,
With the sound of moorings slacking,
Suddenly there came a cracking
As of pack-ice closer packing—
    Crowding in toward the shore—
    All of this and then some more.

Fiala, roused by this commotion
In the lonely Arctic Ocean,
Instantly, with optic psychic,
    Saw that ghost he saw before.

Quoth he "Man or devil, hark'ee—
Speak to me from out thy parkee—
Tell me—(if thou knowest, mark'ee)—
    Tell me this now, I implore—
    Only this, I ask no more:

"Can she twice withstand the crushing
Of the pack upon her rushing—
Lying here at outer ice-edge,
    Far from the protecting shore?"
Spake the ghost, with grin ungainly—
"Listen—I will tell thee plainly
That thou strivest to save her, vainly
    Her bones share with mine this shore,
    Here they'll rest forever more."

Anthony, with eyeballs starting,
Thro' his pale lips slightly parting
Breathed a prayer—then humped himself
    As he had never humped before.
While the "Chief" cursed the timbers crashing,
The "Old Man," with bull's eye flashing,
Down the narrow gangplank dashing
    Dragged "chronometer" ashore.
    Only this?—well, perhaps more.

Later, Hartt with tears surprising,
Muttered that the water, rising,
Made the ship unsafe to stay on—
    Something he'd ne'er said before,
To Fiala—"You show sand, sir;
But I'm now in full command, sir;
And I order you to land, sir.
    Be so good to climb ashore,
    I am last—." And then some more.

Those at home may have a notion
That the mystic Arctic Ocean
Offers deeds of valor only,
    To our manhood's precious store;
But all those who—joyed or grieving—
Saw our little party leaving,
Realize that I'm not weaving
    Fiction in with History's lore—
    This there is—and then some more.

Thus, dismantled, crushed and dying,—
But with colors bravely flying—
Our good ship lies on the ice pack,
    Doomed to sleep on Teplitz shore.
On the bridge, the parkee spirit
Shouts his order 'till we hear it
All about the ship or near it,
    Sometimes we can hear his roar
    From our cabin on the shore—
    Sometimes his—and sometimes more.

Robert W. Chambers

Out of the Depths

ROBERT W. CHAMBERS (1865-1933) *might be best known today for "The King in Yellow," much admired by H. P. Lovecraft. Prior to the publication of "Out of the Depths" in the Christmas* Colliers *of* 1904, *the magazine teased it as "a very modern ghost story," also stating the author "is never more at home than when in the realm of the occult." In* 1907 *it and other short stories of his were repurposed as chapters of* The Tree of Heaven, *threaded together upon a slender plot as a literary note at the time described, but his artistry making it work.*

D UST AND WIND HAD SUBSIDED, there seemed to be a hint of rain in the starless west.

Because the August evening had become oppressive, the club windows stood wide open as though gaping for the outer air. Rugs and curtains had been removed; an incandescent light or two accentuated the emptiness of the rooms; here and there shadowy servants prowled, gilt buttons sparkling through the obscurity, their footsteps on the bare floor intensifying the heavy quiet.

Into this week's-end void wandered young Shannon, drifting aimlessly from library to corridor, finally entering the long room where the portraits of dead governors smirked through the windows at the deserted avenue.

As his steps echoed on the rugless floor, a shadowy something detached itself from the depths of a padded armchair by the corner window, and a voice he recognized greeted him by name.

"You here, Harrod!" he exclaimed. "Thought you were at Bar Harbor."

"I was. I had business in town."

"Do you stay here long?"

"Not long," said Harrod slowly.

Shannon dropped into a chair with a yawn which ended in a groan.

"Of all God-forsaken places," he began, "a New York club in August."

Harrod touched an electric button, but no servant answered the call; and presently Shannon, sprawling in his chair, jabbed the button with the ferrule of his walking stick, and a servant took the order, repeating as though he had not understood: "Did you say two, sir?"

"With olives, dry," nodded Shannon irritably. They sat there in silence until the tinkle of ice aroused them, and——

"Double luck to you," muttered Shannon; then, with a scarcely audible sigh: "Bring two more and bring a dinner card." And, turning to the older man: "You're dining, Harrod?"

"If you like."

A servant came and turned on an electric jet; Shannon scanned the card under the pale radiance, scribbled on the pad, and handed it to the servant.

"Did you put down my name?" asked Harrod curiously.

"No; you'll dine with me—if you don't mind."

"I don't mind—for this last time."

"Going away again?"

"Yes."

Shannon signed the blank and glanced up at his friend. "Are you well?" he asked abruptly.

Harrod, lying deep in his leather chair, nodded.

"Oh, you're rather white around the gills! We'll have another."

"I thought you had cut that out, Shannon."

"Cut what out?"

"Drinking."

"Well, I haven't," said Shannon sulkily, lifting his glass and throwing one knee over the other.

"The last time I saw you, you said you would cut it," observed Harrod.

"Well, what of it?"

"But you haven't?"

"No, my friend."

"Can't you stop?"

"I could—now. To-morrow—I don't know; but I know well enough I couldn't day after to-morrow. And day after to-morrow I shall not care."

A short silence and Harrod said: "That's why I came back here."

"What?"

"To stop you."

Shannon regarded him in sullen amazement.

A servant announcing dinner brought them to their feet; together they walked out into the empty dining room and seated themselves by an open window.

Presently Shannon looked up with an impatient laugh.

"For Heaven's sake let's be cheerful, Harrod. If you knew how the damned town had got on my nerves."

"*That's* what I came back for, too," said Harrod with his strange white smile. "I knew the world was fighting you to the ropes."

"It is; here I stay on, day after day, on the faint chance of something doing." He shrugged his shoulders. "Business is worse than dead; I can't hold on much longer. You're right; the world has hammered me to the ropes, and it will be down and out for me unless——"

"Unless you can borrow on your own terms?"

"Yes, but I can't."

"You are mistaken."

"Mistaken? Who will——"

"I will."

"You! Why, man, do you know how much I need? Do you know for how long I shall need it? Do you know what the chances are of my making good? *You!* Why, Harrod, I'd swamp you! You can't afford——"

"I can afford anything—now."

Shannon stared. "You have struck something?"

"Something that puts me beyond want." He fumbled in his breast pocket, drew out a portfolio, and from the flat leather case he produced a numbered check bearing his signature, but not filled out.

"Tell them to bring pen and ink," he said.

Shannon, perplexed, signed to a waiter. When the ink was brought, Harrod motioned Shannon to take the pen. "Before I went to Bar Harbor," he said, "I had a certain sum——" He hesitated, mentioned this sum in a low voice, and asked Shannon to fill in the check for that amount. "Now blot it, pocket it, and use it," he added listlessly, looking out into the lamp-lighted street.

Shannon, whiter than his friend, stared at the bit of perforated yellow paper.

"I can't take it," he stammered; "my security is rotten, I tell you——"

"I want no security; I—I am beyond want," said Harrod. "Take it; I came back here for this—partly for this."

"Came back here to—to—help *me!*"

"To help you. Shannon, I had been a lonely man in life; I think you never realized how much your friendship has been to me. I had nobody—no intimacies. You never understood—you with all your friends—that I cared more for our casual companionship than for anything in the world."

Shannon bent his head. "I did not know it," he said.

Harrod raised his eyes and looked up at the starless sky; Shannon ate in silence; into his young face, already marred by dissipation, a strange light had come. And little by little order began to emerge from his whirling senses; he saw across an abyss a bridge glittering, and beyond that, beckoning to him through a white glory, all that his heart desired.

"I was at the ropes," he muttered; "how *could* you know it, Harrod? I—I never whined——"

"I know more than I did—yesterday," said Harrod, resting his pale face on one thin hand.

Shannon, nerves on edge, all aquiver, the blood racing through every vein, began to speak excitedly: "It's like a dream—one of the blessed sort—Harrod! Harrod!—the dreams I've had this last year! And I try—I try to understand what has happened—what you have done for me. I can't— I'm shaking all over, and I suppose I'm sitting here eating and drinking, but——"

He touched his glass blindly; it tipped and crashed to the floor, the breaking froth of the wine hissing on the cloth.

"Harrod! Harrod! What sort of a man am I to deserve this of you? What can I do——"

"Keep your nerve—for one thing."

"I will!—you mean *that*!" touching the stem of the new glass, which the waiter had brought and was filling. He struck the glass till it rang out a clear, thrilling, crystalline note, then struck it more sharply. It splintered with a soft splashing crash. "Is *that* all?" he laughed.

"No, not all."

"What more will you let me do?"

"One thing more. Tell them to serve coffee below."

So they passed out of the dining room, through the deserted corridors, and descended the stairway to the lounging room. It was unlighted and empty; Shannon stepped back and the elder man passed him and took the corner chair by the window— the same seat where Shannon had first seen him sitting ten years before, and where he always looked to find him after the ending of a business day. And continuing his thoughts, the younger man spoke aloud impulsively: "I remember perfectly well how we met. Do you? You had just come back to town from Bar Harbor, and I saw you stroll in and seat yourself in that corner, and, because I was sitting next you, you asked if you might include me in your order—do you remember?"

"Yes, I remember."

"And I told you I was a new member here, and you pointed out the portraits of all those dead governors of the club, and told me what good fellows they had been. I found out later that you yourself were a governor of the club."

"Yes—I was."

Harrod's shadowy face swerved toward the window, his eyes resting on the familiar avenue, empty now save for the policeman opposite, and the ragged children of the poor. In August the high tide from the slums washes Fifth Avenue, stranding a gasping flotsam at the thresholds of the absent.

"And I remember, too, what you told me," continued Shannon.

"What?" said Harrod, turning noiselessly to confront his friend.

"About that child. Do you remember? That beautiful child you saw? Don't you remember that you told me how she used to leave her governess and talk to you on the rocks——"

"Yes," said Harrod. "*That*, too, is why I came back here to tell you the rest. For the evil days have come to her, Shannon, and the years draw nigh. Listen to me."

There was a silence; Shannon, mute and perplexed, set his coffee on the window sill and leaned back, flicking the ashes from his cigar; Harrod passed his hands slowly over his hollow temples: "Her parents are dead; she is not yet twenty; she is not equipped to support herself in life; and—she is beautiful. What chance has she, Shannon?"

The other was silent.

"What chance?" repeated Harrod. "And, when I tell you that she is unsuspicious, and that she reasons only with her heart, answer me—what chance has she with a man? For you know men, and so do I, Shannon, so do I."

"Who is she, Harrod?"

"The victim of divorced parents—awarded to her mother. Let her parents answer; they are answering now, Shannon. But their plea is no concern of yours. What concerns you is the living. The child, grown to womanhood, is here, advertising for employment—here in New York, asking for a chance. What chance has she?"

"When did you learn this?" asked Shannon soberly.

"I learned it to-night—everything concerning her—to-night—an hour before I—I met you. *That* is why I returned. Shannon, listen to me attentively; listen to every word I say. Do you remember a passing fancy you had this spring for a blue-eyed girl you met every morning on your way down-town? Do you remember that, as the days went on, little by little she came to return your glance?—then your smile?—then, at last, your greeting? And do you remember, once, that you told me about it in a moment of depression—told me that you were close to infatuation, that you believed her to be everything sweet and innocent, that you dared not drift any farther, knowing the chances and knowing the end—bitter unhappiness either way, whether in guilt or innocence——"

"I remember," said Shannon hoarsely. "But that is not—cannot be——"

"That is the girl."

"Not the child you told me of——"

"Yes."

"How—when did you know——"

"To-night. I know more than that, Shannon. You will learn it later. Now ask me again, what it is that you may do."

"I ask it," said Shannon under his breath. "What am I to do?"

For a long while Harrod sat silent, staring out of the dark window; then, "It is time for us to go."

"You wish to go out?"

"Yes; we will walk together for a little while—as we did in the old days, Shannon—only a little while, for I must be going back."

"Where are you going, Harrod?"

But the elder man had already risen and moved toward the door; and Shannon picked up his hat and followed him out across the dusky lamp-lighted street.

Into the avenue they passed under the white, unsteady radiance of arc lights which drooped like huge lilies from stalks of bronze; here and there the front of some hotel lifted like a cliff, its window-pierced façade pulsating with yellow light, or a white marble mass, cold and burned out, spread a sea of shadow over the glimmering asphalt. At times the lighted lamps of cabs flashed in their faces; at times figures passed like spectres; but into the street where they were now turning were neither lamps nor people nor sound, nor any light, save, far in the obscure vista, a dull hint of lightning edging the west.

Twice Shannon had stopped, peering at Harrod, who neither halted nor slackened his steady, noiseless pace; and the younger man, hesitating, moved on again, quickening his steps to his friend's side.

"Where are—are you going?"

"Do you not know?"

The color died out of Shannon's face; he spoke again, forming his words slowly with dry lips:

"Harrod, why—why do you come into this street—to-night? What do you know? *How* do you know? I tell you I—I cannot endure this—this tension——"

"*She* is enduring it."

"Good God!"

"Yes, God is good," said Harrod, turning his haggard face as they halted. "Answer me, Shannon, where are we going?"

"To—her. You know it! Harrod! Harrod! How did you know? I—I did not know myself until an hour before I met you; I had not seen her in weeks—I had not dared to—for all trust in self was dead. To-day, downtown, I faced the crash and saw across to-morrow the end of all. Then, in my journey hellward to-night, just at dusk, we passed each other, and before I understood what I had done we were side by side. And almost instantly—I don't know how—she seemed to sense the ruin before us both—for mine was heavy on my soul, Harrod, as I stood, measuring damnation with smiling eyes—at the brink of it, there. And she knew I was adrift at last."

He looked up at the house before him. "I said I would come. She neither assented nor denied me, nor asked a question. But in her eyes, Harrod, I saw what one sees in the eyes of children, and it stunned me . . . What shall I do?"

"Go to her and look again," said Harrod. "*That* is what I have come to ask of you. Good-by."

He turned, his shadowy face drooping, and Shannon followed to the avenue. There, in the white outbreak of electric lamps, he saw Harrod again as he had always known him, a hint of a smile in his worn eyes, the well-shaped mouth edged with laughter, and he was saying: "It's all in a lifetime, Shannon— and more than you suspect—much more. You have not told me her name yet?"

"I do not know it."

"Ah, she will tell you if you ask! Say to her that I remember her there on the sea rocks. Say to her that I have searched for her always, but that it was only to-night I knew what to-morrow she shall know—and you, Shannon, you, too, shall know. Good-by."

"Harrod! wait. Don't—don't go——"

He turned and looked back at the younger man with that familiar gesture he knew so well.

It was final, and Shannon swung blindly on his heel and entered the street again, eyes raised to the high lighted window under which he had halted a moment before. Then he mounted the steps, groped in the vestibule for the illuminated number, and touched the electric knob. The door swung open noiselessly as he entered, closing behind him with a soft click.

Up he sped, mounting stair on stair, threading the narrow hallways, then upward again, until of a sudden she stood confronting him, bent forward, white hands tightening on the banisters.

Neither spoke. She straightened slowly, fingers relaxing from the polished rail. Over her shoulders he saw a lamp-lighted room, and she turned and looked backward at the threshold and covered her face with both hands.

"What is it?" he whispered, bending close to her. "Why do you tremble? You need not. There is nothing in all the world you need fear. Look into my eyes. Even a child may read them now."

Her hands fell from her face and their eyes met, and what she read in his, and he in hers, God knows, for she swayed where she stood, lids closing; yielding hands and lips and throat and hair. She cried, too, later, her hands on his shoulders where he knelt beside her, holding him at arm's length from her fresh young face to search his for the menace she once had read there. But it was gone—that menace she had read and vaguely understood, and she cried a little more, one arm around his head pressed close to her side.

"From the very first—the first moment I saw you," he said under his breath, answering the question aquiver on her lips—lips divinely merciful, repeating the lovers' creed and the confession of faith for which, perhaps, all souls in love are shriven in the end.

"Naida! Naida!"—for he had learned her name and could not have enough of it—"all that the world holds for me of good is here, circled by my arms. Nor mine the manhood to win out, alone—but there is a man who came to me to-night and stood sponsor for the falling soul within me.

"How he knew my peril and yours, God knows. But he came like Fate and held his buckler before me, and he led me here and set a flaming sword before your door—the door of the child he loved—there on the sea rocks ten years ago. Do you remember? He said you would. And he is no archangel—this man among men, this friend with whom, unknowing, I have this night wrestled face to face. His name is Harrod."

"*My* name!" She stood up straight and pale, within the circle of his arms; he rose, too, speechless, uncertain—then faced her, white and appalled.

She said: "He—he followed us to Bar Harbor. I was a child, I remember. I hid from my governess and talked with him on the rocks. Then we went away. I—I lost my father." Staring at her, his stiffening lips formed a word, but no sound came.

"Bring him to me!" she whispered. "How can he know I am here and stay away! Does he think I have forgotten? Does he think shame of me? Bring him to me!"

She caught his hands in hers and kissed them passionately; she framed his face in her small hands of a child and looked deep, deep into his eyes: "Oh, the happiness you have brought! I love you! You with whom I am to enter Paradise! Now bring him to me!"

Shaking, amazed, stunned in a whirl of happiness and doubt, he crept down the black stairway, feeling his way. The doors swung noiselessly; he was almost running when he turned into the avenue. The trail of white lights starred his path; the solitary street echoed his haste; and now he sprang into the wide doorway of the club, and as he passed, the desk clerk leaned forward, handing him a telegram. He took it, halted, breathing heavily, and asked for his friend.

"Mr. Harrod?" repeated the clerk. "Mr. Harrod has not been here in a month, sir."

"What? I dined with Mr. Harrod here at eight o'clock!" he laughed.

"Sir? I—I beg your pardon, sir, but you dined here alone to-night——"

"Send for the steward!" broke in Shannon impatiently,

slapping his open palm with the yellow envelope. The steward came, followed by the butler, and to a quick question from the desk clerk, replied: "Mr. Harrod has not been in the club for six weeks."

"But I dined with Mr. Harrod at eight! Wilkins, did you not serve us?"

"I served you, sir; you dined alone——" The butler hesitated, coughed discreetly; and the steward added: "You ordered for two, sir——"

Something in the steward's troubled face silenced Shannon; the butler ventured: "Beg pardon, sir, but we—the waiters thought you might be—ill, seeing how you talked to yourself and called for ink to write upon the cloth and broke two glasses, laughing like——"

Shannon staggered, turning a ghastly visage from one to another. Then his dazed gaze centered upon the telegram crushed in his hand, and shaking from head to foot, he smoothed it out and opened the envelope.

But it was purely a matter of business; he was requested to come to Bar Harbor and identify a useless check, drawn to his order, and perhaps aid to identify the body of a drowned man in the morgue.

Wallace Irwin

Old Nick and Saint Nick

WALLACE IRWIN (1875-1959), *originally of New York, was versatile across many forms and genres, from musicals to silent film screenplays, but was particularly admired as a humorist— some of which humor has aged badly. His poem anticipates other Santa-nappings like Tim Burton's* The Nightmare Before Christmas, *and the unintended results of gift substitutions. It was given a whole page in the Christmas* Collier's *of* 1906.

OLD Satan on a Christmas eve
    Went forth to tempt and to deceive.
So on the housetops snowy white
He lingered through the starry night
Until there chanced to come that way
Old Santa in his jolly sleigh.
"Halt!" shrieked the Fiend until in fear
The Saint reined in his restless deer,
And Satan, further to confound him,
Seized him at wrists and shins and bound him,
Possessed himself of Santa's pack,
And whipped the prong-horned steeds *snick-snack.*
"Ha, ha!" he howled, "these gifts shall be
Distributed, as we shall see,
That all the world shall feel dismay
And none rejoice on Christmas Day."

So Satan, in the Saint's disguise,
    Slid nimbly down the sooty flues.
At every home he left a prize
    Meant most to anger and confuse.
Beside the Gambler's soft repose
    A pious book of hymns he dropped,
And in the Pastor's saintly hose
    A pack of greasy cards he popped.
He gave the Anarchist a bomb,
    He dowered the rich with needless riches,
Gave lavish gifts to naughty Tom
    While docile Dick got naught but switches.
A phonograph of pleasant tone
    To deaf old Grandpa Smith he carried,
And gave the Spinster sour and lone
    Portraits of men she might have married.
Beside the Infant's cot he thrust
    A work entitled "Famous Battles"
And wise Professor Dryasdust
    Received some woolly lambs and rattles.
"Aha!" cried Satan when 'twas done,
    "Good morrow, gentlemen and ladies!"
Then chuckling at his demon fun
    He drove his reindeer down to Hades.

Now good old Santa, when he found
His hands and feet securely bound,
Bethought him of a magic word
Which oft at Christmas he had heard.
So o'er the roofs of snow and ice
He shouted "Merry Christmas!" thrice
And all the world, when it awoke,
Beholding the Satanic joke,
Responded with a Yuletide will

And felt the Christmas spirit still.
The Rich Man, when he saw his gift,
Resolved the Poor Man to uplift,
The Infant, when he chanced to look
At that profoundly weighted book,
Smiled, softly, opened wide his eyes
And said: " 'Twill help me to be wise."
The Anarchist renounced his bomb,
And even naughty, wanton Tom
Divided all his presents rich
With docile Dick who got the switch.
The Gambler thought the hymns sublime
And was converted in due time.
And when the pastor saw the pack
Of cards that dropped from Satan's sack
He said: " 'Tis Christian to forgive—
Let us be merry while we live."
Thus Santa Claus had won his case
And put Sir Satan in his place.

MORAL

Though Christmas blessings oft misfit,
The Saint is not to blame for it.
The thankful heart frost can not shrivel—
Let's praise the Day and shame the Divvil!

Robert W. Service

The Cremation of Sam McGee

This poem by ROBERT WILLIAM SERVICE *(1874-1958) first
appeared in his collection* Songs of a Sourdough *in 1907.
Born in England, he left for Canada at twenty-one and wandered the continent through Mexico, the western United States,
and British Columbia, but his move to the Yukon in 1904 proved
to be especially defining. Service's poems easily lend themselves
to recitation—the reader may even be familiar with this one,
though the fact that it was set around Christmas and the days
following must have escaped the memory of Christmas ghost
story anthologists.*

———

> There are strange things done in the midnight sun
>   By the men who moil for gold;
> The Arctic trails have their secret tales
>   That would make your blood run cold;
> The Northern Lights have seen queer sights,
>   But the queerest they ever did see
> Was that night on the marge of Lake Lebarge
>   I cremated Sam McGee.

Now Sam McGee was from Tennessee, where the cotton
blooms and blows.
Why he left his home in the South to roam round the Pole,
   God only knows.
He was always cold, but the land of gold seemed to hold him
   like a spell;

Though he'd often say in his homely way that he'd "sooner live
in hell."

On a Christmas Day we were mushing our way over the
Dawson trail.
Talk of your cold! through the parka's fold it stabbed like a
driven nail.
If our eyes we'd close, then the lashes froze, till sometimes we
couldn't see;
It wasn't much fun, but the only one to whimper was Sam
McGee.

And that very night as we lay packed tight in our robes beneath
the snow,
And the dogs were fed, and the stars o'erhead were dancing
heel and toe,
He turned to me, and "Cap," says he, "I'll cash in this trip, I guess;
And if I do, I'm asking that you won't refuse my last request."

Well, he seemed so low that I couldn't say no; then he says with
a sort of moan:
"It's the cursed cold, and it's got right hold till I'm chilled clean
through to the bone.
Yet 'tain't being dead—it's my awful dread of the icy grave that
pains;
So I want you to swear that, foul or fair, you'll cremate my last
remains."

A pal's last need is a thing to heed, so I swore I would not fail;
And we started on at the streak of dawn; but God! he looked
ghastly pale.
He crouched on the sleigh, and he raved all day of his home in
Tennessee;
And before nightfall a corpse was all that was left of Sam McGee.

There wasn't a breath in that land of death, and I hurried, horror driven,
With a corpse half-hid that I couldn't get rid, because of a promise given;
It was lashed to the sleigh, and it seemed to say: "You may tax your brawn and brains,
But you promised true, and it's up to you to cremate those last remains."

Now a promise made is a debt unpaid, and the trail has its own stern code.
In the days to come, though my lips were dumb, in my heart how I cursed that load.
In the long, long night, by the lone firelight, while the huskies, round in a ring,
Howled out their woes to the homeless snows—O God! how I loathed the thing.

And every day that quiet clay seemed to heavy and heavier grow;
And on I went, though the dogs were spent and the grub was getting low;
The trail was bad, and I felt half mad, but I swore I would not give in;
And I'd often sing to the hateful thing, and it hearkened with a grin.

Till I came to the marge of Lake Lebarge, and a derelict there lay;
It was jammed in the ice, but I saw in a trice it was called the "Alice May."
And I looked at it, and I thought a bit, and I looked at my frozen chum;
Then "Here," said I, with a sudden cry, "is my cre-ma-tor-eum."

Some planks I tore from the cabin floor, and I lit the boiler
fire;
Some coal I found that was lying around, and I heaped the fuel
higher;
The flames just soared, and the furnace roared—such a blaze
you seldom see;
And I burrowed a hole in the glowing coal, and I stuffed in
Sam McGee.

Then I made a hike, for I didn't like to hear him sizzle so;
And the heavens scowled, and the huskies howled, and the
wind began to blow.
It was icy cold, but the hot sweat rolled down my cheeks, and
I don't know why;
And the greasy smoke in an inky cloak went streaking down
the sky.

I do not know how long in the snow I wrestled with grisly
fear;
But the stars came out and they danced about ere again I ventured near;
I was sick with dread, but I bravely said: "I'll just take a peep
inside.
I guess he's cooked, and it's time I looked," . . . then the door I
opened wide.

And there sat Sam, looking cool and calm, in the heart of the
furnace roar;
And he wore a smile you could see a mile, and he said: "Please
close that door.
It's fine in here, but I greatly fear you'll let in the cold and
storm—
Since I left Plumtree, down in Tennessee, it's the first time I've
been warm."

There are strange things done in the midnight sun
  By the men who moil for gold;
The Arctic trails have their secret tales
  That would make your blood run cold;
The Northern Lights have seen queer sights,
  But the queerest they ever did see
Was that night on the marge of Lake Lebarge
  I cremated Sam McGee.

Christmas ghost stories will soon be out. They will be cut on the old style this season, with the skeptical guest, the haunted room, the creaking stair and all other proper appurtenances.
  Democrat and Chronicle (Rochester, N.Y.), Dec. 8, 1883

Dear old Santa Claus.—A couple of murders, a few suicides, half a dozen robberies and some good elopements with no more ghost stories thank you, is the wish of
                    FRANK K. ALBRIGHT [City Editor].
                    Wichita Star (Kan.), December 26, 1888

We are inclined to believe that the Memphis Avalanche is poking fun at us in the subjoined paragraph: "Col. H. M. Doak's Christmas ghost story in THE NASHVILLE AMERICAN didn't get the first prize, but it scared Carmack and the other boys out of their wits. The proof-reader of THE AMERICAN took to the woods and has not yet been captured."
                    Daily American (Tenn.), December 30, 1889

Amorel Sterne

Xmas

Appearing in the December 24, 1908 African-American news-paper The New York Age, *this might be the first published poem of* Amorel Elizabeth Sterne O'Kelly Cooke (*c. 1881-1927*). *It might also be autobiographical, as the 1910 U.S. Census shows she had three deceased children at that time, and four living. Part of her 1909 "Christmas Time" poem for the same paper also referenced death in the family. In 1918 she would become the founding president of the Women's Volunteer Service League, a branch of the Newark, N.J. mayor's committee of the Woman's Council of National Defense that provided a five-story building as a canteen and school for soldiers and sailors, and to teach technical trades to young women.*

I T is Xmas time and my heart is sore,
    And my eyes are dim with tears.
For 'twas Xmas time in the days of yore
That my heart grew sick with fears.

When the yule-tide comes and the clean New Year
When over the earth falls the snow,
And the merry bells of the sleigh we hear,
I think of just two years ago.

For 'twas Xmas time and Santa Claus came,
And the presents he brought us all,
For brother a wagon and sister a game
And baby a rattle and ball.

And dear little Madeline a pair of shoes,
And a dolly with golden hair,
And a tiny tea set, a silver cup,
And a cute little "Teddy Bear."

And the child was filled with a great delight,
And her dimpled sweet face so fair
With a smile unearthly would seem to light,
As she cried, "See my Teddy Bear."

And "Yook at my 'hoes. Oh! mamma, see,
Des 'ou yook at my pitty tup;
Ole Tanta Taus he binged 'em to me
And I don't want to put 'em up."

But right in the midst of our mirth and zest
A spectre stood outside the door;
A grim unwelcome, an unbidden guest,
His shadow cast over the floor.

And sick grew our child and a fever burned
On her brow, and her pulse was great,
Yet all of the while for her toys she yearned,
And so patiently bore her fate.

I worked and we prayed, and the Doctor came;
He looked and gravely shook his head,
"You are very sick, my dear little child,
But we'll do what we can," he said.

As I bent o'er the child she smiled at me,
And a great fear did seize my heart.
And I said, "Oh Dear Christ, it cannot be
That my darling and I must part!"

And then, when the snow fell over the earth,
All over the land far and wide,
And the clean-shaven New Year had found its birth,
My darling called "Mama!" and died.

We folded her hands o'er her little breast,
And my heart grew cold as stone;
And I told the children she'd gone to rest;
The Master had taken His own.

And so in the Springtime another He sent
To warm up my heart icy cold—
A dear little Angel He graciously lent
From out His cherubeum fold

It is Xmas time and my heart is sore,
And broken with grief and pain;
That grim-visaged spectre has crouched at my door,
Reflecting his shadow again.

And now he has taken my Angel child
And left me in Rachel-like woe,
And the Xmas tide brings but tears to me
And sorrows that overflow.

Kate Masterson

A Cubist Christmas

Dickens had "scary ghost stories and tales of the glories of Christ-mases long, long ago," a tension between a romanticized past and a ghastly future. In the December 25, 1913 issue of the humor magazine Life, CATHERINE "KATE" KELLY MASTERSON *(c. 1864-1927) dreamed of an undead, non-Euclidean monstros-ity, the horror of Modernism. Cubist art had begun in the decade prior. Literary efforts appear to have been less common, though examples include Max Weber's* Cubist Poems *and Gertrude Stein's* Tender Buttons, *both 1914. A 1938 Chicago Trib-une item described a card titled "A Christmas Adventure in Surrealism" reading: "Electric lights on blue tweed rabbits,/ Pastel sieves in riding habits,/Corkscrews flee from pelting rain,/ Merry Christmas once again." When Salvador Dali designed Christmas cards for Hallmark in 1948, the results were not well-received by the public. Times having changed, they find admirers and collectors today.*

T HE snow popped up and rattled like rice
    In the low, lush mistletoe marsh
The chimes swung thick on a sickle of ice
And jangled a discord harsh
And the herring bone in the pickle jar
Why *that* was a Christmas tree
And the glibbering, globular glint was a star
But not to you and me.

And off to the right where the candles grew
Was a goglet that made you glare
Pink and yellow and green and blue
It was something descending the stair
Carrying a slosh of sugar of lead
Powdered with spangled ink.
You couldn't say if 'twas living or dead
But wouldn't it make you *think!*

That centipede doing the turkey trot
It seems was a Christmas kiss
You should keep one eye on the nineteenth leg
And the other eye shut, like this
And oh—the moon in the oilcloth glow
And the bath-spray burst in bloom
'Twas holly and evergreen all in a row
If the artist had had more room.

Oh, where is the blazing pudding of plum
And dear old Santy C——
Who skidded over the rooftops some
On his annual Christmas spree
And where is the trusty Yule log's flare
That we used to read about
They are all in that lunatic diagram there
The thing is—to find them out!

Anonymous

Desuetude

A Ghost Story

The flash fiction of "Desuetude," containing a strikingly eccentric story of under 280 characters, sits between earlier genres like fin de siècle literature and nonsense poetry and later ones like surrealism and Fortianism. It appeared in February 1914 in the El Paso Herald's column "The Daily Novelette." The title means protracted cessation, and is also a legal concept whereby an unenforced law may be abrogated by protracted disuse. The malaise expressed in the story might be familiar to modern readers.

(Editor's note—We wish to call our readers' busy attention to a few psychological facts in support of the veracity of this unusual but absolutely true story. On August 11, 1545, Auguste Stindenpfeifer discovered the remarkable theory that souls, winging their way to heaven at the approximate rate of four million and a quarter miles a second, often contract serious colds as a result of the prodigious rush of air. Late in the year 1456 Felix Shizzilkopf found that if an angleworm is cut in half and the halves removed to opposite ends of the earth, the two pieces, after a day or two, do not seem to miss each other. On the 14th of January, 1654 A. D., it was discovered by Michael Worser, that a Chinese baby of two weeks, if nursed for seven years by a healthy Indian woman, has by that time generally attained the age at which children are commonly admitted into the primary school. Lastly, Raymond Wunker, in the fall of 1765, ascertained that an empty bottle that has been placed by the bedside of a dying man will emit a hollow sound if tapped at certain angles with a piece of ordinary kindling wood.)

Desuetude.
(A Ghost Story.)

"Isn't Christmas a little early this year!" she said, a trifle nervously.

"Yes," he answered, "I never remember its coming in May before."

Darkness closed in on them.

Anna Alice Chapin

The Christmas Ghost

New Yorker ANNA ALICE CHAPIN (1880-1920) *was the co-author of the fairy story* Babes in Toyland *in* 1904, *the adaptations of which—Laurel and Hardy's in* 1934, *Shirley Temple's in* 1960, *and Disney's in* 1961—*have been Christmas favorites for some. Like Lucy Comfort, the author of the other story in this volume titled "The Christmas Ghost," she was already publishing when still in her teenage years. This tale appeared, with slight textual variations, in at least five different American newspapers during the Christmas season in* 1915.

"AND IT'S GOING to be a real Christmas Eve party—old fashioned you know; with an open fire, and ghost stories, and punch with baked apples in it, and——"

"And a flash-light!"

"Who told you? A flash-light! How beastly!"

"No; what fun! What a lovely idea! Was it one of Candace's?"

"I think it was. She wants a record of the evening, and we are all to have copies of the pictures to keep as souvenirs."

They were all merry, and chattered like young birds, all except Myra Randall. She smiled, and was cheerful enough in a way, but she had never seemed quite carefree since the breaking of her engagement to Max Atwood, two years before.

Candace Jewett, the young hostess tonight, had been trying for months to bring the two together again, and had gone so far as to include them both in her Christmas Eve party, but neither Max nor Myra had acted at all comfortably. They had been singularly cool and calm and polite to each other, but nothing more.

Candace was disappointed enough to cry. Getting Myra off in a corner while the others were laughing and discussing the best games, for twelve people, she took her guest's pretty slim shoulders into an affectionate though exasperated grasp.

"Myra, you little pig!" she said, with that ghost of a stammer which her many adorers found so irresistible, "why don't you make up with Max? I'm sure anyone ought to be willing to.

"He's a darling," concluded Candace.

Myra was tall and daintily made, with grey eyes, and a vast quantity of smooth, red brown hair. She was a girl who rode to hounds a great deal and looked it. She was equally perfect in a riding habit and in full evening dress, but never showed up to advantage in shirt-waists or in frills.

Now she raised her level brows with a slightly mocking expression.

"Sorry, my dear," she said, "but I can't do it, even to oblige you. Max is attractive."

She looked down the room and through the door to the young man, who was joking and flirting to the top of his bent with Letty Lovell. They were fixing up some mysterious game, weaving string round every conceivable object.

"He is attractive," repeated Myra reflectively. "But frankly, Candy, I can't marry a man who has no more heart than than—than a crocodile."

"Myra Randall!" gasped Candace with sincere indignation. "How dare you compare our Max to a c—crocodile? He has the warmest, kindest, nicest understandingest heart in the world!"

"Candace," said Myra, quietly looking straight in front of her—and Candace saw her slender, strong hands clench hard at her sides—"Beatrix loved Max; and he loved her—and said so. And yet within one year of her death he can joke and play at love like that."

Candace nearly fell into the fire in surprise. Myra was the most unexpected person.

"Beatrix?" she repeated almost stupidly. "Beatrix! Who died last Christmas time?"

"Yes," said Myra. "My cousin Beatrix. Didn't you ever suspect? They cared for each other; that was why I broke the engagement."

"But—did he—did she tell you? I don't see how——"

"I heard Beatrix telephone him from here that Christmas Eve two years ago when we were all together. You remember?"

"Rather! Our first house-party since we were all grown up and out and so on."

"Well, you know Max had sent word he couldn't get out until Christmas day. On the afternoon of the day before Christmas I was curled up there—" Myra pointed to the little room opening out of the big library where they all were—"dozing over a book; and"—she laughed very bitterly—"thinking of Max. I adored him you see then—

"I heard a little rustle and Beatrix passed the half-open door and went to the telephone in the hall. She did not see me, and it never occurred to me to let her know until I heard her say:

"'Oh, Max! Oh, darling! Is it you? Yes; they are all upstairs dressing. No; there's no chance of her overhearing.'

"And so on—and so on—I—I can't repeat it all."

Myra's clear color faded perceptibly at the memory, but she went steadily on.

"They agreed to meet in London that evening, for the last time. They had agreed to give each other up, you see. Do you remember that Beatrix was called to town suddenly that evening?"

"To see her aunt who was ill. Yes."

"And came back next day on the same train with Max?"

Candace nodded speechless.

"Well," said Myra, "that was all—except that I broke the engagement."

"Did you ever tell them?"

"No; I tried to save their feelings."

Myra laughed again and shrugged her shoulders.

"You see," she added simply, "I was fond of them both. I was quite sorry when it never came to anything between them in spite of my setting Max free. I suppose they must hare quarreled. And a year later she was dead."

"And you can wear mourning for her?" broke out Candace irrepressibly.

"Why not?" said Myra in faint surprise, looking down at her black dinner-dress. "She was first my cousin, and I loved her dearly. Beatrix was such a splendid, vital creature, with such will and poise. And to think that she is dead!"

Candace left her silently and went across to where Letty and Sibyl were talking in low tones.

"You seem very solemn girls!" she said, trying to speak lightly.

"Sib was saying how Beatrix would have loved it tonight," said Letty again.

Candace started uncomfortably.

"Beatrix seems to be in the air!" she said almost impatiently.

"Well," said Sibyl, "she said she would be, you know."

"What on earth do you mean?" exclaimed Letty.

"Why, don't you remember, how she used to laugh and say: 'If I die first girls, I'll come back and haunt you! I'll never be quiet in my grave.'"

"We were just an even dozen then, counting Beatrix, at our party two years ago," said Letty. "We are only eleven now, aren't we?"

"No; still twelve," said Candace. "My kid brother is old enough to join us now. And with Gracie's brother Jimmy, and Max and Rudolph, the two Graves boys and Colin Clay we're an even dozen still. It's going to be just the old crowd.

"I didn't want to ask an extra girl," she added hesitatingly. "Somehow, on Beatrix's account, I thought I'd let Jack be the twelfth."

She went off to superintend the bringing in of the great bowl of steaming punch in which the baked apples floated in the true old English style.

Corny Grange had been given over to the young people that Christmas Eve. Candace's father had repaired to his study at the back of the house, that her guests might be at liberty to make merry until the dawn if they liked.

And, of course, they took advantage of it to romp and laugh and pretend they were school children again. They played games, and sang carols, and told fortunes. Finally Candace suggested playing "Oracles."

No one knew anything about it.

"You play it this way," she explained. "Each of us writes a question and folds it up and writes a number outside; and then everyone draws from a hat a slip of blank paper with a number written on it and writes an answer to an imaginary question.

"Just any foolish thing you like: 'Yes,' or 'Not at all,' or 'They are better with onions'; or you can put mysterious prophecies or sentimental messages—anything that occurs to you.

"Then you put them into a hat or bowl or something, and take them up to the Oracle. And then people go up one by one and read their number, and the Oracle hands them the answer corresponding, and they have to read out the question and answer. It is awfully funny sometimes!"

It was an absurd game, of course, but young people at Christmas time can get fun out of anything. So they appointed Jimmy Markwell the Oracle, and jestfully settled down to the game.

After they had written all the papers they turned all the answers over to Jimmy, who sat in a mysterious corner behind a fire screen.

They put out all the lights except one ghostly candle. Then one by one they went up and received their messages from Fate. Some of the combinations of questions and answers were ridiculously incongruous, and they had one or two good laughs before it came to Myra Randall's turn.

She walked the length of the dark room, almost invisible in her sombre gown.

"Number eleven," she said in a very low tone.

She felt now that the question she had written had been a foolish one; no, more than foolish—indiscreet. She dreaded having to read it aloud.

The Oracle handed over a slip. She approached the one candle. It spluttered so that she could hardly see to read.

"Question—Should one believe one's own eyes and ears when one does not want to?"

"Hold on! The draught is getting worse," struck in Max. "I'll draw the curtain."

Myra put her hand to her throat. She went on:

"Answer—The eyes and ears of the living are dulled by earth."

She stopped short, appalled. How could so pat an answer have come by chance? Someone must have read her question before writing the answer.

"By jove!" said Rudolph uncomfortably.

"There's no fun if it comes out as well as that! Who wrote it anyway—the answer, I mean? Don't all speak at once."

No one spoke.

The candle had stopped flickering, and now was burning with a clear, steady light. In its rather ghostly rays the faces of the twelve friends looked pale and unnatural.

Candace was the first to speak.

"I—I don't think it's proving a very funny game," she said nervously. "Let's do something more amusing."

"Lord yes!" said Rudolph. "Let's tell ghost stories, or go and visit the graveyard, or do something really lively and cheerful."

"Next!" called the Oracle. "We might as well finish, Candy. It's your turn, anyway; you're the only one left."

"Twelve!" stammered Candy.

Her question was about making the offer. The answer— easily traceable to Sibyl Lee—was concerned with some rules for deportment. It was not a particularly amusing combination, but they all laughed rather hysterically. Myra's coincidence had been a little depressing.

"So that's your old game!" said Sibyl—scornfully. "Well, I don't think much of that—"

"No. 13," said someone.

They all jumped.

"Who on earth said that?" demanded the Oracle.

"Somebody's fooling," said Max at once. "The game's over. There are only twelve of us here."

"But there's a paper here—there are two papers here!" protested the Oracle.

"Oh, well, I suppose it's Rudolph!" said Candace. "He's always playing jokes."

She spoke quite as if Rudolph were not in the room.

"I swear I didn't," he protested.

"Read them out, Jimmy," said Max.

"I can't see to read over here," said the Oracle crossly. "Bring me that confounded candle."

The candle was misbehaving again, but in a moment it stopped and burned clearly once more. Max carried it across the room and held it while Jimmy read out slowly and with many pauses.

"Number thirteen. Question—What was Beatrix doing on Christmas Eve two years ago?"

"Oh, Jimmy, that is too much!" gasped Candace, shocked. "Beatrix, who is dead! Oh, no one should drag her name into this nonsense!"

"I can't help it," said the misjudged Oracle indignantly. "That's what's on the paper here. Someone's written it!"

"Then someone has very bad taste!" put in Sibyl.

"Do you want to hear the answer?" asked Jimmy.

Candace hesitated, but to everyone's surprise Max spoke.

"Yes, please," he said quietly. "Let's have the answer."

And Jimmy read:

"Number thirteen. Answer—On Christmas eve, one year before she died, Beatrix went to the telephone at Gorby Grange and pretended to call up Max. She knew that Myra was in the next room, and she let her think that she was exchanging words of love with the man Myra was engaged to.

"She made believe she was agreeing to an appointment in town that evening and Myra saw her leave for the evening train. She and Max came to Corby Grange together next day, and Myra broke the engagement. Myra did not know that Beatrix had not spoken to Max for weeks until she met him on the train that morning—"

"I can hardly read this," Jimmy said. "It's so scrawly and queer—as if it had been written in a tearing hurry.

"'——nor that——the receiver—'

"I think it's 'receiver'; yes, of course.

"'—nor that the receiver had never been taken off the hook.'"

Dead silence in the room; then suddenly without warning the candle went out.

Candace screamed outright. Sibyl clung to Rudolph. Grace and Lotty Lovell had both burst into tears. Myra did not cry, but she shook from head to foot with a strange excitement that was not entirely terror. Someone touched her hand softly in the darkness. Instinctively she knew it was Max.

"It's all right," he said nervously in her ear. "They'll find a match in a minute. Just an absurd, rather rotten joke of someone's."

"Joke!" Myra gasped. "Oh Max, was it true what the thirteenth paper said?"

"I suppose so," he said gently. "I never received a telephone message from Beatrix in my life."

"Max!" she whispered, and he had time to draw her near him and kiss her before a rather tremulous match flared up.

"See here," he said as he lighted—not the candle, but the gas. "I've had enough of this Oracle business."

"It was ghostly," said Candace, tearfully. "Who could have written those things?"

"I frankly suggest," said Jimmy earnestly, "that we don't ever try to find out."

A knock sounded at the door.

"Were they ready for the flash-light?"

They welcomed the diversion gratefully, but it was twelve rather solemn young faces that faced the man with the camera.

"One of you moved, didn't you, during the flash?" asked the photographer.

"Oh, I don't think so," one of the group returned.

"But just as I touched off the flash, I thought I saw a pale young woman in a white dress sitting next to the tall gentleman, and, as you see, she is not there now."

Candace started.

"No lady here tonight is wearing a white dress," she said as she caught her breath.

"Oh, my mistake!" murmured the mystified photographer. "It—it might have been a window shade or—or—a curtain."

"Yes, of course," agreed Candace hastily.

★ ★ ★

The pictures were never sent around as souvenirs. The plate was discovered. For in the group in the photograph there was a thirteenth person, and the face was the face of Beatrix, who had been dead a year.

Stephen Leacock

Merry Christmas

Comedians Jack Benny and Groucho Marx were both admirers of Canadian STEPHEN BUTLER LEACOCK (1869-1944). *A group of his friends created a Stephen Leacock Memorial Medal for Humour "awarded annually since* 1947 *for the best Canadian book of literary humour published in the previous year." Leacock's figures in this story, first published in* Hearst's *Magazine in December* 1917, *come closest to the Ghosts of Christmas Past, Present, and Future variety, likewise providing guidance, and it lends a cautiously optimistic note on which to end this volume and this unusual, challenging year.*

"MY DEAR YOUNG FRIEND," said Father Time, as he laid his hand gently upon my shoulder, "you are entirely wrong."

Then I looked up over my shoulder from the table at which I was sitting and I saw him.

But I had known, or felt, for at least the last half-hour that he was standing somewhere near me.

You have had, I do not doubt, good reader, more than once that strange, uncanny feeling that there is some one unseen standing beside you—in a darkened room, let us say, with a dying fire, when the night has grown late, and the October wind sounds low outside, and when, through the thin curtain that we call Reality, the Unseen World starts for a moment clear upon our dreaming sense.

You *have* had it? Yes, I know you have. Never mind telling

me about it. Stop! I don't want to hear about that strange presentiment you had the night your Aunt Eliza broke her leg. Don't let's bother with *your* experience. I want to tell mine.

"You are quite mistaken, my dear young friend," repeated Father Time, "quite wrong."

"*Young* friend?" I said, my mind, as one's mind is apt to in such a case, running to an unimportant detail. "Why do you call me young?"

"Your pardon," he answered gently—he had a gentle way with him, had Father Time—"the fault is in my failing eyes. I took you at first sight for something under a hundred."

"Under a hundred?" I expostulated. "Well, I should think so!"

"Your pardon again," said Time, "the fault is in my failing memory. I forgot. You seldom pass that nowadays, do you? Your life is very short of late."

I heard him breathe a wistful hollow sigh. Very ancient and dim he seemed as he stood beside me. But I did not turn to look upon him. I had no need to. I knew his form, in the inner and clearer sight of things, as well as every human being knows by innate instinct the unseen face and form of Father Time.

I could hear him murmuring beside me: "Short—short, your life is short," till the sound of it seemed to mingle with the measured ticking of a clock somewhere in the silent house.

Then I remembered what he had said.

"How do you know that I am wrong?" I asked. "And how can you tell what I was thinking?"

"You said it out loud," answered Father Time, "but it wouldn't have mattered, anyway. You said that Christmas was all played out and done with."

"Yes," I admitted, "that's what I said."

"And what makes you think that?" he questioned, stooping, so it seemed to me, still further over my shoulder.

"Why," I answered, "the trouble is this: I've been sitting

here for hours, sitting till goodness only knows how far into the night, trying to think out something to write for a Christmas story. And it won't go. It can't be done—not in these awful days."

"A Christmas story?"

"Yes; you see, Father Time," I said, glad with a foolish little vanity of my trade to be able to tell him something that I thought enlightening, "all the Christmas stuff, stories and jokes and pictures, are all done, you know, in October."

I thought it would have surprised him, but I was mistaken.

"Dear me!" he said, "not till October! What a rush! How well I remember in ancient Egypt—as I think you call it—seeing them getting out their Christmas things, all cut in hieroglyphics, always two or three years ahead."

"Two or three years!" I exclaimed.

"Pooh," said Time, "that was nothing. In Babylon they used to get their Christmas jokes ready—all baked in clay—a whole solar eclipse ahead of Christmas. They said, I think, that the public preferred them so."

"Egypt?" I said. "Babylon? But surely, Father Time, there was no Christmas in those days, I thought."

"My dear boy," he interrupted gravely, "don't you know that there has always been Christmas?"

I was silent. Father Time had moved across the room and stood beside the fireplace, leaning on the mantel. The little wreaths of smoke from the fading fire seemed to mingle with his shadowy outline.

"Well," he said presently, "what is it that is wrong with Christmas?"

"Why," I answered, "all the romance, the joy, the beauty of it has gone, crushed and killed by the greed of commerce and the horrors of war. I am not, as you thought I was, a hundred years old, but I can conjure up, as anybody can, a picture of Christmas in the good old days of a hundred years ago: the quaint old-fashioned houses, standing deep among the evergreens, with the light twinkling from the windows on the snow—the warmth and comfort within—the great fire roaring on the hearth—the merry guests grouped about its blaze and the little children with their eyes dancing in the Christmas firelight, waiting for Father Christmas in his fine mummery of red and white and cotton wool to hand the presents from the Yule-tide tree. I can see it," I added, "as if it were yesterday."

"It was but yesterday," said Father Time, and his voice seemed to soften with the memory of bygone years. "I remember it well."

"Ah," I continued, "that was Christmas indeed. Give me back such days as those, with the old good cheer, the old stage-coaches and the gabled inns and the warm red wine, the snap-dragon and the Christmas-tree, and I'll believe again in Christmas, yes, in Father Christmas himself."

"Believe in him?" said Time quietly, "you may well do that. He happens to be standing outside in the street at this moment."

"Outside!" I exclaimed. "Why don't he come in?"

"He's afraid to," said Father Time. "He's frightened and he daren't come in unless you ask him. May I call him in?"

I signified assent, and Father Time went to the window for a moment and beckoned into the darkened street. Then I heard footsteps, clumsy and hesitant they seemed, upon the stairs. And in a moment a figure stood framed in the doorway—the figure of Father Christmas. He stood shuffling his feet, a timid, apologetic look upon his face.

How changed he was!

I had known in my mind's eye from childhood the face and form of Father Christmas as well as that of Old Time himself. Everybody knows, or once knew him—a jolly little rounded man, with a great muffler wound about him, a packet of toys upon his back and with such merry, twinkling eyes and rosy cheeks as are only given by the touch of the driving snow and the rude fun of the North Wind. Why, there was once a time, not yet so long ago, when the very sound of his sleigh-bells sent the blood running warm to the heart.

But now how changed!

All draggled with the mud and rain he stood, as if no house had sheltered him these three years past. His old red jersey was tattered in a dozen places, his muffler frayed and raveled.

The bundle of toys that he dragged with him in a net seemed wet and worn till the cardboard boxes gaped asunder. There were boxes among them, I vow, that he must have been carrying these three years past.

But most of all I noted the change that had come over the face of Father Christmas. The old brave look of cheery confidence was gone. The smile that had beamed responsive to the laughing eyes of countless children around unnumbered Christmas trees was there no more. And in the place of it there showed a look of timid apology, of apprehensiveness, as of one who has asked in vain the warmth and shelter of a human home—such a look as the harsh cruelty of this world has stamped upon the faces of its outcasts.

So stood Father Christmas shuffling upon the threshold, fumbling his poor tattered hat in his hand.

"Shall I come in?" he said, his eyes appealingly on Father Time.

"Come," said Time. He turned to speak to me, "Your room is dark. Turn up the lights. He's used to light, bright light, and plenty of it. The dark has frightened him these three years past."

I turned up the lights and the bright glare revealed all the more cruelly the tattered figure before us.

Father Christmas advanced a timid step across the floor. Then he paused, as if in sudden fear.

"Is this floor mined?" he said.

"No, no," said Time soothingly. And to me he added in a murmured whisper, "He's afraid. He was blown up in a mine in No Man's Land between the trenches at Christmas time in 1914. It broke his nerve."

"May I put my toys on that machine-gun?" asked Father Christmas timidly; "it will help to keep them dry."

"It is not a machine-gun," said Time gently. "See, it is only a pile of books upon the sofa,"—and to me he whispered— "they turned a machine-gun on him in the streets of Warsaw. He thinks he sees them everywhere since then."

"It's all right, Father Christmas," I said, speaking as cheerily as I could, while I rose and stirred the fire into a blaze, "there are no machine-guns here and there are no mines. This is but the house of a poor writer."

"Ah," said Father Christmas, lowering his tattered hat still further and attempting something of a humble bow, "a writer? Are you Hans Andersen, perhaps?"

"Not quite," I answered.

"But a great writer, I do not doubt," said the old man, with a humble courtesy that he had learned, it well may be, centuries ago in the Yule-tide season of his northern home. "The world owes much to its great books. I carry some of the greatest with me always. I have them here—"

He began fumbling among the limp and tattered packages that he carried. "Look! The House that Jack Built—a marvelous deep thing, sir—and this, The Babes in the Wood. Will you take it, sir? A poor present, but a present still—not so long ago I gave them in thousands every Christmas time. None seem to want them now."

He looked appealingly toward Father Time, as the weak may look towards the strong for help and guidance.

"None want them now," he repeated, and I could see the tears start in his eyes. "Why is it so? Has the world forgotten its sympathy with the lost children wandering in the wood?"

"All the world," I heard Time murmur with a sigh, "is wandering in the wood." But out loud he spoke to Father Christmas in cheery admonition: "Tut, tut, good Christmas," he said, "you must cheer up. Here, sit in this chair—the biggest one—so—beside the fire—let us stir it to a blaze—more wood—that's better—and listen, good old friend, to the wind outside—almost a Christmas wind, is it not? Merry and boisterous enough for all the evil times it stirs among."

Old Christmas seated himself beside the fire, his hands outstretched toward the flames. Something of his old-time cheeriness seemed to flicker across his features as he warmed himself at the blaze.

"That's better," he murmured. "I was cold, sir, cold, chilled to the bone: of old I never felt it so; no matter what the wind, the world seemed warm about me. Why is it not so now?"

"You see?" said Time, speaking low in a whisper for my ear alone, "how sunk and broken he is? Will you not help?"

"Gladly," I answered, "if I can."

"All can," said Father Time, "every one of us."

Meantime Christmas had turned toward me a questioning eye, in which, however, there seemed to revive some little gleam of merriment.

"Have you, perhaps," he asked half-timidly, "schnapps?"

"Schnapps?" I repeated.

"Aye, schnapps. A glass of it to drink your health might warm my heart again, I think."

"Ah!" I said, "something to drink?"

"His one failing," whispered Time, "if it is one. Forgive it him. He was used to it for centuries. Give it him if you have it."

"I keep a little in the house," I said, reluctantly perhaps, "in case of illness."

"Tut, tut," said Father Time, as something as near as could be to a smile passed over his shadowy face. " 'In case of illness!' They used to say that in ancient Babylon. Here, let me pour it for him. Drink, Father Christmas, drink!"

Marvelous it was to see the old man smack his lips as he drank his glass of liquor neat after the fashion of old Norway.

Marvelous, too, to see the way in which, with the warmth of the fire and the generous glow of the spirits, his face changed and brightened till the old-time cheerfulness beamed again upon it.

He looked about him, as it were, with a new and kindling interest.

"A pleasant room," he said, "and what better, sir, than the wind without and a brave fire within!"

Then his eye fell upon the mantelpiece, where lay among the litter of books and pipes a little toy horse.

"Ah," said Father Christmas almost gayly, "children in the house!"

"One," I answered, "the sweetest boy in all the world."

"I'll be bound he is!" said Father Christmas, and he broke now into a merry laugh that did one's heart good to hear. "They all are! Lord bless me! The number that I have seen, and each and every one—and quite right too—the sweetest child in all the world. And how old, do you say? Two and a half all but two months except a week? The very sweetest age of all, I'll bet you say, eh, what? They all do!"

And the old man broke again into such a jolly chuckling of laughter that his snow-white locks shook upon his head.

"But stop a bit," he added. "This horse is broken—tut, tut,—a hind leg nearly off. This won't do!"

He had the toy in his lap in a moment, mending it. It was wonderful to see, for all his age, how deft his fingers were.

"Time," he said, and it was amusing to note that his voice had assumed almost an authoritative tone, "reach me that piece of string. That's right. Here, hold your finger across the knot. There! Now, then, a bit of beeswax. What? No beeswax? Tut, tut, how ill-supplied your houses are to-day. How can you mend toys, sir, without beeswax? Still, it will stand up now."

I tried to murmur my best thanks. But Father Christmas waved my gratitude aside.

"Nonsense," he said, "that's nothing. That's my life. Perhaps the little boy would like a book too. I have them here in the packet. Here, sir, Jack and the Beanstalk, a most profound thing. I read it to myself often still. How damp it is! Pray, sir, will you let me dry my books before your fire?"

"Only too willingly," I said. "How wet and torn they are!"

He stood bowed over his little books, his hands trembling as he turned the pages. Then he looked up, the old fear upon his face again.

"That sound!" he said. "Listen! It is guns—I hear them!"

"No, no," I said, "it is nothing. Only a car passing in the street below."

"Listen," he said. "Hear that again—voices crying!"

"No, no," I answered, "not voices, only the night wind among the trees."

"My children's voices!" he exclaimed. "I hear them every-where—they come to me in every wind—and I see them as I wander in the night and storm—my children—torn and dying in the trenches—beaten into the ground—I hear them crying from the hospitals—each one to me, still as I knew him once, a little child. Time, Time," he cried, reaching out his arms in appeal, "give me back my children!"

"You see?" said Time. "His heart is breaking, and will you not help him if you can?"

"Only too gladly," I replied. "But what is there to do?"

"This," said Father Time, "listen."

He stood before me grave and solemn, a shadowy figure but half seen though he was close beside me. The firelight had died down, and through the curtained windows there came already the first streaks of dawn.

"The world that once you knew," said Father Time, "seems broken and destroyed about you. You must not let them know—the children. The cruelty and the horror and the hate that racks the world to-day—keep it from them. Some day he will know"—here Time pointed to the prostrate form of Father Christmas—"that his children, that once were, have not died in vain: that from their sacrifice shall come a nobler, better world for all to live in, a world where countless happy children shall hold bright their memory for ever. But for the children of To-day, save and spare them all you can from the evil hate and horror of the war. Later they will know and understand. Not yet. Give them back their Merry Christmas and its kind thoughts, and its Christmas charity, till later on there shall be with it again Peace upon Earth, Good Will toward Men."

His voice ceased. It seemed to vanish, as it were, in the sighing of the wind.

I looked up. Father Time and Christmas had vanished from the room. The fire was low and the day was breaking visibly outside.

"Let us begin," I murmured. "I will mend this broken horse."